"We've f[...]

Abby sank to the [...] wanted to guzzle [...] and sipped. Handing it to him, she sighed. "Heaven. Pure heaven."

He eased down by her and sipped until the water was gone. "This is better than sex."

"You think so?"

He lifted an eyebrow. "At this exact moment, yes."

He filled the pitcher three times. The third time they didn't drink much. Ethan poured the last bit over his head and water ran down his face and onto his chest. Droplets clung to swirls of dark chest hairs. Without thinking, without judging herself, she leaned over and licked the drops from his warm skin.

He stiffened. She didn't stop.

"Abby."

Her lips touched his. He groaned, cupped her face and kissed her like she'd never been kissed before.

Dear Reader,

I'm excited to start a new trilogy for Harlequin Superromance: Willow Creek, Texas. The stories are about three friends, Ethan, Carson and Levi, who grew up in the small town and one way or another find their way back to their roots.

Like most authors I'm often asked where I get my ideas. Everywhere is usually my answer, from TV to movies to the news and everyday life. In 2011, Texas suffered through the worst drought in its history. Lakes, stock tanks and creeks dried up. Ranchers had no grass so they either sold their cattle for next to nothing or had hay trucked in from other states.

It was a scary time as wildfires were rampant. One was not far from our house. We could see smoke billowing to the sky and I thought about the people who had to evacuate their homes, and how traumatic that must be for them. I prayed no one was trapped in the fire. Every day there seemed to be news of another fire, another evacuation. In the summer of 2011, the germ of an idea began. I would write about a wildfire, and the story for *A Texas Hero* was born.

Ethan and Abby are two complete strangers thrown together by extraordinary circumstances. The story is about surviving in tragedy and in love. I hope once you start reading you'll be entertained to the very end.

With love and thanks,

Linda Warren

P.S. You can email me at Lw1508@aol.com or send me a message on Facebook (authorlindawarren) or Twitter (@texauthor). You can also write me at P.O. Box 5182, Bryan, TX 77805 or visit my website at www.lindawarren.net.

A Texas
Hero

———

Linda Warren

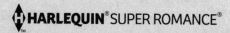

ISBN-13: 978-0-373-71861-0

A TEXAS HERO

HARLEQUIN®

™ www.Harlequin.com

Printed in U.S.A.

ABOUT THE AUTHOR

Linda Warren is addicted to happy endings, and to get her fix she spends her days weaving happy-ever-after love stories for Harlequin. She's a bestselling, two-time Rita®-nominated author and winner of the *RT Book Reviews* Reviewers' Choice Award, the National Readers' Choice Award, the Holt Medallion, the Booksellers' Best Award, the Book Buyers Best Award and the Golden Quill, but her readers and their support are her greatest reward. You can reach her at www.lindawarren.net.

Books by Linda Warren

HARLEQUIN SUPERROMANCE

HARLEQUIN AMERICAN ROMANCE

*The Belles Of Texas
**The Hardin Boys

ACKNOWLEDGMENTS

I would like to thank the many long-suffering people who answered my pesky questions about banks, robbery, wildfires, child custody, parental rights and police procedure. And especially to Melody for sharing her beautician skills. I learned something important while doing research: never ask a banker how to unlock the front door or open the vault. Not a good question to ask. All errors are strictly mine.

DEDICATION

I dedicate this book to the people of Texas who endured the drought of 2011. And to everyone who has dealt with the wrath of Mother Nature. God Bless.

CHAPTER ONE

ABBY BAUMAN BELIEVED in real forever love.

Until she got married.

That's when fantasy and reality collided like a chemistry experiment gone awry, stinking up the room and blowing out windows. That described her two-year marriage. It stunk. And blew all her dreams to hell.

Douglas Bauman, her ex-husband, did not know the meaning of the words *forever* and *monogamy*. Nor did he grasp the concept of the word *divorce*. After a year, he was still trying to weasel his way back into her life by manipulation, using their three-year-old daughter as leverage.

She swerved in and out of traffic like a Formula One driver, which she wasn't. If she got one more ticket she wouldn't be able to afford insurance. But thanks to her conniving ex, she was late.

Doug had Chloe every other weekend, and this was his weekend. As per his pattern, something had come up and he couldn't pick up their daughter until noon. She told him to forget it and that she would be talking to her lawyer on Monday to change the custody agreement. Hanging up before he could respond gave her little satisfaction. Once again, she had to call her father to ask him to babysit, which took a strip off her pride because she did not get along with her stepmom, who was a Sue Sylvester of *Glee* double. Gayle shouldn't be allowed around children.

Since Abby had to be at work at 8:15 a.m. and Doug had called at 7:15, she had few options. And it was a Saturday. Her friends had other plans or liked to sleep in on the weekends. As did Gayle.

Her dad lived twenty-five minutes away in Barton Springs, while she lived near downtown Austin, Texas. She had to ask him to pick up Chloe because there was no other way if she was to make it to work on time. As usual, he agreed. He was a sweetheart. She just hated to cause friction in his marriage. But frantically looking for a babysitter would change once she spoke to her lawyer on Monday. She wasn't putting up with any more of Doug's crap.

The light ahead was yellow. She pressed on the gas, zooming through, hoping no cops were in sight. This wasn't the first time Doug had bailed on keeping Chloe. It would be his last, though.

Her cell on the console buzzed and she pushed speaker phone. "Hi, Hol."

"Hey, girl. You ready for tonight? Wear something low-cut and short."

"I can't go." Since Doug had Chloe for the weekend, she and her friend had planned a girl's night out. She'd known Holly all her life. They'd met in kindergarten.

"Don't tell me he did it to you again?"

"Yes. I wish I had known you were up this early. I'd have dropped Chloe at your apartment. I had to call Dad again and you know how that goes."

"Sorry. You need a better lawyer, that's all. Someone who is not intimidated by the wealthy Baumans."

"I was thinking the same thing. Since you're a cop, maybe you can get me the name of a good lawyer just in case the one I have gives me any flak."

"You bet."

"Come over this afternoon and we'll take Chloe swimming in the apartment complex pool. Bring your rubber duckie."

"Oh, gee, I can hardly contain my excitement."

"Damn!"

"What?"

"I missed my turn." Without thinking, she slammed on the brakes. A loud thump followed that jarred her car.

"Damn!"

"What's going on?"

"Someone just rear-ended me. I'll call you later." She jumped out into traffic to see a man inspecting the damage to the front of his truck. He turned to glare at her.

"Why the hell did you stop?"

The early-morning August sun beamed down on them, but more heat seemed to be emanating from the stranger, rolling off his tall, lean body in waves of controlled anger. And it was directed at her.

"I missed my turn and…"

"So you just stopped on a busy highway?" She could almost read *stupid woman* in his narrowed dark eyes. He flung a hand toward his truck. "You're going to pay for this. This thing is new and you've scratched my bumper with your insane driving."

"Your bumper? Look at my trunk!" She lost her cool for a second but she quickly corralled her rising temper. Glancing at her watch, she realized she had eight minutes to get to work. That put everything into perspective. She needed her job. "Follow me to that bank." She pointed across the freeway. "I work there, and we can exchange information." Turning on her heel, she marched to her car.

In her rearview mirror she saw the what-the-hell look on his etched-in-granite face. His dark hair was slicked back and wet as if he'd just gotten out of the shower or had an early-morning swim. He was dressed for the heat in cargo shorts, Crocs and a white T-shirt that had Don't Mess With Me emblazoned on it. Yeah, she got the message. Jerk.

A slight clang echoed as she pulled away. She probably wouldn't be able to open her trunk now and she'd have to ask her dad for help. She really needed to find a handy boyfriend, but these days she viewed most guys as jerks. Good guys were out there and she wasn't giving up on finding one. But lately, that feeling of hope needed a resurrection. Maybe she could talk Holly into taking a mechanics class. Then she could fix her own vehicle. No man required.

She pulled into the parking lot of one of the branch convenient banks scattered across Austin. Mr. Harmon, the manager, pulled in beside her in his Buick. No sign of the big silver truck or the furious stranger. Had she lost him? That would be a stroke of luck, but luck was more inclined to slap her in the face.

"It's going to be another scorcher today, Abby," Mr. Harmon said as they walked to a side door. The man was in his sixties and after over thirty years in banking, he planned to retire in October and move to Florida to be near his daughter. He was easy to work for, and she would miss him.

"The weatherman said one hundred and two for the high today," she replied.

"Oh, heavens. It's a good thing we have air-conditioning."

The silver truck pulled into the parking area and the stranger strolled toward them with long, sure strides. He exuded strength, power and control. From his sun-kissed skin to his amazing biceps, he was obviously a man of action and loved the outdoors. Or maybe he spent a lot of time in a gym and a tanning salon. Either way, the arrogant Neanderthal was not her type.

As the stranger approached, Mr. Harmon said, "I'm sorry, sir. Only the drive-through is available on Saturdays. It will be opened shortly and you..."

"Oh, sorry." Abby hurried to explain. "I had a minor accident on the way here and I just needed to give him my insurance information." She dug in her purse for her business card, found a pen and scribbled the info on the back. Handing him the card, she said, "Call me Monday and we'll get everything straight." *And fix your itty-bitty scratch,* she added as an afterthought in her head. She didn't even want to think about her insurance rate going up.

He nodded and turned to walk away. The screech of tires drew their attention. A battered white van swerved into the lot and backed to the curb. The double doors flew open and two guys in Halloween masks holding handguns jumped out and ran to them.

"Open the door. Open the door!" they shouted.

A robbery!

Abby's heart jackknifed into her throat. Mr. Harmon's hand shook as he punched in the code and used his key to open the door. The robbers pushed them all inside.

The one wearing a gorilla mask pointed a gun at Mr. Harmon. "Open the vault. Now!"

Mr. Harmon's fair skin turned even paler, but he managed to open the vault. The bank didn't carry large amounts. Just enough to cash payroll checks, but it was probably more than the two would see in a lifetime.

The robber shoved Walmart bags at her. "Fill these up. Fast. And don't push any alarms and no color bombs. You got it?"

Abby nodded, entered the vault and threw wrapped twenties into the bag. Her hands shook and she kept repeating what she'd learned in classes for just this type of situation. *Stay calm. Do as asked. Do not risk your life.*

The last one stuck in her mind as she pushed the silent alarm. It was hard to detect and she flicked her hand across it as she pulled out stacks of twenties. She handed the guy two bags and just then a siren wailed in the distance.

The gorilla-masked guy shoved a gun in her face. She trembled. "Did you push an alarm?"

"N-o, no. You watched me the whole time."

He pressed the end of the barrel against her temple. The cold steel on her skin propelled rolls of shivers through her.

"If you did, bitch, it'll be the last thing you do." The odor of sweat mixed with marijuana clogged her nostrils.

"O-oh. Oh." Mr. Harmon clutched his chest and crumpled to the floor.

"Mr. Harmon!" She fell down by him to see if he was okay. He was so still. She wasn't sure he was breathing.

"Man, we gotta go," the one with the clown mask shouted. "The cops are coming."

The other robber grabbed her arm and yanked her to her feet. "We'll take her as a hostage. If she set off the alarm, she's gonna pay for it."

"Let's go! Let's go!"

The guy dragged her out of the vault. She couldn't think. Her mind was wrapped around a cold ball of fear.

"Come on, man," the stranger spoke up, cool as ice water. "She's a woman. She'll only slow you down. Take me."

"C'mon," the clown guy at the door yelled. "We're losing time. The cops will be here any second."

"We're taking both of them," the other robber decided, pushing them toward the door and to the van.

Never get into a van. Never get into a van. The warning ran through her mind and she dug in her heels. "I'm not getting in."

The gorilla guy slapped her hard across the face and knocked her halfway into the van. The stranger jumped him but was stopped when the man shoved a gun into his ribs.

"Get her into the van," the guy growled. "I'll deal with you later."

The stranger lifted her inside. He was gentle. That was the only thing that registered besides the sense of doom clogging her lungs. The doors slammed shut and they roared away onto the freeway.

The clown guy drove and the other one sat in the back with them. The van was dark. It took a moment for her eyes to adjust. A piece of dirty, stained carpet was on the floor and heat rose up from the hot highway, warming her backside. That was the least of her worries. Her jaw ached and she couldn't think clearly. *Chloe.* Her precious baby. Would she ever see her again?

Suddenly, the siren was closer and the wail was deafening. "Lookie there, Rudy, it's an ambulance. She didn't alert the cops."

"Shut up, you idiot. Now they know my name."

"So? Dead people don't talk."

The stranger moved beside her. "Stay calm," he whispered.

"What did you say to her?" Rudy demanded.

"It's damn hot in here," the stranger retorted. "Doesn't this thing have air-conditioning?"

Rudy waved the gun. "Shut your trap." He reached behind him and pulled out a roll of duct tape. "Tape his wrists together," he said to her.

She didn't move. The heat and gas fumes hampered her breathing.

"Now!" he screamed.

She dragged in air and reached for the tape. The stranger held his wrists together and she nervously wounded the tape around them. His hands were strong, his fingers lean.

"Tighter," Rudy yelled.

She pulled until her arms hurt and then she used her teeth to rip into it. The stranger's dark eyes watched her. There was something in them she couldn't define. A message, maybe. *Trust me.* Or was she reading what she wanted to see?

"Holy shit, Rudy," the driver called. "There go four police cars and a SWAT van. The old man must have woken up and called them. Too bad, suckers. We're long gone."

The van rolled to a stop.

"What the hell you stopping for?"

"Red light, dude."

"Watch the man so I can tie up the woman."

The vehicle was basically a shell with two seats. The driver pointed a gun at them and Rudy whipped the tape around her wrists. He still had on the mask and all she could see were his dull green eyes staring at her from behind a gorilla face. Goose bumps popped up on her skin.

"Hey, dude, we got a looker here. I might keep her." He ran his hand up her arm and she jerked away. "She's feisty, too."

"Leave her alone," the stranger snapped

"Shut up," Rudy hissed, "or I'll tape your mouth."

"There's a cop car behind us," the driver said as they moved through the light.

"What the frickin' hell?" Rudy looked out the small back windows. "His light's blinking. Don't stop."

"No way. I can lose him," the driver bragged.

"He's going around us."

"Yeah, Rudy. He's turning around up ahead. Must be heading to the bank to give assistance. Sucker! Cops are idiots."

"Turn off this damn highway," Rudy ordered. "And follow the route I told you."

The van swerved onto another road and then another and Abby knew they were miles away from the bank…away from safety. Suddenly they turned onto a dirt road and bounced along on uneven ground, knocking her against the stranger, except he didn't feel like a stranger anymore.

He watched the gunman as if waiting to catch him off guard. But what could he do? His hands were tied, literally.

The van hit a pothole and her body slammed against the stranger's. Her shoulder pressed into his and her thigh molded to his tight muscles. His strength radiated to her and her grip of fear lessened. She wasn't in this alone. He was her ally. Her prince? Oh, God, had the heat twisted her brain? But he would be her only hope in the hours ahead.

And she didn't even know his name.

ETHAN JAMES WATCHED the robber, reading him like he had so many other criminals. His teeth were yellow, his fingertips yellower and his eyes were dull and bloodshot. A drug-head.

Which meant he was capable of anything—and he was dangerous. Ethan had to be careful.

The woman was holding up well. No crying, screaming or panic attacks. She had to stay calm if they were going to make it out of this ordeal alive. The odds were against them. Two armed druggies, and one of them had his eye on her. This was a highly volatile situation, and there was nothing he could do but try to protect her.

Would he risk his life for hers? He had a daughter at home to think about—a kid who was a stranger to him and seemed to hate him. But since he'd won full custody, he was trying to be a good father. He'd never had that chance before.

He promised to take Kelsey horseback riding this morning. Another promise broken. His whole life was riddled with them, and most of them were out of his control. Because he always put his job first.

He glanced at the woman who sat in a petrified state. Why in the hell had she stopped short? Now he might never see his daughter again. The woman was beautiful, he'd give her that. A blue-eyed blonde with inviting curves like he'd seen in numerous magazines—made to look at but not touch.

Her hair hung to her shoulders and dripped with sweat, as his did. A sleeveless green top was cut low, too low for guys with trouble on their minds. The filth in the van stained her white slacks. He was annoyed with her, yet empathetic at the same time. This kind of situation wasn't easy for the strongest of women. Or even the strongest of men.

He tried to gauge how long they'd been on the road, but wasn't quite sure. On and on they rode. Branches rubbed against the van so he knew they were in a remote area. That wasn't good. Too much could happen away from civilization. They came to a sudden stop and the double doors opened. "Get out," Rudy shouted.

Ethan scooted to the door and stood. He turned to help the woman but she was right behind him. After the semidarkness of the van, the sun was blinding. He blinked several times to adjust his eyes. The woman stumbled but maintained her balance.

A run-down shack was in front of him. Dried dead weeds surrounded it. No one had been here in a long time. Rudy shoved them toward a broken step. The door was half open, the lock rusted shut. Floorboards creaked as they went inside. A rat the size of a raccoon ran across the floor.

"Oh." The woman stepped back, but didn't scream or fall apart. He admired that. The rat was a little too big for his comfort zone, too.

"Sit down," Rudy ordered.

The dirty floor was uncomfortable, but they were out of the hot van and able to breathe. Ethan took in the tiny room at a glance. Part of the roof had caved in over the sink. The refrigerator looked rusted shut, too. Two steel bunk beds with rotted mattresses stood in a corner. Junk littered the wobbly plank floor, and the glass in the two windows was broken out. An abandoned deer-hunter's cabin, was his thought. How were the two hoods connected to it?

"Don't even think about moving," Rudy warned and walked out the door.

Ethan eased to his feet to listen and maybe get a glimpse of their faces. The masks had to be hot. He heard their voices.

"I'm sweating bullets in this mask." That was the driver.

"Take it off. We don't need them anymore," Rudy told him.

"What are we gonna do?"

"This sounded good last night when I was high." Rudy removed his mask. "Man, the boss is gonna be pissed."

"Who cares? We've got the money and we'll head to Houston and get lost."

"I'm taking the woman with me." Rudy made that clear.

"You're stupid, man. I didn't agree on no kidnapping. She'll get us caught."

"Shut up."

Ethan took a quick peep. They stood by the van. Rudy was white, the other guy black, but he already knew that from their hands. He had to get the woman out of here and fast. Rudy was determined to have her.

He stepped over beer cans to the window and saw nothing but thick woods. This was their way out and they had to take it quickly.

"What are you doing?" the woman whispered.

"We're crawling out this window," he whispered back.

"Our hands are tied."

"A minor problem," he replied. "C'mon. We have to go before they come back."

After a bit of a struggle, she got to her feet and walked to him.

"Balance with your hands and swing your legs over the sill. I'll help."

"I can do it," she snapped.

"Lady, I'm the only friend you got so don't be short with me."

"Sorry. I'm just on edge."

"We don't have time for this. Go! Once outside, run into the woods, and don't look back, even if they capture me, even if they shoot at you. Keep running. Hide. Anything to save yourself because, lady, you don't want to experience what these guys have in mind for you."

She visibly paled.

"Go!"

She slid one long leg over the dust-covered ledge, balanced with her clasped hands and slid out kind of sideways, but she'd done it. Thank God she wore flats. High heels would have made running away impossible.

He followed and had to bend low to get his body through the hole. Then he was off running behind her. Shots rang out, disturbing the stillness of the trees. Disturbing his equilibrium. He caught up with her.

"I can't breathe," she gasped.

He had that problem, too. The heat was suffocating, and he knew they had to stop or collapse from it. They came to a gully and slid down it. He took her clasped hands and pulled her up the other side. They gulped in hot air.

Voices echoed through the trees.

"We have to go. Walk on the leaves. Try not to disturb them." She followed orders easily and he liked that. The woods grew thicker and difficult to get through. "We have to find a hiding place."

"Where?" She looked at the dense woods all around them.

He pushed through thick yaupons and saw a felled oak tree with more yaupons growing around it. "C'mon." The tree was big and had been dead for some time. "We'll hide behind this." He pulled back some branches and they crawled in. "Lie lengthways against the trunk, your taped hands out in front, and don't make a sound." She stretched out against the trunk and he joined her—their hands inches apart.

Voices rumbled through the dense woods.

"Have you found them?" Rudy shouted.

"No, man. Let's get the hell out of here. This ain't part of our plan."

"Screw the plan." Rudy's voice rose. "Shoot the guy. The woman is mine."

CHAPTER TWO

ABBY HUGGED THE rotted tree trunk with her body. Dust clogged her nose, and dirt coated her skin and clothes. Vivid terror held her captive like a ball and chain clamped to her. It beat a rapid warning in her chest.

She inched her fingers along the ground, through the leaves to touch the man's hands. He clutched hers. He was there... with her. The thought gave her courage, which she feared she would need in the next few minutes.

"They have to be here somewhere," Rudy said. "Help me look."

"I'm done, man. I'm taking the money and leaving."

"You better not."

"The woman's only trouble. She'll get us caught, Rudy, and I'm not going back to prison."

"You sorry bastard."

"So long, sucker."

"Devon!"

A gunshot rang out followed by a curse. Then a barrage of bullets slammed into the woods. A couple of shots hit the tree and the dried wood splintered over them. Neither moved or made a sound, but she gripped the man's fingers tighter.

"You sorry sons of bitches, I hope you die out here," Rudy screamed, and then the pounding of footfalls receded into the distance. Still neither one of them moved.

Neither wanted to die.

Silence was crucial.

Creep-crawly bugs swarmed out of the tree, covering their

arms. Were they termites? Did they bite? The feel of them on
her skin made her want to scream, but she knew her very life
depended on her not responding.

The silence stretched. A soft rustling was the only sound.
Sweat ran from her hair onto her neck and the heat was stifling. Breathing was difficult. She had to get out of here. Away
from the bugs. The heat. Panic rose in her chest, but reality
kept her grounded.

She lifted her head from her arm. "Are they gone?" came
out barely audible.

"I'll check." He looked over the trunk and surveyed the
scene. Then they both heard the sound—the revving of a motor.
"They're leaving."

"Both of them?"

"I'm not sure, but we have to get this tape off our hands."
They shook off the bugs and crawled through the yaupons into
a small opening. They sat in the dirt while he kept one eye on
the woods, in case Rudy was lurking behind a tree.

With his teeth, he caught the edge of the tape on his wrists
and pulled. Scooting closer, she used her fingers to help undo
it. Then he helped her free her hands. The tape left open welts
on her skin, but she was glad to be free of it.

"Now what?" she asked, instinctively knowing he would
know what to do.

"We start walking." He rose to his feet, as did she. Slowly,
they trekked through the woods, down the gully and back to
the shack. The van was gone and the dried grass torn apart
where the men had sped away. "They're gone," he said. "I guess
Rudy decided to go with the money."

Sweat rolled down her back and pooled at her waistline.
She was miserable, but at his words relief washed over her.

They were gone.

All the courage she had mustered and the fear she'd bottled
up inside burst forth into an array of weakness she couldn't
control. Her body trembled and tears rolled from her eyes.

"Hey." He touched her arm. "No tears. It's dehydrating. Take a deep breath and keep all that moisture inside. You can't fall apart now."

"I...I..." She couldn't form a sentence and she felt so weak in front of this strong man.

"C'mon. Let's sit under a shade tree and figure out what we need to do."

She sank down under a huge live oak, willing the tears away as she tried to regain control of her emotions. "I'm so thirsty," she murmured.

"Me, too." He sat beside her and drew up his knees. His legs and arms had scratches from the trees and she realized her arms were scratched, too. Yet he seemed cool as ever, unruffled about what they'd been through.

"Who are you?"

He looked at her and his dark eyes were tired, the first signs of stress she'd noticed. "Ethan James."

"Thank you" was all she could say. After a moment, she found more words. "I'm so grateful you insisted on coming. I don't know what would have happened to me if you hadn't."

He lifted an eyebrow. "I wanted to make sure I get my bumper fixed."

Through all her agony, she smiled. "I'll fix it with my own two hands."

They stared at each other for a long time and Abby felt a connection like she'd never felt before—a connection of trust and friendship. And above that she knew she could depend on him. Words like *honor, loyalty* and *hero* floated through her mind. She didn't think there were men like him left. Of course, she could be delusional. But she still wanted to know more about him.

"What do you do, Ethan James?"

"I'm a detective for the Austin Police Department. I work homicide."

It fit. "That's why you're so cool and collected."

"I was in the Marines, too. The first thing you learn is to never show fear."

"You have that mastered."

"On the outside. Inside is a different story." He leaned forward, scanning the landscape, and she knew he wasn't going to talk anymore about himself. "We have two goals—to find water and a way out."

"The police will be looking for us."

"Yeah, but they don't have a clue where we are. Our only hope is that there are surveillance cameras in the bank and…"

"Inside and out," she said.

"Good. Then maybe that van will show up on the cameras and the cops can trace it. But that doesn't help us unless Rudy or Devon tells them where they left us. They'll deny it at first. All criminals do. The detectives will have to apply pressure and that will take time."

"You mean we could be out here overnight?"

"Yes." He got to his feet. "I'm guessing this is an old deer-hunter's cabin that hasn't been used for a while. The gully is probably a creek that dried up from the drought. But I'm hoping the hunters had access to another water supply. I'll take a look around."

He walked toward the shack and she had the urge to run after him. But she knew he wouldn't leave her here. Strange, how she was so sure of that. She leaned her head against the tree and wondered if her father had been notified. Her heart ached at what he must be going through. He was strong, though, and would take care of Chloe. She was sure of that. Just like she was sure Ethan James would get them out of this nightmare.

The hot sun bore down like a furnace and she guessed it had to be midmorning by now. She'd left the house in such a hurry earlier that she'd forgotten her watch. In the afternoon the sun would be unbearable, and they would not be able to survive without water.

She was tired and thirsty and a feeling of lethargy washed

over her. If she closed her eyes, she'd wake up in her apartment holding Chloe and watching SpongeBob SquarePants. The morning would all be a bad dream. Because men like Ethan James only appeared in women's fantasies. They didn't exist in real life.

"You KNEW WE had plans for the day. Why did you agree to keep Chloe?"

Everett Baines looked up from his paper into the furious face of his wife. "Abby needed help and I'm her father. I will always be there for her."

"But we had plans."

"Picking out new patio furniture? We can do that tomorrow or the next day."

"You always put them before me—your wife."

"Gayle, I'm not having this conversation with you again." He picked up his coffee cup. "I'm going to watch cartoons with my granddaughter."

"I'm still going shopping."

"Fine. Buy whatever you want." He walked into the den, placed his cup on the end table, and picked up his granddaughter from the sofa. Abby had her dressed in pink shorts, a pink-and-white halter top, white sandals and pink bows in her blond hair. Chloe clutched Baby, her favorite doll.

"Is Daddy coming, Grandpa?" she asked.

"No, sweetiepie. Your mom will pick you up."

"'Kay."

Everett had offered to pay for a top-notch lawyer, but Abby always refused. Because of Gayle. This time he wasn't taking no for an answer. Doug's lawyer controlled the situation and the visitation set out in the divorce papers. Which meant nothing to Doug, who did as he pleased. When Abby complained, the lawyers talked but nothing changed. That wasn't acceptable anymore.

Sitting in his chair, he cradled Chloe close. She looked so

much like Abby had at that age, blond curls and big blue eyes. Thank God she didn't look anything like her father.

"Aren't you going to feed her breakfast?" Gayle asked from behind him. "Abby lets her eat all that sugary cereal. It's not good for her."

"Go shopping, Gayle, before I lose my temper."

The doorbell rang before she could get in a retort. "I'll get it," Gayle said. "Maybe it's Doug for Chloe and then we can have our weekend back."

He hated to tell her but he wasn't going shopping under any circumstances. Abby's last words were for him not to let Doug have Chloe. And he would honor her wishes. Doug needed to be taught a lesson.

Two tall men with Stetsons in their hands walked into the den. One had a gun on his belt as well as a badge. A cop. Something was wrong.

"Everett, these men would like to talk to you."

He got to his feet, holding Chloe.

"I'll take Chloe and fix her something to eat," Gayle offered.

"You don't have to do that," he replied, but didn't object as she took the little girl from him.

"Have a seat." He waved a hand toward the sofa and resumed his. "What's this about?"

The men sat, but it was a moment before either spoke. "It's about your daughter, Mr. Baines," the one with the badge told him.

"Abby." He scooted to the edge of his seat, the hollowness in his stomach telling him it was something bad. "She's at work."

"That's why we're here. I'm Ross Logan with the Austin Police Department and this is Levi Coyote, a private investigator."

He shook his head. "What does this have to do with my daughter?"

"I don't know how else to say this, sir, but the bank where your daughter works was robbed this morning."

"Oh, God! My d-daughter. Where's my daughter?"

"She was taken hostage."

"What!" His chest tightened in pain and he leaned back, clutching it.

Both men were on their feet.

"Mr. Baines, are you okay?" Ross asked.

"Everett!" Gayle screamed.

He gathered himself and sat up. "I'm fine."

"No, you're not. I'm calling your doctor," Gayle insisted.

"Do not call my doctor," he warned. "It's just the shock."

"Do you have heart problems, Mr. Baines?" Levi asked.

"No. I had a spell one time, but the doctor said it was anxiety. I have a lot of stress in my life."

"Maybe you should get checked out," Ross suggested.

"No. Tell me what happened."

The detective hesitated.

"Tell me."

Gayle handed him a glass of water. He took a sip and placed the glass by his coffee.

"The silent alarm went off at 8:14 a.m. this morning. Officers arrived at 8:17 a.m. to find the door unlocked and Frank Harmon on the floor in the vault."

"Is he okay?"

"He's had a massive heart attack and is at the hospital. We haven't gotten an update on his condition, but he's critical."

"Good God."

"Your daughter's purse and phone were on the floor of the vault. We're assuming that's where she pushed the alarm."

"Oh, what she must have gone through." Everett put his head in his hands.

"Does your daughter know Ethan James?"

Everett raised his head. "No. I don't recognize the name. Who is he?"

"His truck was found at the bank."

"So he's involved with the robbery?"

"No, sir," Ross replied. "He's my partner and a detective.

His wallet and phone were in his truck, but he's nowhere to be found."

He frowned. "What does this mean?"

"We're thinking Ethan and Ms. Bauman were taken as hostages."

"Why would the robbers do that? I've been in banking all of my adult life and robbers are not known for taking hostages. It's excess baggage and slows them down."

"We're not sure about that, but we'll known more soon."

He looked them in the eye. "Oh, but you do know, don't you? My daughter is very beautiful and they took her for dire reasons."

They didn't dispute that and his blood ran cold.

"Mr. Baines, Ethan is with her and if anyone can get her out of that situation, he can. He's a former marine, tough and smart."

"I admire your confidence, Mr. Logan, but…"

Levi squatted in front of him. "Ethan and I grew up together and I know him well enough to say he will sacrifice his life to save your daughter's. Hang on to that. Be positive. We'll keep you posted and notify you the moment we locate them."

"Thank you. I appreciate that. Could I please have a number to call to get updates?"

Ross scribbled something on a business card and handed it to him. "That's my cell."

"Thank you."

"The investigators are going through the digital video from the surveillance cameras. We're hoping to get an ID of the vehicle they used or anything that can point us in the right direction. We'll be in contact." They walked toward the foyer, but Ross turned back. "We found Douglas Bauman's cell number in your daughter's purse. He didn't answer our call and we didn't leave a message."

"He's her ex and not involved in her life in any way, except with their daughter. Do not waste your time on him."

Ross nodded. "As you wish."

With extreme effort Everett got to his feet. Gayle put her arms around him. "I'm so sorry."

He pulled away. "No, you're not. You're finally going to get your wish, Gayle. The next call I receive might be to tell me my daughter is dead. She'll be out of our lives for good."

"How can you say such a thing?"

"Because it's true." He waved a hand around the room. "We have a four-bedroom, five-bath home and my daughter has never spent one night here. I've asked dozens of times, especially when I keep Chloe so Abby can go out and have fun like other young women, but she refuses. She knows you don't want her here. You don't want my only child in any part of our lives."

"That's not true! She doesn't like me."

"Oh, please. I'm tired of listening to that excuse. I'm just tired of the tension you create. Now I'm going to hold my granddaughter and pray like I've never prayed before." He spared her a glance. "And you can go shopping."

ETHAN CANVASSED THE place, but found nothing useful. Everything was old, rusted and bug-infested. He strolled back to the woman. She'd fallen asleep leaning against the tree, her head tilted to the left. Her hair, matted with leaves and dirt, hung in rattails around her face. The left side of her face was badly bruised where the bastard had hit her. Her arms bore scratches from tree branches and her clothes were filthy. Even with all that, it was hard to disguise her beauty.

He was good at reading people. He'd guess she was a sorority girl who'd led a privileged life. But that didn't quite fit. She worked in a bank, so that meant she was a working girl, supporting herself or her family. And she had an inner strength he'd noticed right away. Not many women would have had the nerve to say to his face that they didn't have time to deal with the wreck and to meet them at the bank. He'd thought of arresting her for being so damn cheeky.

Whoever she was, he knew someone she loved was getting bad news right about now, like his dad and Kelsey. The last thing his kid needed was to have her father go missing.

He eased down by the woman and she instantly woke up, blinked, looked at him and then closed her eyes tightly.

"This isn't a dream, is it?" she asked.

"Afraid not."

She opened her eyes and he was struck by how blue they were. He felt he could see all the way to heaven through them—and he wasn't a poetic man. Since he'd sworn off women about two years ago, he found that odd and disturbing. He wasn't interested in the woman. In his experience, even the nicest of women turned into a bitch once the honeymoon period ended.

"Did you find any water? Anything?"

"Nope. There's an old well, but the rusted pump has caved into it. It's useless."

"So, what do we do?"

"We walk out of here and try to survive in this heat."

"That's impossible without water."

"We have to stay in the shade and take breaks. Who knows—" he added at her despondent look "—there could be a convenience store just beyond those trees."

"Yeah, right."

From her tone, he sensed the woman didn't want him to sugarcoat anything so he'd stick to the facts. "I'm guessing we were in the van from thirty to forty minutes so we're out of Austin and apparently deep into deer country, but where I have no idea. We turned right from the bank. That means we headed south, and then we turned east, but there were so many turns after that I lost track." He looked at her. "I'm sorry. I didn't catch your name."

"Abby Bauman."

"Of the banking Baumans?"

"I married Douglas Bauman, Jr., but we've been divorced for over a year."

"And you have to work?"

"I didn't want anything from him but my freedom and custody of our daughter."

"How did that work out?"

She glared at him. "You're…very abrupt. I guess it comes from your line of work."

He studied the tight lines around her full lips. "I think you meant to say I'm *a bastard,* and you'd be right. A lot of my attitude comes from my job. I deal with the seedier, horrific side of life. And it isn't pretty or uplifting."

"Then why do it?"

"It's who I am. A hard-nosed bastard who's gonna get you if you're stupid enough to cross a line to kill someone and think you can get away with it."

Her baby blues opened wide. "I've come to the conclusion that all men are jerks and you've just proven my point." She wiggled her hand back and forth. "With you, though, it might be borderline insanity."

"You could be right."

"I'm sorry. That was rude." She changed her mind a lot, as most women were known to do.

"Ah, lady, you're…"

"Don't call me lady," she snapped. "My name is Abby."

"Well, Abby, it takes a lot more than that to hurt my feelings. You want to know what really gets me upset? It's when an airhead stops in the middle of a damn highway."

"Don't call me an airhead."

He shrugged, realizing they both were venting their frustrations of the morning on each other.

"I'm sorry I stopped like that. Doug has our daughter every other weekend and he pulled a no-show like he usually does. I had to scramble to call my dad to take care of Chloe and to get to work on time. I was fuming and missed my turn. I'll admit I wasn't thinking, but I'm really grateful you were at the bank this morning. And it was incredibly heroic of you to offer to take my place."

She did the unexpected with her honesty, took him out of his don't-get-involved comfort zone and made him see her as a person with everyday problems. He didn't like that she did it so easily. "Lady, I—" He held up a hand as she made to object. "Abby, I'm not a hero. I'm just trying to get us out of this situation alive."

One eyebrow arched. "You really *are* a bastard."

"Remember that and you and I will get along fine."

"Jerk."

He scooted up against the tree, his shoulder touching hers. "Save all that energy for later."

"What do you mean?"

"We have to walk out of here in the heat."

"How will we know where to go?"

"We'll follow the trail the van made coming in and out. Hopefully, we'll come to a dirt road and we can flag someone down."

"We can do it, right?"

"Yep."

He looked into her concerned blue eyes and saw a lot more than he wanted to. Femininity. Beauty. Strength. Trouble. His defenses were rock-solid against the fairer sex. He'd been burned too many times to let his guard down. But there was something about her that made him feel weak. And that brought out the true bastard in him. There was no way a woman was taking advantage of him again.

CHAPTER THREE

WALTON JAMES GLANCED at the wall clock in the kitchen one more time. After eleven. Ethan had said he'd be home at least by nine and to make sure Kelsey was up and ready to go riding. The poor kid had been in the kitchen three times to ask if Ethan was home.

She didn't call him Dad or Daddy and he supposed that was understandable since they'd just met two years ago, but it grated on the one good nerve he still had. It was just plain disrespectful.

The girl's attitude was a little hard to take, but Ethan had asked him to make an effort to get along. And he'd do anything for his boy, even put the skids on his cussing. He was an old cowboy and cowboys cussed. That was just a fact. Facing seventy, he was doing his best to tame his colorful tongue.

He glanced at the clock again. Where was Ethan?

A knock sounded at the door and he ambled toward it. Ross Logan, Ethan's partner, and Levi Coyote, a friend and neighbor, stood outside.

"What are you boys doing here? Ethan with you?" He looked around them, but only saw Rowdy, his blue heeler, wagging his tail for another biscuit. He'd already given him two. He wasn't getting any more.

"Walt, could we talk to you for a minute?" Levi asked.

"Sure. Come on in." He followed them into the living room and sat on the edge of his recliner while they eased onto the brown tweed sofa. Walt knew trouble. He'd seen it a lot of times in his life. And he was looking square at it in the eyes of Ross and Levi.

"Just tell me about Ethan. Where is he? I know that's why you're here."

"Have you had the TV on this morning? Or a radio?" Ross asked.

"Nope. I had calves to feed and then I fixed breakfast for Kelsey. Ethan said he'd be here by nine and I've been waiting and waiting." He looked directly at Levi because he knew the man would give him a straight answer. "What happened to my son?"

Levi twisted the hat in his hand. "There was a bank robbery off I-35 this morning. Ethan's truck was parked outside, but he's nowhere to be found. A woman teller is missing, too."

"Holy…sh—crap."

Levi's lips twitched. "Still trying to curb those curse words?"

"Yeah. And there's a bunch burning my tongue right now. What was Ethan doing at a bank? He didn't say anything about stopping. He was anxious to get home to Kelsey."

"We don't have any answers yet, but…" Ross's cell rang. He stood as he talked. Closing his phone, he said, "Gotta go. A white van was identified on the security cameras. I want to be with the SWAT team when they make contact with the owner."

"I'll call you later, Walt." Levi followed Ross to the door.

"Just bring my son home safe."

"Ethan's been kidnapped?" Kelsey asked from the hall doorway.

Walt had to blink every time he looked at his granddaughter. Long black hair hung around her face. Dyed black hair. That crazy mother of hers let the child dye her hair with a purple streak. Her T-shirt and jeans were black, as were her fingernails and toenails. It felt like an alien had been dropped among them.

Levi took a step toward her. "We'll do everything we can to find him."

"Like I care." She turned on her heel and marched back to her room, slamming the door.

Walt pointed a finger at Levi. "Find Ethan and bring him home. My patience is wearing about as thin as the hair on my head."

"Try not to worry," Levi told him.

"Yeah. That's what the bobcat said to the chicken right before he took a big bite."

"I'll call as soon as I know anything."

Walt went out the back door to the wood deck Ethan had built for Kelsey, complete with a barbecue pit and lawn furniture so she could have friends over. He'd also installed a trampoline. Kelsey never used any of them. She stayed locked in her room watching vampire movies. He'd always wanted a grandchild, but he never dreamed it would be like this.

He sank into a cushioned redwood chair and buried his face in his hands. His boy had to come home. And then he did something he hadn't done in a long time. He prayed.

ABBY FOLLOWED ETHAN'S rigid back through the woods. Her sweat-soaked body ached, but she trudged on, determined not to slow them down. She hoped her dad wasn't too worried. He'd had a spell with his heart a few months ago and she didn't want it to turn into something more. Dealing with Doug wasn't going to be easy. He'd demand to take Chloe, if only to show the world he was a good father and to prove Abby was inept as a mother.

Her game plan of the morning had changed drastically. Doug would appear all concerned but he would use the morning's events against her when it came to custody of Chloe. Her job was dangerous; he'd said that so many times, especially since there had been a rash of bank robberies lately.

She'd been a vice president in the corporate offices of the Bauman bank. When she had Chloe, she'd stayed at home to be a mom. Even after the divorce was final, Doug continually pleaded for her to come back to her old job where it was safe, but she stuck to her guns of being independent and on her own. Being a teller was a long way from her cushy job.

Instead of thinking of the past, she concentrated on the man ahead of her. He really went out of his way to be rude. Why would he do that? She'd read somewhere that victims often fell in love with their rescuers. That was one concern he didn't have to worry about. She wasn't in the mood to fall in love, especially with a hard-ass like him.

She couldn't help but wonder what had happened in his life to make him so harsh and disillusioned about women. In that area they had a lot in common. She wasn't sure if she knew what love was anymore.

God, she was so thirsty. And hot. When was he going to stop? No sooner than the thought had left her mind, he stopped, and, of course, she ran into him.

"Oh." She stepped back. "You startled me." His back was like a wall of steel. She'd never touched anything that powerful, and she was really glad he was on her side. Or, at least, she thought he was. Sometimes it was difficult to tell.

"Time for a break," he said and slid to the ground beneath a huge oak. He sat, his back against the tree, his arms by his sides, his legs outstretched—totally at rest.

"How far do you think we've walked?" she asked, sitting beside him.

"Maybe two miles."

"And nothing but more woods."

"Yep."

"This is frustrating."

"Yep."

"Do you think our families have been notified?"

"Yep."

She gritted her teeth and immediately stopped when she realized how bad her jaw hurt. "Can't you say something besides *yep?*"

"Nope."

He was one cantankerous man. "It's just you and me out here. You could be a little more cordial."

"This isn't a party." He turned his head and she looked into his dark, dark eyes. It was like staring into the darkest of nights and seeing nothing, but feeling the power all around her. Fear. Frustration. Warmth.

She had to search deep to find the warmth, but it was there. And if she looked long enough she felt she'd find that Ethan James was a soft cuddly puppy inside—all warm and loving. A side this hard-nosed cop never showed to anyone.

"Some woman really did a number on you." She hadn't realized she'd spoken the words out loud until she heard them coming out of her mouth.

"Yep."

She laughed and it startled her. She didn't think she had any laughter left in her.

His eyes narrowed. "You find that funny?"

"Yep," she replied in his stern, husky voice.

The corner of his mouth twitched ever so slightly, but she saw it.

"You know you're not the only one who has had their heart stomped on."

"Listen, lady…"

"You keep calling me lady even though I've asked you not to. Somehow you feel if you say my name it makes our relationship personal. Let me tell you something, we've been through a bank robbery and barely escaped with our lives. That's personal and frightening and anything else you want to tag on to it, but if you think I'm going to fall madly in love with you because of it, you better think again, Mr. Hard As Nails. I've had one jerkface in my life and I'm not looking for another."

"Are you through?"

"No. If you keep yepping me, I'm gonna yep you right back."

He stared at her and she stared back. "I can't imagine anyone taking advantage of you, with your fiery tongue."

"I was very naive back then. Did your mother ever read fairy tales to you?"

"What?"

"Fairy tales. Cinderella? Sleeping Beauty?"

"Hell, no."

"You're lying, Ethan James."

"Well, yeah, she read me stories like Cowboy Billy and horse ones. I didn't pay attention to the others."

"I did. I dreamed of one day finding my prince. He'd be handsome, charming, compassionate, have a great sense of humor and high values and morals. We'd fall madly in love, get married and live happily ever after on Fairy Tale Lane." She stuck a finger in her mouth and pretended to gag. "I can't believe I was that stupid but, sadly, I was a clone of millions of women looking for a prince and ending up with a big toad."

"He cheated on you?"

"Yeah, but not with his heart. Only his body."

"That's an old line."

"Oh, Doug has hundreds."

"How did you find out?"

"Quite unexpectedly. Since Doug is an executive in his dad's banking empire, he travels a lot. He'd returned from a four-day weekend in Florida and he was exhausted. He said it was business meeting after business meeting. The next day I was scrapbooking some of Chloe's baby pictures into an album and I ran out of paper. I went online to order it because I knew they didn't have it at the store. I'd already looked."

She lifted her wet hair from her hot neck and prayed for a breeze to cool the heated emotions churning in her. But the air was still and blistering in the woods.

"I had two emails from someone I didn't know, and usually I would just delete them, but for some reason I opened the first one and received the shock of my life. It was a video of my husband and a woman who works in his office. They were naked and having sex. I sat in a stupor and opened the other one, which was more of the same. I downloaded it to a flash drive and my phone. I then packed my clothes and Chloe's and left. I drove to the bank and withdrew a large sum of money from our checking account. My dad is also in banking so I went to his bank and asked him to deposit the money in his name so the Baumans couldn't touch it."

She drew a long breath. "I left Chloe with Dad and went back to the Bauman bank. I delivered the flash drive to Doug, told him my lawyer would be in touch and not to call me or try to get in touch."

"Your marriage was over just like that?"

"No. It was a god-awful year before it was over. The judge ordered counseling and the Baumans got involved, begging me to forgive Doug's one-time lapse. They wanted me to think of Chloe and how much Doug loved us."

"You didn't bend under the pressure?"

"No. The moment I saw Doug on my computer screen with that woman, he killed whatever love I had for him."

"People do make mistakes. Maybe he regrets his lapse."

She studied the strong lines of his face. "Are you kidding me?"

"You loved him until you saw the video. Anger has just clouded your feelings."

She scooted to her knees beside him. "So, cheating is just something men do. It's part of their nature. Women should overlook it. The poor soul couldn't help himself."

"I didn't say that."

"Oh, I think you did, Mr. Everything Goes Tom Cat."

"Listen, lady…"

"Abby."

"Could you please shut up? We need to conserve our energy."

"Fine." She scooted back against the tree. "I don't want to talk to someone like you, anyway."

Nothing was a said for a few minutes. Abby wasn't so hot or tired anymore. She was just mad at his pompous attitude. She didn't end her marriage because she was hurt. Their marriage vows had been irrevocably broken. She could never trust Doug again and without trust they had nothing.

Then it hit her. She turned to look at the stoic macho male beside her. "You cheated on your wife, didn't you?"

"I've never been married," he said without even looking at her. "But I have a kid."

"Oh." All types of scenarios whizzed through her head.

"I thought you were going to be quiet."

"I lied," she replied tongue-in-cheek. "Women do that. It's in our nature."

"I know."

The way he said that gave her pause. Those two words echoed with a lot of hurt and pain. "Who lied to you?"

He turned to her, his eyes fever-dark and she felt dizzy at all the emotions she saw there. "Abby…"

"Yes, Abby. That's not so hard, is it?"

"I liked it better when you were mad at me."

She lifted an eyebrow. "That can change at any minute."

"Yep."

She poked him in the ribs. "Don't start that." She stood on her knees again and leaned back on her heels. "Tell me about the woman who lied to you."

ETHAN WOULD HAVE sworn on a stack of Bibles that he would never talk about his past, especially to the most aggravating woman in the world, but before he knew it, words tumbled from his mouth.

"I was in the Marines and home on leave. When I returned to the San Diego base, I still had a couple of days left before reporting for duty. My buddy and I decided to have a fun weekend before shipping out to Afghanistan. We hooked up with two girls in a bar. Unfortunately, my date was Sheryl Winger. Two months later I got a letter from her. I don't know how she got my address, but she did. She was pregnant and wanted money. What she really wanted was to have my check mailed to her. That didn't fly. I did send her money and told her I would take care of the baby."

"She gave you the child?"

"Not exactly. I sent her money for three months and then I got a letter saying she'd made a mistake. The baby wasn't mine. I was happy to be off the hook and swam away without giving it another thought. I told my commander about it though and he said it was a scheme to get my check. There really wasn't a baby."

"But there was?"

"Oh, yeah. About ten years later I heard from her again. She wanted ten years of child support. I wanted a DNA test."

"The child was yours?"

"Yep. By then I'd hired a killer attorney and Sheryl received no money and I got full custody of Kelsey. Except Sheryl disappeared with Kelsey. When she knew the cops were closing in, she dumped Kelsey on my doorstep with one suitcase. In front of Kelsey, she said I could have the smart-mouthed kid."

"How awful."

"I did a background check on Sheryl and she'd used Kelsey in several attempts to extort money from marines. Kelsey stayed with Sheryl's mother until she passed away. Kelsey was nine then. The kid has had it pretty rough and is filled with so much anger. I'm not sure I did her any favors by fighting for her." He got to his feet. "We have to move on."

"Ethan, I'm so sorry."

"Yeah. Everybody is. Let's go." He was tired of talking. It served no purpose but to dredge up his own anger.

She fell into step beside him. "I understand your attitude toward women a little better."

"I don't need you to understand me. I need you to follow orders so we can find our way back to our families. Do you think you can handle that?"

He walked off, leaving her with her mouth gaping open. But he didn't care. If not for her, he would be home with his daughter.

Then Abby Bauman would be dead.

The thought splintered through his hard demeanor and shook his resolve. He wouldn't let anything happen to her. He wasn't sure why that was so important. For now, though, they had to work together to survive.

EVERETT MADE PEANUT BUTTER and jelly sandwiches for lunch. It was Chloe's favorite. Gayle cut up fruit, even though he hadn't asked her to. They hadn't spoken since the morning, and she never did go shopping. All he could think about was his daughter. He and Gayle would talk later.

"Time for a nap, sweetiepie."

Chloe rubbed her eyes. "You have to read to me, Grandpa. Mommy does."

"Okay. Let's get one of your books." He carried her into the den and rummaged through the bag Abby had left. A Disney Princess book was on top. Abby and her prince books. She'd always loved them. He often wished he'd talked to his daughter more about the real world. But she had a good head on her shoulders, and he knew she'd choose a husband wisely. He thought she had until Doug showed his true colors.

He cradled Chloe close and opened the book, but his granddaughter was already asleep. Lifting her into his arms, he carried her down the hall to a guest bedroom and placed her on the bed with Baby in her arms. He laid an afghan over her. The air-conditioning was chilly.

"Shouldn't you put some pillows around her?" Gayle asked from the doorway. "She might roll off the bed."

"I can take care of my granddaughter," he replied shortly and walked past her.

"Why are you so mean to me?" She followed him.

He turned to face her. "Gayle, I'm worried out of my mind about Abby and I'm not in a mood to argue with you."

"Everett." She stroked his arm. "I'm worried about her, too. I'm sorry if I sounded crass earlier."

Before he could respond, the doorbell rang. "I'll get it."

Doug stood on the doorstep in white shorts and a yellow-and-white golf shirt. He removed his sunglasses, hooked them on the front of his shirt and stepped inside. "Hi, Everett. I'm here to pick up Chloe." From his sunny attitude Everett knew he hadn't heard about Abby. And why hadn't he? It was on the news, the internet, everywhere.

"What makes you think Chloe is here?"

"Abby always brings her to you."

"When you pull a no-show."

"I had a meeting. I told Abby that."

"Yes. At seven-fifteen this morning. The exact time you were to pick up Chloe. I've been a banker for a lot of years and if you had a meeting this morning, on a Saturday, you knew about it yesterday or the day before."

"Damn it, Everett. If she would take the damn settlement, she wouldn't have to work. If she would forgive me, we could be a family again. I've apologized until I'm blue in the face and I'm in counseling, but Abby refuses to give me a second chance."

"So you use manipulative tricks to bend her to your will."

Doug frowned. "I don't have to explain anything to you. Where's my daughter?"

"You don't know, do you?"

"What?"

"Abby's bank was robbed this morning."

"What?"

"The bank was robbed. I'm surprised you haven't heard about it."

"I haven't." His cool facade slipped a little. "So Abby's here, too? Is she resting?"

"Doug, Abby was taken as a hostage."

"What?" Color drained from Doug's suntanned face.

"The police have identified a white van that was used in the robbery. It belongs to a Calvin Williams of Austin. He said he loaned it to his son, Devon. The van was located in Houston, but there's been no sign of the robbers or Abby."

"Oh, my God." Doug ran his hands through his hair. "Have you told Chloe?"

"Of course not. She's too little to understand."

"She needs to be with me. Where is she?"

"You're not taking her. Abby's last words were for me not to let you have her."

"That's insane. I'm her father."

"Still, she stays here until Abby returns."

"You're crazy, Everett. I'm taking my daughter." Doug pushed past him and headed for the hall doorway.

Gayle stood there with one of his golf irons in her hands. "You better leave, Doug, unless you want a really bad head-ache."

"You're not serious."

"Try me."

"Fine." He held up his hands. "I'll be back with a police-man and you'll have to give her to me." He turned on his heel and slammed out the front door.

Everett eased into his chair, his breathing shallow. "Call Holly and have her come get Chloe."

"Why?"

"I think I'm having a heart attack."

CHAPTER FOUR

ABBY COULDN'T GO ON. Her sweaty clothes clung to her body. Her muscles ached and her skin felt on fire. Dragging hot air into her weak lungs made her dizzy. She sank to her knees.

"E-than" came out as a croak.

He swung around. "Hey, you okay?"

"I have to rest a couple of minutes." She crawled through the leaves and dirt to a tree and leaned against it, praying for a breeze, something to grant a reprieve from the god-awful heat.

"Sure. I'm just going to check things out."

Check things out? Was he nuts? It was trees and more trees, bushes, dirt, leaves and brittle dried grass. The scenery was monotonous and boring. And deadly. The word shot across her brain with chilling foreboding. She scooted up closer to the tree, the bark cutting into her back. She would not give up this easily.

Ethan was some distance away, gazing at the dried grass, and then he glanced toward the sky. What was he doing? Evidently searching for the van tracks. But what was in the sky? He suddenly strolled toward her with long strides. He didn't even seem tired. Whatever exercise program he was on, it worked. His clothes and hair were also sweaty, but he wasn't gasping for breath. The man had stamina. He was probably one of those guys who could make love all night long.

Now, where had that thought come from? Obviously she was losing it.

He plopped down by her. "Better?"

"No. I'm thirsty and tired." She turned her head to stare at him. His dark hair was plastered to his head like a wet cap. A complacent expression etched across the rawboned lines of his face. "Why aren't you tired?"

"I am. I just don't whine about it."

"If I had any strength, I'd smack you."

"Save all that indignation for walking."

"Okay, Ethan James."

"Don't say my name like that."

"How?"

"Condescending."

"Then don't be rude to me."

He groaned and pushed up against the tree. "Could you please be quiet for a few minutes?"

"If you ask nicely."

"Whatever." He leaned back his head and closed his eyes.

With his features relaxed, he was actually quite handsome. Sort of had a Noah Wyle from *Falling Skies* appeal. And she had to stop thinking about him. She turned her thoughts to her dad and Chloe. Hopefully, her dad was coping. Under stress, his blood pressure tended to shoot through the roof. But Gayle would be there to keep a close eye on him.

Had they told Chloe? She'd just turned three and she would be asking for her mommy. Her stomach cramped at the thought of her baby's distress. *Don't worry, Chloe. Mommy will come home.*

Doug was probably there by now and had whisked their daughter away. She hoped he used some discretion if he told her about the bank robbery. Chloe was his daughter and he wouldn't do anything to hurt her. She had to keep telling herself that.

She lifted her foot to look at her shoes. Her Manolo Blahniks were coated with dirt and ruined.

"What are you doing?" he asked.

"Looking at my last big expense before the divorce."

He leaned forward. "I never understood women's obsession with shoes."

She stared directly at him. "And I'll never understand a man's obsession with his truck."

He frowned. "That's different. I use my truck for transportation."

"These shoes were made for walking." She lifted her shoe higher. "And that's what I do in them."

"It's not the same thing," he stressed. "That's like comparing apples to oranges."

"No. It's like comparing a Granny Smith apple to a Red Delicious. And in case you're wondering I'm Red Delicious and you're a tart Granny Smith."

He just stared at her with an irritated expression.

"Okay." She turned to face him. "How do you feel when you get in that big ol' truck?"

"What?" His irritation intensified.

"You probably feel in control. Confident. As if you can take on the world."

"I think the heat's getting to you."

She ignored the snide remark. "When I put on these shoes—" she lifted one so he could see the classy, if dirty, little bow "—I feel pretty. Confident. And ready to take on the world." She paused. "See? Same thing."

He shook his head. "Does anyone ever get anything past you?"

"No. So stop trying." She relaxed against the tree feeling as if she'd scored a point with the hard-nosed cop. Neither said anything for the next few minutes. The woods were quiet. An occasional rustling but nothing else.

"What time do you think it is?" she asked.

He raised his left wrist. "Damn. I can't believe I didn't put my watch on this morning. It's the first thing I do after my shower, but I was in a rush to get home. I gathered up my things and put them in the console of my truck."

"Do you usually work nights?"

"No. My partner and I are working on a murder case and keeping an eye on a person of interest."

"Who keeps your daughter?"

"My dad, and he's not the most patient person. I promised Kelsey we'd spend the day together."

Guilt weighed on her conscience. "Once she finds out what happened I'm sure she will understand."

"No, she won't." He locked his arms around his knees. "She has a chip on her shoulder about the size of the Alamo. It will be just one more time an adult has let her down."

"I'm sorry, Ethan."

"Yeah, well, let's get some rest." He shrugged off her apology as if it meant nothing, and it probably didn't. "I'm guessing it's about four o'clock, the hottest part of the day. We'll stay here for a while and then trek on."

"What were you checking out earlier?"

"I lost the tire tracks. I don't know if they turned right or left or drove straight ahead. It's as if the tracks disappeared into thin air."

"Why were you looking at the sky?"

"I was checking for power lines."

"And?"

"There are none. Fences either."

"And that means?"

"I'm guessing this land is part of a big ranch and this section is leased for deer hunting. Since the cabin's in disrepair and hasn't been used for a while, my thought is that it's up for sale."

"But wouldn't they need electricity?"

"Some guys like to rough it, but if we keep walking we'll reach power lines and water."

"I'd kill for a glass of water."

He leaned back against the tree. "Rest. We'll start walking when it's cooler."

She stretched out her legs and drifted into sleep. When she

awoke, her head was on his thigh. She sat up and rolled her head from side to side, feeling a little better. The heat wasn't so intense, but the need for water hadn't left her.

Sweat trickled from Ethan's hair down the side of his strong face. She was mesmerized by it.

"What would you do if I sucked the sweat off your face?"

With a gleam in his eye, he replied, "Depends how you do it."

Staring into the warmth of his eyes, she felt a heat that had nothing to do with the temperature. It had to do with hormones, chemistry and a titillating attraction between a man and a woman. It was wrong, wrong. Denying that didn't change a thing.

She'd fallen for her rescuer.

EVERETT FELT LIKE a fool. He'd had another anxiety attack brought on by stress. His blood pressure was extremely high, too. A bad combination. The doctor had said he could have a stroke if he didn't reduce the stress in his life. He'd gotten some medication to help, but nothing was going to help until Abby was returned safely.

Through the floor-to-ceiling windows in the den he could see Chloe and Holly playing in the pool. His granddaughter was happy for now, but soon she would be asking for her mother.

"Everett, why don't you lie down for a while," Gayle said behind him. "I'll wake you if the police call."

"I'd rather sit in my chair. Chloe will be in soon and I don't want her to think I'm sick."

"Okay. I'm not going to argue with you."

"I'd appreciate that."

"I'll get you some iced tea."

"Thank you."

Gayle was being calm and rational, and that's what he needed right now. He hated to think he was so weak he would collapse if something happened to Abby. Something *had* happened to his daughter and he was falling apart. That wasn't easy to admit. He was an indoor, quiet guy, a retired banker. He was good at numbers. He often wished he was a rough and tough outdoorsman, but that just wasn't his personality.

As Gayle handed him a glass of tea, the doorbell rang. "That's probably Doug," she said. "Please remain calm."

"I will." Taking a sip, he set the glass on a coaster. He knew the dangers and he wasn't risking his health. He had to stay strong for Abby and Chloe.

Doug and a policeman followed Gayle into the den. Doug's eyes went to the windows and Chloe and Holly playing in the pool.

"What's Holly doing here?" Doug demanded.

Gayle bristled. "I didn't realize we needed your permission to invite people over."

"I didn't mean it that way. Holly hates me and fills Chloe's head with nonsense."

"They're playing, Doug," Gayle told him. "So relax."

Doug moved toward Everett. "I'm here for Chloe."

"I know," he replied. "She's swimming as you can see. I had no right to try to keep you from your daughter." Those were the hardest words he'd ever had to say and it was killing him to let go of his link to Abby.

"I'm glad you see that. I'll get her."

"If that's all you need, I'll be on my way," the policeman said.

"Yes, yes, and thank you." Doug headed for the pool.

"I'm surprised at you, Doug." Gayle crossed her arms over her breasts.

Doug swung back. "What are you talking about?"

"I thought you'd be more concerned about Abby."

"I am. I'm worried out of my mind."

"No. I meant when they find her. She's going to need love, support and a shoulder to lean on. I'd assumed you'd want to be that person. But Everett and I are more than happy to be there for Abby. Under the circumstances, it's probably best, too."

By Doug's stunned expression, Everett could almost read his thoughts. This was his opportunity to be there for Abby. To prove how much he loved her. Everett shook his head in disgust.

"You're right, Gayle," Doug said. "I've been so worried I hadn't thought about Abby needing me."

"You seem to forget about Abby a lot."

Before Doug could respond, Chloe ran in from the sun-room. She climbed into Everett's lap. "Did you see me swimming, Grandpa?"

"Yes, I did." He stroked wet curls from her face. "You swim like a fish."

"That's what Holly said."

Holly walked in with an oversize towel wrapped around her waist. Her eyes zeroed in on Doug. "I didn't know rats came out of the sewer at this time of day."

"Your daddy is here," Everett said quickly before heated words could start.

"Hi, Daddy." Chloe raised a hand, but she made no move to go to him.

Doug squatted by Everett's chair. "Do you want to go to Daddy's house?"

Chloe shook her head. "I have to stay with Grandpa. Mommy's coming to get me."

"Okay, sweetie." Doug leaned over and kissed his daughter's cheek. "Daddy has a lot to do, but I'll come back for you."

"No, Daddy. Mommy's coming." Chloe's little face scrunched up in worry. Even at three she sensed something was not right.

"C'mon, cutie," Holly said. "Time to get dressed."

Chloe gave Doug a hug and ran after Holly.

Doug left without another word.

Everett looked at his wife. "I knew you were crafty, but you've taken devious to a new level. Doug didn't even catch on."

She shrugged. "You didn't want Chloe to leave and I figured out a way to accomplish that."

"Thanks."

"I'm not a monster."

"I know, honey. I said things this morning I didn't mean." He raised his eyes to hers. "Did you mean it when you said we'd take care of Abby?"

"Yes. I'm not the motherly type, but I will try."

"Don't try, Gayle. Let it happen naturally."

She kissed his forehead. "I'll make us a nice dinner."

"Chloe—and Holly, too?"

"Of course."

His cell buzzed and he quickly pulled it out of his trousers. "Hello."

"Mr. Baines, this is Detective Logan."

"Yes, I know. Have you found my daughter?"

"Sorry, Mr. Baines, no. But a SWAT team and the feds have arrested Devon Williams at his girlfriend's."

"And Abby wasn't with him?"

"No. He said the van broke down and he left it on the side of the highway in Houston. He called his girlfriend and she picked him up and they traveled to her apartment in south Houston. The girlfriend verified his story. He said he doesn't know anything about a bank robbery."

"You believe this?"

"Not for a minute. He's being transported back here and I'll get a crack at him. I'll stay in touch."

"Thank you."

Everett stared at his phone and suddenly threw it across the room. It landed with a soft thud on the large Oriental rug.

"Everett!"

He told Gayle what the detective had said. "My daughter is probably lying dead in a field somewhere, and he just didn't want to tell me."

"No. No. Don't say that." Gayle wrapped her arms around him. "We're staying positive. Do you hear me?"

"I think I will lie down."

"No." She kissed his face. "I'll get the checkerboard out and you can play checkers with Chloe. She loves it."

"But you hate it when we make a mess."

"I don't care." She wrapped her arms around him again and he held on tight. "Abby will come home, Everett. We have to believe that."

And he did.

WITH EACH STEP, Ethan cursed himself. One look from her sleepy blue eyes and he'd let his guard down—allowed himself to wonder what it would feel like to have her lips on his skin. He'd come to his senses quickly, telling her they had to keep moving. She'd seemed startled, but complied. Concerning Abby Bauman, he had one goal—to return her safely to her family. That was it. No hanky-panky.

"E-e…"

He swung around to see Abby crumpled to the ground. He fell down beside her and lifted her upper body onto his thigh. "Abby!"

She'd passed out from the heat, and her breathing was shallow. Balancing her on his leg, he whipped his T-shirt over his head and wiped her face with it, running it around her neck trying to cool her.

"That feels good," she murmured, opening her eyes. Lightly touching his chest, she added, "That feels even better."

He slowly removed her hand from his hot skin, even though he had the urge to press it closer.

"What happened?"

"You fainted."

"Oh. I'm so hot." She moved restlessly. "I'm sticky and miserable."

"Maybe take off your bra. It's restrictive and might rub blisters."

Her eyes opened wide. "Oh, you want to get me out of my bra?"

"This isn't personal." He had to make that clear.

"Oh, no, we don't want to get personal. That could get messy, messy..." Her head tilted against his chest.

"Abby, stay awake." He rubbed her face and neck again and she stirred. "Is it a front or back hook?"

"F-ront."

He slid his hand under her top and unhooked her bra, touching unbelievably smooth, soft skin.

"You did that rather easily," she said, watching him.

"It's in my repertoire of skills."

"I bet."

"Can you get it off? Or do you need me to help?"

"I can do it."

Some of her stubbornness was back. She pulled her arms through the sleeveless top and finagled a strap over her arm and then another. Removing it, she threw the lacy beige bra into the leaves. Then she jammed her arms back into the openings.

They both stared at the lacy bra. "Can you imagine the conversation when someone finds that?" she asked.

"Only nocturnal creatures will find it, or birds will use it to make nests." He looked down at her. "Ready to continue on?"

She reached up and touched his face. He froze. There was that thing again between them. He kept pushing it away and it kept coming back. Describing *it* was difficult. Attraction? Sexual awareness? Or gratitude?

He was well aware of all three, but their connection hinged on gratitude. He was positive of that.

A snort and a thrashing rumbled through the trees. Before Ethan could move, a big buck came charging out, leaped over them and disappeared just as quickly.

"What was that?" Abby sat up.

"A deer and I'm betting he's headed for water. We have to follow."

"Oh, water. Do you think it's close?"

"We have to go to find out. Can you stand?"

She pushed to her feet and he slipped into his sweaty T-shirt. With his arm around her waist to steady her, they started off. She didn't stumble or complain so he kept them moving. They stopped as the trees meandered down into a small overgrown valley. In the middle sat an old shack.

"There has to be a creek running by it. Let's go." He started off, but she stayed at the top. Glancing back, he called, "C'mon. What are you waiting for?"

"I've been waiting for you, Ethan. I've been waiting for you all my life."

What? She was delirious. That was the only answer.

"That's crazy," he said before he could stop himself. "C'mon."

She walked toward him and against every sane objection in his head a delusional thought slipped through. *He'd been waiting for her, too.*

The heat had finally gotten to him. He was a hard-nosed, badass cop and he was well insulated from silly, romantic nonsense.

Until Abby Bauman.

CHAPTER FIVE

WALT PLACED A glass of iced tea in front of his friend Henry Coyote, Levi's grandfather. Even though Henry was older by seven years, they were best friends. They were hardworking, hard cussing cowboys who were born and raised in Willow Creek, Texas. Henry had started a family early, while Walt had been thirty-five when Ethan was born. Henry's son had been killed in a car accident and the son's wife had moved to Austin with Levi and his sister. But Levi had returned every chance he got and lived here now. Like Ethan, Levi never strayed far from his roots.

Walt and Henry argued like two-bit lawyers and fought like bobcats. That is, they had in their younger days. They'd been there for each other through the bad times, the deaths of both their wives and the death of Henry's son.

"Sure you don't want to go to the Rusty Spur, drink some beer and play dominoes?" Henry asked.

"Nope. Not going anywhere until my boy comes home."

"Levi is on the case and there ain't nobody better at catching crooks than Levi."

"Except Ethan."

"Ah, shit…let's don't have this argument again."

"Then don't say your grandson is better than my son. And I told you not to cuss in my house."

Henry shook his gray head. "You're getting strange, Walt."

"And you're a baboon."

"Stop using them stupid words you made up. If you mean bastard, say bastard."

"You're a hairy baboon with no manners."

Henry slapped the table with one of his big paws. "That's it. I'm going to the Rusty Spur to drink beer, play dominoes and cuss. Real cuss words that'll burn your ears. Not some stupid ones I made up."

"You better go then."

"I'm going." Henry shoved his worn hat onto his head and got to his feet. "I don't understand why not cussing is so important to you."

"Because Ethan asked me not to. He wants to have a good environment for his daughter."

Henry leaned in and whispered, "She's twelve. I know she's heard cuss words."

"It's what Ethan wants and I'm doing it."

"Well, don't call me a baboon. That's insulting. If you can't say bastard, just call me Henry."

"Goodbye, Henry."

His friend tapped the table with his arthritic knuckles as if to make a point. "I'm sorry about Ethan."

"I know."

Henry ambled to the door and Walt took the glasses to the sink. Henry's head was as hard as Walt's, but they understood each other most of the time. If Henry thought not cussing was easy for him, then he'd better think again. Walt's tongue was about to fall out of his mouth from sheer lack of use.

"Hey."

Walt turned to see Kelsey standing there. As always, it took a moment for his eyes to adjust. His last good nerve snapped at the word *hey.* He pointed to a chair. "Sit down."

She scurried to a chair and he sat facing her. "Let's get something straight. Whether you like it or not, I'm your grandpa. You can call me Grandpa, Gramps, Pop or whatever you're comfortable with, but you will not call me Hey. It's disrespectful. You got it?"

She raised her head and looked at him, something she rarely

did. Long black hair partially covered her face, but Ethan's brown eyes stared back at him. "Yeah, but you will not call me girl, gal or alien. You will call me Kel or Kelsey."

Damn! She'd heard him say that. His gut knotted tight with guilt.

"Deal." He extended his hand across the table. It took a moment, but she finally shook it. "I apologize for calling you an alien. That was out of line. I give you my word as your grandfather I will never do that again."

"Deal." She nodded. "Did they find Ethan?"

"No. They arrested one of the robbers and they're questioning him now. I'll let you know if I hear anything."

"Okay." She stood and twisted on her flip-flops. "Can I have some ice cream?"

"Kelsey, this is your home now, and you can have any food we have."

She shrugged. "I didn't know. My grandma didn't have a home and we lived with her older sister. She didn't like me eating her food. When my grandma died, my mom and me lived in motels or rented rooms."

Lordy, Lordy. What a life for a young girl—his granddaughter. A load of guilt hit him right between the eyes as powerful as a butt of a Colt .45. For Ethan's daughter, he had to do better.

"You have a home now and can eat whatever you want."

She opened the freezer, took out an ice-cream bar, and ran to her room.

Walt went out onto the deck and sank into a chair. Rowdy lay at his feet. He gazed past the chain-link fence to his pastureland. Cows lay in the shade of several big live oak trees out of the stifling heat. He'd check the water troughs later to make sure they had enough to drink. In this heat, they needed constant water. Wherever Ethan was, he prayed he wasn't in the heat.

Walt leaned forward, bowed his head, and clasped his hands

together. *"Lord, I've been talking to You a lot in the past few hours and You might find that strange since I haven't talked to You in years. Maureen, my wife, was a religious woman, and she talked to You daily. I figured that pretty much covered the bases for me. But there comes a time in a man's life when he has to confront his maker alone. For me, that's today. My boy's been taken by some thugs. You probably know that, right? He's a good man. You know that, too. He has a twelve-year-old daughter who needs him. I don't know a thing about little girls, but I'll do my best until You return Ethan to us. That's all I'm asking, Lord. Watch over Ethan. Kelsey needs him. I need him, too. Thanks for listening."*

He got up and went back into the house with a purpose—to forge a bond with his granddaughter. It didn't matter what she looked like on the outside. Inside she was a scared little girl needing a home, family and love. Wrestling a steer to the ground might be easier than reaching Kelsey. But grandpas didn't give up. And that's who he was—Grandpa.

THE LIGHT-HEADEDNESS CONTINUED and Abby floated in and out of the clouds. Ethan's hand rested on her hip as they walked and she knew she was okay. Weird thoughts ran through her head. Had she told Ethan she'd been waiting for him all her life? No. She hadn't said that out loud. She was almost positive. Besides, she'd only known him a few hours. But inside her heart was a certainty that their souls had connected.

Ethan stopped and she glanced up. They'd reached the small weatherworn wood cabin. There was nothing but dirt around it. What little grass had been there had died. It wasn't as run-down as the other cabin, and a porch graced the front. She sank onto the stoop.

"Rest," Ethan said. "I'll check things out."

She lay on the wood flooring, totally spent. Suddenly a slight breeze touched her skin. Opening her eyes, she sat up.

The breeze continued. She pulled the wet blouse from her skin and fanned it. Heavenly. After a moment, her mind cleared.

"Ethan."

He strolled from the side of the cabin. "What?"

"The wind."

"Yeah. It's picked up." He glanced toward the sun. "It's probably about seven o'clock and the sun is going down."

"We get a break."

"Yeah." He eyed her. "Do you feel better?"

"Yes." There was something different in his gaze. Was he worried about her? She cleared her dry throat. "Did you find anything?"

"There's an old-timey well out back with a rope and a bucket. The bucket is cracked and the well handle's rusted, but I'm hoping I can find something in the cabin to use for oil."

She followed him inside. The flooring was sturdy and the roof hadn't caved in like the other one. Bunk beds occupied two walls. Faded sheets were still on them. A small cabinet with a makeshift sink and window took up another wall. A refrigerator stood in a corner.

"Without electricity, how do they run a refrigerator?"

"They bring a generator."

"Oh."

Ethan opened drawers and cabinet doors. "Not much here. Must be why animals haven't overrun this place." He yanked wide the doors beneath the sink. "Wait. What's this?" He pulled out a large plastic container. "Peanut oil. Not much left, but it should be enough." He reached for something in the top cabinet. "This stoneware pitcher is heavy and has a handle. We might be able to use it for a bucket."

She trailed behind him out the side door to the well. It looked like so many she'd seen in landscaped yards. Of course, this one was very rustic. But it had a roller bar across the top with a rope and a crank handle. The bucket lay on the ground, useless. The housing around the hole was made of wide, weatherworn boards. The opening was covered with a heavy-looking metal object.

Ethan took a small scrub brush from his pocket. She hadn't even seen him remove it from the cabin. He poured peanut oil on it and began to scrub the rusty crank. The well was in the open and the sun showered them with waves of heat, but it wasn't as intense. Sweat rolled from his face. He had to be exhausted, too, but he never stopped. She wanted to help him. Using her better judgment, though, she just watched, marveling at the muscles working in his arms and the total concentration on his face.

She could imagine him pursuing a killer with everything in him. She'd never been this impressed with anyone in her life. And she wasn't delusional.

"Hot damn," he shouted as the crank began to move. After more elbow grease it made a complete circle. Then another.

"It's working," she cried.

"All it took was a little muscle."

"And you've got those."

He gave her a dark-eyed glance.

"What?" She lifted an eyebrow. "Is that a secret?"

"Stop distracting me." He continued to work the crank.

"Oh, I didn't realize I was doing that."

He turned to face her. "One minute you're half-conscious and the next you're flirting."

"I am not flirting," she insisted.

"Whatever." He went back to working on the well.

Maybe she was flirting, but he didn't have to be so grouchy. And he wasn't really as grouchy as he appeared. She knew that now. He was a nice guy with a big heart, which he kept hidden with his brusqueness. Ethan was one of the good guys. Even knowing that didn't keep her from getting mad at him.

"Okay." Ethan sank to the ground with the pitcher and the end of the rope. "The rope isn't thick, so that's good. The trick is to tie the rope to keep the pitcher from tilting. It has a narrow neck and a rounded bottom. If I tie to the handle, it will tilt. The best bet would be to use the narrow neck."

He was talking to himself. She'd allow him that foible. After looping the rope around the neck, he tied a knot and then another.

"Is the rope strong?" she asked.

"I'm hoping. I pulled to test it and it didn't break." He placed the pitcher aside and got to his feet. "I have to remove the lid."

"Can you? It looks heavy."

With a wicked glint in his eyes, something she thought she would never see from him, he said, "That's what these muscles are for." And to dispel the notion that he might be flirting, he added, "Besides, I removed it earlier."

He plucked off the heavy cover as if it weighed no more than a board. Placing it against the well housing, he stuck his head over the open hole and took a deep breath. "Ah, I smell water."

"Water doesn't smell."

"Stick your nose over here, Ms. Doubtful."

She leaned over and took a whiff. Her whole body vibrated with yearning. "Oh, oh, Ethan. There's water. Hurry! We have to bring it up. I'm dying for a drink."

"Patience." He removed his shirt and attempted to wipe dust from the rope.

"Will that do any good? Your shirt is dirty and sweaty."

"The well probably has bacteria in it anyway and cleaning the rope with a dirty shirt was the lesser of two evils I was thinking."

"How will we know if it has bacteria?"

"When we get sick."

"Oh, great."

"But we don't have much choice. Without water, we can't survive in this heat."

Abby licked her parched lips. "Let's do it."

Ethan laid his shirt on top of the cover and picked up the pitcher. With one hand he lowered it into the well hole and cranked it lower with the other hand. "Keep your fingers crossed the rope doesn't break."

Abby crossed her fingers, held her breath and watched the pitcher disappear into the dark hole.

"We've hit water," Ethan said. "We'll give it a minute to fill and then I'll pull it up."

Slowly he cranked the pitcher upward. "It's heavier so it must be full." When it reached the top, he reached out and grabbed the neck of the pitcher. Water spilled onto his hand. Her heart beat so fast she could barely breathe. He handed the pitcher to her and she took a sip and then a gulp.

He grabbed the pitcher. "Hey, go slow. You'll make yourself sick."

She sank to the ground. Even though she wanted to guzzle it, she sipped and sipped. Handing it to him, she sighed. "Heaven. Pure heaven."

He eased down by her and sipped until the water was gone. "This is better than sex."

"You think so?"

He lifted an eyebrow. "At this exact moment, yes." He stood to refill the pitcher and she wondered about his sex life. Someone as virile as Ethan had to have a regular girlfriend. Or maybe not. Considering what had happened to him, he was probably very choosy about whom he slept with. And she had a feeling Ethan didn't stay around for much sleeping.

He filled the pitcher three times. The third time they didn't drink much. Ethan poured the last bit over his head. Water ran down his face and onto his chest. Droplets clung to swirls of dark chest hairs. Without thinking, without judging herself, she leaned over and licked the drops from his warm skin.

He stiffened. She didn't stop.

She licked up his chest to his strong chin. His skin tasted of salt, sweat and granules of sand. But it wasn't off-putting. Just the opposite. It was the most sensual experience her mouth had ever encountered. The tip of her tongue throbbed from the taste, texture and sensuality of him.

"Ab-by."

Her lips touched his. He groaned, cupped her face and kissed her as she'd never been kissed before. His lips were strong, powerful and she didn't weaken under the onslaught to her senses. She reveled in it, meeting his fervor with her own. She ran her hands along the strong muscles in his shoulders and neck.

The kiss went on and on. He held her head in place as he ravaged her lips and spiked her blood pressure. His thumbs stroked her jawline and she purred like a satisfied cat. The sound startled her until she realized it was her.

Slowly, he released her. "We have to stop this."

"Yes," she replied, but inside she was wanting much more.

"Look." He waved a hand. "The sun has gone down."

While they'd been otherwise engaged, it certainly had. A yellow glow invaded the woods.

"It will be completely dark soon, so we have to find a place to bed down." He stood, placed his T-shirt over one shoulder and fitted the lid over the well. He placed the pitcher on top.

She followed him into the almost completely dark cabin. "My stomach is complaining and I'm starving."

"It's the cool water on an empty stomach. It's reminding you of how empty it is. Try not to think about it." Handing her his shirt, he tested one of the mattresses. "They seem okay. It's better than sleeping on the ground." He dragged one outside and placed it on the porch and then went back for another. He situated them about twelve feet apart, making it more than clear that kissing wasn't happening again.

He plopped onto a mattress, removed his shoes, and stretched out. "Ah, this feels good. I can get a good night's rest."

"You're kidding, right? Snakes could be inside the mattresses."

"I'm exhausted and going to sleep. You can stand guard and watch out for snakes."

"Ethan."

"Mmm."

"What do you want me to do with your shirt?"

"Lay it out on the floor to dry."

"I'm not your maid."

"Fine. Throw it to me."

She aimed for his face and he caught it effortlessly. Darkness crept around them, hiding the dry, parched earth. The only illumination was the moon, which hung high in the sky like a huge night-light. She slid down to the mattress and tested it. Bouncy and soft. That was good.

Slipping off her shoes, she tried to relax. She was being testy for no reason. That was Ethan's department, but his cavalier attitude about their out-of-this-world kiss annoyed her. He acted as if it was just another kiss. It wasn't. Or was it? She drew a deep breath. Due to the circumstances, she was blowing this way out of proportion. And being a complete bitch, she couldn't let it go.

"Are you seeing someone?"

After a long moment, he replied, "No."

"I'm not either, if that matters."

"It doesn't."

"I thought you might be feeling guilty."

"I'm not. Now, go to sleep."

"I'm not sleepy."

"Lie down and close your eyes. That's what most people do."

She thought of doing that, but her mind was filled with thoughts about the day, the heat, Ethan and the night. Not to mention her dad and Chloe. She hoped her dad wasn't worried too much. How could he not be? His only child had been taken hostage in a bank robbery.

The warm wind brushed across her face, reminding her that she was alive. And soon her dad would know that, too.

With water, there was no doubt they could make it to safety. She'd say goodbye to Ethan and they'd go their separate ways.

She touched her lips and remembered the kiss. Maybe she could say goodbye in another way. Did she have that much nerve?

"Ethan."

CHAPTER SIX

ETHAN IGNORED THE soft voice that triggered emotions he'd rather not have. Shouldn't have. But he had to admit for the first time in years his resistance to the opposite sex had reached an all-time low. Against his better judgment, he'd kissed her. And didn't want to stop. She was as tempting as a drink of water from the pitcher and he couldn't get enough.

After the comment about sucking the sweat from his chest, he couldn't get that image out of his head. And he was a man who didn't fantasize. Ever. Except in his teens and early twenties. And occasionally since then. Okay, he was lying to himself now. He didn't want to be attracted to Abby. As a police officer, he considered her under his care and protection. It was hell having to remind himself of that.

"Ethan."

"Go to sleep."

"I'm worried about my little girl."

"I'm sure she's fine. Doesn't your dad have her?"

"Doug probably has her by now. I don't want him to tell her what happened. She'll be scared."

"He's a father. He won't do that."

"I guess." She jumped up at a chirping sound. "What's that?"

"Crickets. They're harmless."

"I know, but they're very loud." She pulled the mattress closer to his. "It might be something else."

"It isn't. Lie down and go to sleep."

She sat on the mattress, but didn't lie on it. "Aren't you worried about your daughter?"

He sighed. "What do you hear when I say go to sleep?"

"I'm sorry. I feel as if I've had a double espresso. I'm wired and restless. Could we talk for just a minute? It might help me to relax."

"Why do women always want to talk?"

"Oh, I don't know, why do men want to drink beer and watch sports?"

"So we don't have to talk."

"Too bad. We're talking."

He groaned, wondering if he was ever going to win with this woman. She should have been a lawyer.

"Is your daughter okay with your dad?"

He wasn't going to answer. Putting his hands behind his head, he stared out at the dark sky. A wide swatch of black velvet with millions of twinkling rhinestones covered it, or so it seemed. The moon hung like a big spotlight enhancing the glow of the rhinestones. It was beautiful. Relaxing.

Before he knew it, he began to speak. "Kelsey's…"

"What a pretty name."

"I didn't pick it."

"Mmm. So she's okay with your dad?"

"Maybe. Maybe not."

"What does that mean?"

"It means it's complicated. Now…"

"No, I'm not going to sleep," she snapped. "Tell me about your dad and your daughter."

He turned to gaze at her through the darkness. "You can be annoying."

"Do you want me to tell you what you're like?"

"No. I know what I'm like."

"Good. So continue."

He stared at the starry rhinestones, wondering if he could bore her to sleep if he kept talking. He understood her anxieties. There were a lot of dangers out here, but he couldn't dwell on that. They had to rest for the walk tomorrow.

"My dad is a country cowboy, born and raised in Willow Creek, Texas. He has a ranch and works the land like his father before him. He's a simple man and not too knowledgeable about today's teenagers. When my daughter arrived with her long dyed-black hair with a purple streak, black jeans and T-shirt, painted black nails and toenails with three earrings in each ear, it was a bit of a shock."

"Oh, my."

"The first thing he said was, 'Son of a bitch, the aliens have landed.'"

"Oh, no."

"I had to have a talk with him. His vocabulary is a bit colorful and I asked him to curb his swearing around Kelsey. I wanted to create a better environment for her."

"Did he do it?"

"Oh, yeah. He made up new words to use. Instead of saying son of a bitch, he now says things like sunny beaches or son of a beady-eyed bitty or son of a dipstick or anything that comes to mind. For goddamn he says shazam. For shit he says shih tzu."

"That's a dog."

"Yes, and bull shih tzu sounds even worse. As does baboon or buffoon for bastard."

"What does he use for the f word?"

"He's an old cowboy and doesn't use that word."

"That's a relief." He could almost see her smiling. "She'll stay at his house until you return?"

"I live with my dad. I guess I didn't make that clear."

She laughed. A soft melodious sound that under other circumstances would have excited him. Now it irritated him.

"You find that funny?"

"Oh, yeah. Mr. Macho Cop living with his dad just doesn't fit."

"I'm macho enough to make it work."

"I bet you are." She laughed that sound again. "Have you always lived at home?"

"I had an apartment in Austin, but my mom died about five years ago and I started going out to the ranch more and more because I knew my dad was lonely. He's getting older and I noticed how much he's slowed down. On my days off, I started helping him on the ranch. When it was late, I'd stay the night. I was using my apartment very little so I decided to move home. When I found out about Kelsey, I was glad I had a real home for her."

She jumped up again at a soft hoot. "Oh, oh, what's that noise?"

"It's an owl. Haven't you been in the country before?"

"Once. When I was a Girl Scout. I think I was eight." She pulled the mattress closer to his. He could reach out and touch her, which he wouldn't.

"I'm sorry about your situation, but I'm sure your dad and Kelsey will adjust, especially since they're both worried about you."

"Not likely. Kelsey tends to ignore us. She stays in her room watching vampire movies and only comes out to eat."

"How sad."

"She'd agreed to go horseback riding this morning. That's why I was in a hurry to get home."

"I'm so sorry for stopping on the highway like that. Everything was my fault."

He sat up, feeling restless and edgy. "In life things happen, so don't beat yourself up too much." He didn't know why he was letting her off so easily. Maybe because there was no way to change what happened. And Abby would, if she could.

"That's the nicest thing you've said to me."

"Mmm. I'm not known for niceness."

"How about with Kelsey?"

He wrapped his arms around his knees. "I'm trying, but at this late date I'm not sure if we can form a father-daughter connection. I've enrolled her in school, but I worry how she'll fit in. Willow Creek is a country school with country kids who wear Wranglers and boots. Some wear the low-rider jeans and T-shirts, but none have a purple streak in their hair."

"They wouldn't dare make fun of Macho Cop's kid."

"Bullying has even made it into country schools, so I'm not taking anything for granted. We're supposed to meet with the principal soon. Kelsey's grades are awful, barely passing. It's not that she's slow or has a learning problem. She reads all the time. She's been in fifteen different schools as she was shuffled back and forth from her grandmother to Sheryl. She hasn't spent a whole year in any school. If I can't give her anything else, I want to give her a stable home where she can have family and friends."

The owl hooted through the trees, making them aware of where they were.

"Are you sure that's an owl?" She pulled the mattress until it touched his.

"Positive. And does that make you feel safer?"

"Yes."

He tightened his arms around his knees, marveling at how much he'd told her. He'd never opened up this much to any woman, including his mom. It had to be the night and the circumstances. Or it could be her. She was easy to talk to. Sometimes. Other times she drove him crazy. And he'd known her less than twenty-four hours.

"Since you have me wide-awake, tell me about your storybook life." Did he just ask her to talk? They were never going to get any sleep. His macho demeanor didn't work on her.

"Why do you think I've had a storybook life?"

"You have that Princess-Barbie-sorority-girl look that comes with wealth and privilege."

"I resent that." She came right back at him just as he knew she would.

"What was your life like, then?"

"Okay, maybe at first it was. My dad was president of a bank and we lived a good life. And, yes, they probably spoiled me."

"Probably?"

"Shut up. I didn't interrupt you."

He held up his hands. "Okay. Okay."

"My mom died in childbirth when I was ten. My baby brother died, too. She started hemorrhaging in her seventh month and the doctors couldn't stop it. Dad and I were devastated. Mom was the foundation of our lives, and we didn't know how to live without her. But eventually we had to start living again."

"That couldn't have been easy for a ten-year-old."

"No, but time slowly coated the pain with lovely memories. It drew my dad and me closer. When I was fifteen, he started dating. That was a shock." He could feel her moving restlessly. "The first time I met the woman I hated her. I thought she was after my dad's money, but then I found out she had money from her wealthy first husband. So I told her she could never take my mother's place and she would never be my mother."

"Wow. You must have been a real bitch at fifteen."

"I was hurt and I guess I thought if I hated her enough, he'd stop seeing her."

"And he didn't?"

"No. I apologized to both of them, but things never got better. When I moved into a dorm at the University of Texas, they got married and Gayle moved into our home. She slept in my mother's bed. That drove me crazy."

"Why?"

"I don't know. It was my mom's dream house. She designed it, decorated it. It was hers."

"Did you get over that feeling?"

"Well, Dad finally sold the house and built Gayle her own home."

"Because of your feelings."

"Yes. I'm an awful person. Aren't you glad you dragged that out of me?"

"Nope, but I'm seeing you in a whole new light."

"As a bitch?"

"Sort of."

She leaped onto his mattresses and punched him in the shoulder. "Oh, crap, that's like hitting a wall." She rubbed her hand.

"Then don't do it."

"Then don't call me a bitch." She sank down by him, her hip touching his thigh, which was too close for his comfort. Way too close.

"I didn't. You did," he pointed out and knew he should move away. But he didn't. "I hope things got better."

"I grew up and realized Dad deserved a life of his own. I got caught up in college life, dated, met Doug, the man of my dreams, or so I thought. Gayle and I maintain an amicable truce. Chloe and I have dinner with them once a week and Dad keeps Chloe when I need someone. Like this morning."

"Since you're big on talking, have you tried it with Gayle?"

"Yes, but the battle lines were drawn with my teenage behavior and Gayle can't seem to forget that. I hate that my dad gets caught in the middle. I've often thought of finding another sitter for Chloe, but Dad loves her and Chloe adores her grandpa."

"How often do you go out?"

"Maybe once a month."

"That shouldn't be too much to ask."

"I wish life wasn't so complicated and tense. I wish we could live together as a happy, loving family. But the teenage jealous bitch in me destroyed that."

"Don't be so melodramatic. Your problem with your stepmom is minor compared to what I see on a daily basis. Parents killing their children. Children murdering their parents in their sleep. For your dad, beg for your stepmom's forgiveness.

Beg until she caves and your problem is solved. Someone has to bend and since you started the battle, you have to. For your own sanity, make it work." He stretched out. "Now I'm going to sleep. Tomorrow's going to be a long, hot day."

He closed his eyes, but she didn't move. In the few hours he'd known her she'd continued to surprise him. He hoped she wasn't going to surprise him now.

ABBY LISTENED TO the chirps of crickets mingling with the hoots of the owl. The sounds of the night surrounded her and gave her courage. She'd wanted to do this earlier, but lost her nerve. There was something about the darkness that freed her inhibitions.

She was touched by his story and his determination to build a life with his daughter. He was different than any man she'd ever met. And she was attracted to him. Even after all they'd been through, she was very aware of him as a man.

"Ethan."

"Go to sleep, Abby."

"Can I ask you a personal question?"

"No."

"It's personal for me, not you."

"The answer is still no."

"I'll go to sleep if you answer."

He groaned. "What is it?"

"Um…" Her courage faltered for a second. "Um…when we kissed, was my response cold?"

"What?"

"You heard me."

"It's a stupid question, and I'm not answering."

She chewed on her lip trying to find the right words. "When I found out Doug was cheating and our marriage blew up, he blamed me. He said I was cold, unresponsive in bed and it was like making love to a mannequin."

"You didn't fall for that, did you?"

"Well…"

"He's trying to make you feel guilty for his misdeeds."

"I realized that, but there was a small part of me that felt it was true."

"Why?"

"I was very naive. I had a couple of sexual experiences in college that weren't satisfactory. Then I met Doug and he was nice, gentle and kind, and…"

"And what?"

She didn't know if she could continue. She'd never told the intimate details of her marriage to anyone. Not even Holly. The darkness once again gave her courage.

"Sex wasn't as I'd imagined between two people in love. I was usually glad when it was over. I kept telling myself it would get better after we were married. How stupid was that?"

He didn't say anything. She should stop before she made a fool of herself, but somehow she couldn't.

"Doug was my husband and I wanted to please him, but there was never an 'Oh, my God' moment for me. After Chloe was born, I lost all interest in sex. Chloe was a fussy baby and cried a lot. I was exhausted from taking care of her. Doug wanted to hire a nanny. I refused. That's when our marriage really started to deteriorate. So you see, I'm partly to blame. I drove him to other women."

"Did you try talking to him?"

"Yes. He said everything was fine. It wasn't, though. I'm afraid I'm one of those women who don't enjoy sex."

Complete silence followed her declaration and from some secret place in her she found the nerve to continue. "I'm very aware of you as a man."

"Don't go there, Abby."

"Why not? We're both over twenty-one. Adults. Unattached. And free to do what we want. No strings. No attachment. Just sex."

"I'm not having unprotected sex, especially under these circumstances."

"I have a diaphragm."

"It doesn't matter. The only rise you're getting out of me tonight is my temper. Please go back to your mattress and go to sleep."

"Okay. Okay." She crawled to her spot, feeling rejected and about as low as she could get. She couldn't even seduce a man.

"When you get home, see a therapist and work through your issues about sex. Sometimes sex is more in the brain than in the genitals."

"Gee, I should have that printed on a T-shirt."

"Abby." He sighed. "We've only known each other a few hours and most of that time we've been at each other's throats. I'm not trying to hurt you. I just think it's not wise for us to get emotionally involved."

"You're right," she admitted grudgingly. "After everything we've been through, I fear I'm losing it."

"You're not. You're just punch-drunk from exhaustion. Try to sleep. That will help."

"I'm afraid to close my eyes. If I do, I'll be back in the bank with that gun pressed against my temple, or lying against that log with bugs crawling over me waiting for the blast of a gun."

"Close your eyes and you'll simply go to sleep. You're too tired to dream."

His words were comforting. She lay back and felt miserable. "My clothes are filthy and sweaty and I'm dirty from head to toe. I can feel sand between my toes. I can't sleep like this."

"Just don't think about it."

She sat up. "I'll wipe my body with my top. Maybe I'll feel better."

"Whatever. You don't need to tell me what you're doing."

She pulled her damp top over her head and wiped her neck, breasts and arms. The wind touched her skin. "Ah, that feels good."

"Mmm" was his sleepy reply.

A loud howl echoed in the distance.

"What's that?" She leaped onto his mattress right on top of him, their arms and legs entangled.

"It's a coyote. For heaven's sakes, I know you've heard a coyote before."

"On TV and in movies, but not this up close and personal."

"He's miles away and not a threat. I'm about to lose my patience, Abby."

"And you're touching my breast."

"I know." His thumb stroked her nipple until an ache began in her lower belly and dribbled lower.

"You said…ah…" His mouth replaced his thumb and all thought left her. With each suckle, she felt wicked, sinful and ridiculously free. From what, she wasn't sure, but she went with the delicious emotions building in her.

"E-than."

"Shh. Don't talk, Abby. Just don't talk."

His hand slid around her neck and pulled her face to his, their lips met in an explosive kiss, their tongues meeting, dancing, discovering. Abby had never experienced anything this primitive before and she wasn't holding back or freezing up. She was giving as well as taking. Maybe she was punch-drunk.

Effortlessly, they discarded their few remaining pieces of clothing, and then they were skin on heated skin. Ethan caressed every sensitive area on her body and she returned the favor by stroking his strong muscles and feeling the power of him in her hands. When his fingers touched her intimately, she moaned, wanting more. Opening her legs, she welcomed him, but the moment she felt his hardness against her, she stiffened. A reaction she couldn't seem to control.

Ethan's mouth found hers and after a drugging kiss, he whispered, "Relax. Let go." One hand gently stroked from her breast to her hip. "Let go. Don't be afraid."

At his soothing words, her body went limp with need. He

thrust inside her and she marveled at the beauty of the coupling, but her thoughts quickly spun out of control as each thrust heightened her need and awareness that something beautiful was happening. Feeling brazen, she wrapped her legs around him and held him tight until her body dissolved into a shuddering mass of pleasure like nothing she'd ever experienced in her life. Ethan collapsed on top of her in a spasm of release.

Her last thought was, "Oh, my God." She'd just experienced her first orgasm.

CHAPTER SEVEN

ETHAN WOKE UP at dawn and stared down at the woman in his arms. She lay against him, her body curled against his. Her beautiful features were relaxed in sleep…blissful sleep. Red marks from his beard streaked her mouth, neck and breasts. Oh, God, what had he done?

He'd crossed a line—a line as big as Dallas. *Do not get personally involved. Keep a cool head at all times.* Cop rules, and he'd never had a problem maintaining them. Until last night. The moment her naked breasts touched his chest, he'd forgotten everything but her.

The early-morning light showcased the error of his ways— her breasts. They were gorgeous: round, soft, perky. And, oh, so touchable. Damn. He had to get a grip. Having sex with someone in his care was a big no-no and he didn't intend to make that mistake again, even though it was an experience he wouldn't soon forget. She was anything but cold. Maybe a little hesitant and inexperienced. She learned quickly, though. Her ex must be a total douche bag if he couldn't coax a response out of her. But then, dealing with a pregnancy and postpartum depression couldn't have been easy either.

All he knew was that he had to set some ground rules and stick to them. That shouldn't be a problem, since they now had to deal with the heat of the day again. Survival would be their top priority, as it should have been last night. In a way, though, he felt Abby was struggling to find her feminine side. That's why she'd talked about it. He shouldn't have been sucked into her insecurities. And he should have kept his hands to himself. But her breasts were so tempting. They still were.

He resisted the urge to kiss each one to wake her. That would be pure disaster. Taking one last glance at the twin peaks, he eased his arm from under her. He found his underwear and shorts on the floor and jerked them on. They were dry now, so it was easier to dress. He yanked his T-shirt over his head and slid his feet into his shoes.

He made his way to the well for water. After filling the pitcher he slowly drank every drop. When Abby woke up she'd want water, so he went back into the cabin to look for a container to carry her some. He didn't want to untie the rope attached to the pitcher. He found an old glass, rinsed it and then filled it.

On his way to the porch, he heard a loud scream. "Ethan!"

He ran, the water spilling onto his hand. He stopped short at the sight in front of him. Abby was on her knees, her tight butt and curvy backside facing him. He had to force himself to look away. She clutched her top to her breasts. A possum sat on the other end of the porch, watching her.

"Ethan, what is it?"

"It's a possum. Shoo." He picked up a small rock and threw it at the possum. "Shoo." The marsupial ambled to a porch post, crawled down and scurried into the woods.

"I brought water." He held up the glass.

She dropped her top and reached for it. He looked everywhere but where he wanted to. "Put your clothes on first."

"Ethan."

"Clothes first," he insisted, for his own sanity.

She picked up her top and slipped it on, as well as her bikini panties and slacks. He did his best not to look, but he couldn't resist a peek at all those sensitive places he'd touched last night: her flat stomach, the blond triangle of curls between her legs and her smooth white skin. The moment he did that he knew he was in trouble. This wasn't him. She had him acting like a seventeen-year-old.

He handed her the glass and she sank back on her heels, sipping the water and staring at him over the top of the glass.

He had to make a stand. Now. "Abby, last night things got out of control. I apologize for that."

Drinking the last of the water, she stared at him. "You know you get these little lines at the edge of your eyes when you're serious. They're very sexy."

"Abby…"

"I can read your mind."

"You can not." He sat on the porch and rested his back against a post, hoping sincerely that she couldn't.

"How's this?" She cocked her head. "Last night was a mistake. It will never happen again. You're a cop sworn to protect or whatever and you broke some sort of sacred vow the moment you touched me…in that way. You're riddled with guilt and dishonor."

Maybe she *could* read his mind.

"We're two adults, Ethan, and free to do what we want. We didn't hurt anyone. And, as far as I know, you're not on duty."

"It was still out of line." He had to make that clear.

"I instigated it and I'm not ashamed that I did. I've been struggling with a lot of things lately, mostly feelings about my marriage and my part in its failure. I blamed Doug for a lot, but I was at fault, too. The marriage, pregnancy and the post-partum depression took a toll on me and I lost a part of myself that I thought I could never get back. Last night you showed me I could be a woman with deep, sensual, passionate feelings. I feel better about myself and the future ahead."

He had nothing to say. Once again she'd surprised him.

"So you see, I expect nothing from you, and I promised not to stalk you when we get back."

"You're very adult about this."

"I've been angry about Doug's betrayal for a long time, but

being out here where nothing matters but staying alive, I have to admit that I betrayed him, too. When I return home, I'll be able to talk to Doug without all the anger."

"You think you might get back together?" Why did those words taste so bitter on his tongue?

She shrugged. "I don't know. Doug's been wanting to, but I absolutely refused. Our sex life was so unsatisfying I couldn't understand why he would even consider it. Now I see it was only unsatisfying for me."

"So last night was an experiment?"

She glanced toward the awakening horizon with a dreamy expression. "I'll remember last night for the rest of my life. The night I discovered an important part of myself with a hard-nosed macho cop who just happened to be a wonderful man. I don't regret a second of it, and I hope you don't either."

"Nah. It's been my life's goal to awaken unsatisfied women." He was being flippant, but deep down he felt a little used and a little sad. He didn't understand that. Before she'd opened her eyes, he'd been sweating bullets about what she'd expect from him. Obviously nothing. That should be a big relief. Why wasn't it?

And to prove he was the good guy she thought he was, he added, "I hope you can work it out with your ex. It would be best for your little girl." The words came out of his mouth, but he didn't feel them in his heart.

"Yes, but I plan to take things slowly. I'm not sure if we can go back. I'm only sure we need to talk without all the bad feelings."

He swung his feet to the ground. "The sun will be up soon, and we need to walk while it's cooler."

She followed him to the well and they drank more water. "I saw some plastic soda bottles in the cabin. We can fill them with water and carry them with us. Maybe I can make a back-pack out of something."

He found an old knife in a drawer and ripped up a sheet to make a pouch and straps by making holes and tying knots.

"You're very resourceful," she said.

"You learn that on a ranch and in the Marines." He fished the bottles out from under the sink and they went back to the well. "Drink all you want and then we'll fill the bottles."

"Here." She handed him the pitcher and cupped her hands. "Pour some into my hands. I want to wash my face."

He did as requested and she splashed the cool water on her face and rubbed with her hands. The water trickled from her face to her neck and made wet spots on her dirty top. His eyes were drawn to her nipples outlined by the wet fabric. Drawing a deep breath, he went back to drawing water to fill the bottles. He ignored all those feelings stirring inside him. He wasn't a randy teenager, but she sure made him feel like one. Maybe the heat was affecting him more than he thought.

He placed the bottles in the makeshift backpack and slipped his arms through the straps. He tested the weight on his back and asked, "Ready?"

"Yes, but I'm so hungry."

"Mmm. A cheeseburger would do."

"That possum is beginning to look good."

He laughed, and he hadn't done that in a very long time. Not since he learned about Kelsey. "I'm not sure they're edible."

"Ethan?" He glanced into her worried blue eyes. "We are going to make it, aren't we?"

"Sure. We should come to a road or a farmhouse soon. And we have water, so let's start making tracks."

They set off and he looked back at the cabin. He wasn't a deep-thinking man or too sentimental, but he knew enough to know that last night would be a memory he wouldn't soon forget.

EVERETT WOKE UP and looked around for Chloe. She wasn't in the king-size bed. Neither was Gayle. He had insisted Chloe sleep with them because she was scared alone in a big bed away from Abby.

He got out of bed and reached for his phone. No calls. Why hadn't the cops called? It was morning and they still hadn't located his daughter. He'd phone as soon as he knew Chloe was okay. He reached for his robe and headed for the kitchen.

When he reached the den, he heard Gayle and Chloe in the breakfast room.

"I've fixed you some whole wheat pancakes with blueberries," Gayle told Chloe. "Eat up, they're good for you. And drink your milk."

He could see Chloe sitting in her booster chair still in her pink-and-white cotton nightgown, clutching her doll in one arm. She took a bite of pancake and made a face. "It don't taste good."

"Eat it," Gayle said in a sharp tone and plucked the doll from Chloe's arm. "You can't eat holding a doll."

Chloe's bottom lip quivered and tears rolled from her big blue eyes. "You're mean. I want my mommy."

What was Gayle thinking? He would not have her acting like this toward his granddaughter. He was about to step in when he saw the stricken look on Gayle's face.

Suddenly, she stroked Chloe's hair. "Don't cry. Please. You don't have to eat it. Here." She put the doll back into Chloe's arms. "Would you like some Froot Loops? Grandpa buys those for you."

Chloe nodded.

For the first time, he realized his wife knew nothing about children. Her wealthy first husband died after two years of marriage and she'd worked at the bank as long as he could remember, more for something to do than for the money. She later became his secretary and helped him get over the death of his wife. Gayle was a smart woman, but clueless when it came to kids. She didn't get how harsh she sounded sometimes or how her stiffness put people off. That had been the catalyst of Gayle's and Abby's problem.

Anna, his first wife, had been soft and loving, and Gayle was the complete opposite. Gayle's good qualities were there, but she hid them, and a teenage girl was not going to find them unless Gayle made an effort, which she never did. It was his fault. He should not have married Gayle until all the family problems had been resolved.

"Is that better?" Gayle asked as Chloe spooned cereal into her mouth.

Chloe bobbed her head.

"I cut up strawberries and cantaloupe, too."

"I like strawberries," Chloe said around a mouthful of cereal.

"Good. Eat all you want." Gayle pulled a chair closer to Chloe and sat down. Chloe pushed the plate of pancakes toward her and Everett smiled.

Gayle picked up a fork and took a bite of the pancake. She frowned. "Oh, my, that's awful. No wonder your grandfather complains."

Chloe giggled and Gayle stared at her with a wondrous expression on her face, as if she was seeing Chloe for the first time. His wife was having a major meltdown of the good kind. With kids, a kind word and a gentle touch worked much better than orders and strictness.

"Where's Grandpa, Gayle?"

"He's right here." He walked in and gave Chloe a kiss on the cheek. "How my girl?"

"Good. Gayle made me Froot Loops." And without missing a beat, she asked, "Is Mommy coming?"

"I'm not sure, but we'll have lots of fun until she does."

"'Kay."

He went into the kitchen for a cup of coffee. Gayle followed. "I'll take my coffee into the den. I want to call Detective Logan. Can you watch Chloe?"

"Yes. No problem."

"We should have heard something by now. This isn't good."

Gayle wrapped her arms around his waist and hugged. "I know, but we have to remain strong. You make your call, and I'll take care of Chloe."

"Thank you." He started to mention what he'd heard and to reiterate that he would not tolerate her being mean to Chloe. But he was positive she'd come to that epiphany on her own.

Detective Logan didn't have much to say. They were still interrogating the suspect. He was sticking to his story, and so far they hadn't been able to break him. And the search for Abby and Mr. James had turned up nothing.

Everett hung up with a hollow feeling in his gut. His daughter's chances of being found alive were very slim. How did he accept that? How did he go on?

Chloe crawled into his lap. "Can we watch cartoons, Grandpa?"

"Yes." He held his granddaughter close, knowing he had to stay strong for her.

WALT DRUMMED HIS fingers on the table. It was almost nine, and Kelsey still hadn't come out of her room for breakfast. He'd called her at eight and gotten no response. Now what? He was worried about Ethan and didn't have the patience to put up with an ill-mannered little girl.

They finally knew why Ethan was at the bank. One of Ms. Bauman's friends said she'd been talking to her just before the robbery and someone had rear-ended her. There was a scratch on Ethan's bumper, so the cops assumed it was Ethan and he was at the bank to exchange insurance information and got caught in the robbery.

He'd talked to Levi at four this morning and the slimeball robber wasn't budging on his story. Levi was in Houston following a lead on the second robber. The FBI had said the tip was phony, but Levi was double-checking. Ross was handling the interrogation in Austin. Either way, Ethan was still missing and that was getting harder and harder to take.

He marched down the hall to Kelsey's door and banged on it. "Get up. It's breakfast time."

No response.

He started to bang again when he heard a sound. Was that a sniffle? Was she crying? Oh, Lord.

"Kelsey, open the door."

"It's not locked."

Well, he hadn't thought of that. He turned the knob and went in. She sat at the foot of the bed in a black T-shirt, her head down, her hair covering her face.

Something was wrong. He sensed it. He'd play it slow and easy, like a cagey hunter. He didn't want to spook her.

"Breakfast is ready."

"I'm not hungry," she mumbled.

He wished she had told him that two hours ago. "How about some milk or juice?"

"No. Just leave me alone."

Slow and easy wasn't working so he got straight to the point. "Why are you crying?"

"I'm not," she denied.

"If you're worried about Ethan…"

"Why would I worry about him? He never cared anything about me."

"You have to know about someone before you can worry about them. Ethan's been fighting for custody since the moment he found out you were his. That doesn't sound like someone who doesn't care."

"He only did it to get back at Sheryl."

"He could care less about getting back at your mom. He did it so his kid could have a decent life and not be shuffled around like a piece of luggage."

"You don't know what you're talking about. You're just a crazy old man."

"Look at me!" he shouted. "Now."

She raised her head and all he saw was a red blotchy face and a whole lot of hurt. "You can be sullen and pout all you want, but you will not be disrespectful in this house. Do you understand me?"

"Yes," she blubbered.

"Now, why are you crying?"

"Leave me alone."

"Kelsey."

"I got my period, *okay?*" she spat.

Got her period? What the hell did that… Oh, Lord, no! He didn't know anything about the internal workings of girls. Oh. Lord, no. He took a long breath that seared the nitty-gritty of his backbone. Walking out of the room seemed the best choice. But he couldn't do that.

"Do you want to call your mother?"

"She's on a cruise somewhere with her new boyfriend, and she said not to call her."

"Did you talk about this with her or your grandmother?"

She shook her head. "Sheryl told me it would happen, but she never told me what to do. I don't know what to do and I'm scared." She put her face in her hands and started to cry again.

Walt sat by her. "There's no need to cry. We can figure this out. Ethan has a computer in his room. We can look it up on the internet and read all about it."

"I know about it. We learned in school."

"Oh." He must have misunderstood.

"I just don't have any stuff, and I don't know what to do."

"Did you try some toilet paper?"

"Yeah, but it goes through."

"Make it bigger and we'll go to the H.E.B in Dripping Springs. The grocery store should have what you need."

"Okay." She hurried across the hall to the bathroom and he slowly made his way back to the kitchen, wondering what else was going to churn his gut into fish bait.

Thirty minutes later they were in the store and looking at all the products for feminine hygiene. He'd rather be in the hot sun bulldogging a calf than here. This was way out of his realm of expertise, and Kelsey seemed to be lost, too.

Being wise and knowing this was over his head, he decided they needed help. A lady in her forties rounded the corner pushing a basket.

He removed his hat. "Ma'am."

"Yes." She looked at him with cautious eyes.

"I need a woman…"

"Get away from me, you pervert." She hurriedly pushed the cart away from him.

What did he do? He glanced at Kelsey and she was giggling with a hand over her mouth. First time he'd ever seen a smile on her face. She'd put her hair into a ponytail and she looked pretty. He never noticed that before because her hair was always hanging in her face.

"What's so funny?"

"You said it wrong, Grandpa."

She'd called him grandpa in the feminine products aisle at the H.E.B. He wanted to laugh, too. With joy.

"What'd you mean?"

"You said you needed a woman."

"Oh. So that's what she got her dander up about. Stupid bitty. She didn't let me finish."

"It's okay. I figured out what I need." She pulled a package off the shelf. "This will work."

"Get two packages so you'll have enough."

"Okay."

They walked toward the checkout counter and Walt knew he'd remember this day for the rest of his life—the day his granddaughter had called him Grandpa.

He had a lot to tell Ethan.

CHAPTER EIGHT

ABBY FOLLOWED ETHAN through the woods, staring at the make-shift backpack. It looked heavy, and she wanted to offer to carry it for a while, but she knew the answer would be a big *no*. Of that, she was sure. She knew him well—all in a matter of a few hours.

As she walked, last night kept replaying in her mind. She'd never been that bold or brazen before in her life. Ethan brought out the vixen in her and she liked it. She'd kept so much bottled up inside, and it was freeing to let go and just feel without any thoughts of disappointing him. And, wow, did she feel.

This morning she'd wanted to say so many things to him, but she'd said what he wanted to hear. More like what he needed to hear to make him feel better about making love. She'd missed her calling. She should have been an actress. All she wanted to do was throw her arms around his neck and thank him and ask if they could see each other after they were rescued. But that would make him uncomfortable, so she didn't. She'd played it cool.

In the clear light of day she could see what they'd done was a mistake on so many levels. She'd put Ethan in a difficult position, professionally and ethically. It seemed as if someone had taken over her mind and body. Normally she would never act in such a way. She'd often listened to her girlfriends' sexual escapades and wished she had the nerve to flirt without guile, without regret and without thought. Holly would be proud of her, but Holly would never know. No one would.

Her right calf muscle cramped but she kept walking. The

heat was intense again, and her body was soaked with sweat. They'd stopped a couple of times for water, and she was dying for another drink.

"Oh." Another cramp brought her to her knees. Ethan was immediately at her side.

"What is it?"

"Leg cramps."

He removed the backpack. "Stretch out and relax."

She lay in the leaves, uncaring that her hair was in the dirt.

"Which leg?"

"Right."

He pushed her slacks to her knee and began to massage her calf with his big hands.

"Ouch," she cried when her muscles protested.

"You're not relaxed."

"It's hard to relax when the muscle keeps pulling. Your hands are not helping."

She thought he'd stop at her testiness, but he pushed her leg up and ran his fingers lightly down the back of it.

She sighed. "Ah...that feels good." Now that she could handle.

He kept stroking her leg and she relaxed, drifting into sleep. When she awoke she was disoriented for a moment, and frightened, but then she turned her head and saw Ethan sitting against a tree, resting. His face was lined with worry. She crawled to him and sat cross-legged.

"How's the leg?" he asked.

"Better. I didn't mean to go to sleep."

"You were tired and it was time to rest." He pulled a bottle out of the pack and handed it to her. She took a big swallow and gave it back. He took a swig and gazed off into the distance.

"Ethan?"

"Hmm?"

"What's wrong? I can see something is."

"They should have caught those two-bit crooks by now and gotten our location out of them."

He was clearly frustrated and that threw her. She didn't think anything could shake his confidence.

"We should have come across something by now, too—a house, a road, something."

"We just have to keep walking. Soon we'll reach safety. I trust you to get us out of here."

His narrowed eyes stared into hers. "Don't trust me, Abby. Don't trust me."

He was referring to last night and she didn't know how else to reassure him. How could one man carry so much guilt? About his daughter and now about her.

Suddenly, he tensed. "Don't move," he whispered.

"Wh—" Then she heard it. A low growl followed by a hiss.

"There's a bobcat on a branch above me to my left. Remain calm."

Calm? Her heart was thumping so loud she couldn't think, but she sneaked a peek. A huge, grayish mottled cat lay perched on a limp. Another threatening hiss rumbled from his throat. Chills shot up Abby's spine.

Ethan's hand closed around a rock the size of a baseball. Slowly, he lifted his arm and threw. The rock hit the cat and it fell to the ground in a cloud of dust, leaped to its feet and hightailed it into the woods.

"Oh." She sighed in relief. "Was it going to attack us?"

"I don't know. To be out this time of day he must be scrounging for food. We're a little big for his tastes, but it's better to be safe than sorry."

"We should go, then."

"No. Rest your legs. We'll start again in a few minutes."

She lifted her wet top from her skin to let air in. The breeze of last night was long gone and it was like breathing inside an oven.

"May I ask you a personal question?"

"Personal, huh?" She tilted her head and tried hard not to flirt. She just wanted to ease his dark mood.

"Yeah, and I don't want you to take it the wrong way. It's just something I need to know."

"Oh, that sounds ominous." She made a face. "Fire away."

He scooted up closer to the tree and wrapped his arms around his knees. "You do have a diaphragm, right?"

Guilt was about to kill him. "Yes." She placed her hand on his forearm. "I wouldn't lie to you about something like that."

"This is none of my business, but why? Since you're divorced and…"

He was definitely a cop. Always questioning. Making sure. After what he'd been through with Sheryl, that didn't bother her. He had a right to question.

"I have a friend, Holly, who has made it her goal to get me back into the dating scene."

"The once-a-month outing?"

"Yes. We go to clubs, have a few drinks and meet guys. We were planning to go last night. If I met someone special, I didn't want to be unprotected so I kept using my diaphragm. But I guess I have to be…"

She paused as the unspoken words hit her in the face like a slap. *I guess I have to be in love.* She wasn't in love with Ethan, and they'd had sex. Her mind whirled with unsettling thoughts.

"You have to be what?"

"Uh…" What could she say? Would an insanity plea work? "Uh…I guess I have to be suffering from heat exhaustion to have sex." At the strange look on his face, she removed her hand from his hot skin. "Please don't worry about what happened."

"I'm not." He pushed to his feet. "We better get moving."

Once again she followed him, all her thoughts turned inward. She couldn't love Ethan. Love took time to grow, build and to develop into something everlasting. They barely knew each other, and love didn't happen that quickly.

Maybe she knew what was important, though. Ethan would give his life for hers. He'd protect her with his dying breath. He was honorable and respected her. She trusted him and… Oh, she was in so much trouble. She had to stop thinking about Ethan and concentrate on getting home safely to her daughter. Once there she would see these feelings for what they were—foolish and false.

But no matter how she tried to justify her actions she knew one thing—she would always be grateful to Ethan and never cause him any undue stress. When they reached safety, she would disappear out of his life as quickly as she'd stopped in front of him yesterday.

But his memory would linger.

EVERETT SAT IN his chair, his cell on his lap, waiting. Gayle was on the floor with Chloe, playing with Barbies. Dolls and clothes were strewn all over the white-and-mauve Oriental rug they'd spent a small fortune on. Gayle didn't even like people walking on it. Yet his wife was playing dolls with a three-year-old on the rug. There was something definitely wrong with the picture, but he wasn't questioning it. He was glad she'd adjusted her attitude—all because Chloe had called her mean.

The doorbell rang and an eerie feeling came over him. He'd rather not know if something bad had happened to Abby. He'd rather keep waiting.

Gayle got to her feet. "I'll get it."

Doug strolled into the room and Everett stood. "I wasn't expecting you."

"Daddy." Chloe ran to him and Doug picked her up.

"Get your things. You're coming with Daddy."

"Why?"

"Don't ask questions. Just get your stuff."

"I'll help you," Gayle offered and took Chloe to the bedroom.

"You could have given me some notice," Everett said.

"I'm sorry." Doug ran a hand around the back of his neck. "I've been up most of the night talking to the police."

"So go home and get some rest. Leave Chloe here."

"I can't. I've called my father and he and my mom have cut their vacation short and are returning home to be here for Chloe and me. Abby's been missing for over twenty-four hours and from the cops and a criminal lawyer I know, they say it's a very slim chance Abby will be found alive."

"How dare you say that?" Everett's chest tightened in pain.

"Everett, we have to be prepared. If something has happened to Abby, I want Chloe with me and my family. I have to be the one to tell her."

"Get out of my house."

Gayle came running. "What's going on?"

"Get him out of here." Everett turned away, unable to say anything else.

"I ready," Chloe called, dragging her Barbie suitcase.

Everett gathered her into his arms and hugged her. "I love you, sweetiepie."

"I love you, too, Grandpa."

"Let's go," Doug said, and picked up the suitcase.

Gayle stroked Chloe's hair. "Bye, sweetie."

"Bye."

As the door closed behind them, Gayle turned to him. "What happened?"

"He said Abby was probably dead and he wanted Chloe with him so he could tell her. Of course, he'll take Chloe to his parents to show his father how responsible and mature he is."

"Come on, Everett. Don't let him get to you." She put an arm around his waist. "We believe she's alive and we will continue to believe that."

"I'm trying, but it's been so long." He walked back to his chair. "It's lonely without Chloe."

"Mmm." She squatted in the den. "Help me pick up all these toys. It will get your mind on something else."

"I don't…"

"Please." She looked up at him with a loving expression and he found himself on his knees putting Barbies back into a big box.

"Thank you for being more lenient with Chloe."

She paused in putting a dress on a doll. "It's eye-opening to see yourself through the eyes of a child." She placed the doll in a box. "I don't want to be that mean person."

From her expression and the tone of her voice he knew she meant it from her heart. "You're not, honey. You need to relax a little and not be so stern."

"I'm trying, and I plan to do better with Abby, too."

"Thank you." He sat back on his heels, feeling better. His wife supported him and that made all the difference in the world.

His cell buzzed and he reached behind him to get it. It was Detective Logan.

"Mr. Baines, I have good news."

"You found my daughter."

"Not yet, but the FBI arrested the second robber in Houston. He still had most of the money on him and the bank's wrappers were on the stash. Of course, he said he found it. They're transporting him to Austin and as soon as he gets here we plan to crack him open like a piñata."

"Did he say anything about Abby?"

"At the moment, he's denying everything, but that will change."

"How can you be so sure?"

"Mr. Harmon passed away about thirty minutes ago and the charges have been upgraded."

"Oh, I'm so sorry. Abby really liked him."

"His family is here from Florida and it's really hard for them, but keep the faith, Mr. Baines. We're getting close to finding your daughter and Ethan."

"Please contact me the minute you know something."

"I will."

He clicked off and wrapped his arms around his wife. "They're close, Gayle. Oh, God, please bring Abby home."

WALT WALKED THROUGH the back door and hung his worn hat on a rack in the kitchen. His cows had water and were doing well in the heat. The radio said it was one hundred and five today. That was too damn hot for man and beast.

His stock tanks had dried up from the drought, and he had to depend on the windmills and well water for his cows. Luckily, Ethan had found hay in Nebraska and it had been delivered last week. He had enough hay for now, but if the drought continued he'd have to sell his cows. He couldn't afford to keep them. Things hadn't been this dry since the 1950s.

The house was quiet. He'd left Kelsey on Ethan's computer reading about her cycle. He figured that was the best way for her to learn. If he had to tell her stuff, it would scare the hell out of her. The only thing he knew was that his wife had went nutty about once a month, and he'd avoided her at all costs during that time. He felt sure Ethan didn't want him telling Kelsey that.

He found her in Ethan's room sitting on the edge of his bed staring at something in her hand.

Walking in, he asked, "What'cha got?"

"This was on his nightstand." She held up a framed picture of herself. "Where did he get it?"

She wasn't calling him Ethan anymore. Just *he*. Walt sat beside her. "He took it the first time he met you at that motel in Dallas."

"I didn't see him take any pictures."

"You and your mom were standing outside and he took it with his phone before he got out of his truck."

"That's the day we took the DNA test. He didn't know I was his daughter then."

"He watched you for a long time. He studied your facial features and noticed your brown eyes and hair. See?" He poked the picture. "You didn't have your hair colored then, and he just knew you were his."

"Really?"

"Yep."

"I colored my hair to…"

"To what?"

"I thought if I looked gross, he'd leave me alone."

"Oh." A lot of things became clear—a young girl's rebellion at what had been done to her life.

"Did you want to stay with your mom?"

She shrugged. "I just didn't want to live with someone I didn't know."

"I know that's hard for you, but I hope you'll give your dad a chance. He's a good man. I raised him and I know him inside and out, and then some. Make an effort and he won't disappoint you. You have my word on that."

She didn't respond, but gently, almost reverently, placed the photo back on the nightstand. "Can I stay on the computer for a while?"

"Sure."

"I have a couple of friends in Dallas and I want to check their Facebook pages and let them know where I'm living now."

He stood. "Tell them you're home."

"Okay." She slid into Ethan's desk chair.

"Tell them you're home with your dad and your grandpa."

"Okay." Her fingers flew over the keyboard.

At the door, he added, "And don't do anything illegal. Your dad's a cop."

She lifted her head, a slight smile on her face. "I won't."

He was beginning to like that smile.

Before he could make it to the kitchen, a knock at the door sounded. Carson Corbett stood on the porch, his Stetson in his hand. Carson was a good friend of Ethan's. They'd grown up together. A former marine, Carson was now the constable of Willow Creek and surrounding areas.

"Hey, Carson, come on in."

"Thanks, Walt, but I don't have a lot of time. Levi wanted me to stop by and give you the news in person."

He drew a long breath, bracing himself.

"They arrested the second robber."

"I know. I talked to Levi a little while ago."

"Once the charges were upgraded, Devon Williams cracked quickly. He finally told them they didn't kill Ethan or the woman. They left them on the Old Mill Ranch south of Bastrop."

"Thank the Lord."

"I'm going to Austin to join the search after Williams pinpoints exactly where they were left."

"That shouldn't be too hard, should it?"

"It's a five-thousand-acre ranch that's been for sale for years. The heirs are up north, so the place has been abandoned."

"But Ethan's alive?"

"We hope so, but Williams said they didn't leave any water and it was one hundred and two yesterday."

"That son-of-a-bitching bastard. How does that lowdown piece of shit think a person can survive without any water?" Familiar cuss words erupted from his throat and it was too late to yank 'em back. He was just so angry.

Carson placed a hand on his shoulder. "Ethan's resourceful. We all know that. Just keep thinking he's alive. Choppers will be in the air as soon as we have the location and rescuers will go in on foot. We'll find him, Walt. Stay strong."

"Call me as soon as you know anything."

He closed the door and saw Kelsey standing in the doorway. "They don't know if he's alive or dead, do they?"

"No, but your father is strong. Everything will be okay."

"You don't know that!" she screamed and ran to her room, slamming the door.

Lordy, Lordy. He trudged to the kitchen and sank into a chair. *I'm sorry, Ethan. The cuss words just flew out of my mouth. I'll do better.*

He stood up and then sat down again. Fear made him antsy, but what could he do? He couldn't sit here and think about his son dying from heat exhaustion. He had to do something.

"Kelsey," he shouted.

No response.

"Kelsey, get out here. I need your help."

"What?" Her eyes were red. She'd been crying.

"I want you to look up something on the computer."

"What?"

"Old Mill Ranch."

"Isn't that where…"

"Yep. Let's find out how to get there from here."

"You mean we're…"

"Yep."

"Cool."

After he had directions, he and Kelsey filled three five-gallon water coolers and he planned to stop at the convenience store and buy all the bottled water and Gatorade he could. Volunteers and rescue workers would be there, and they'd need water.

As he stored the last container in the back of his truck, Henry Coyote came around the corner of the house.

"Hey, Walt, I've been knocking and knocking. What are you doing?"

"Loading water."

"For what?"

"They know that Ethan and the woman are on the Old Mill Ranch. I'm joining the search."

"Have you lost what little sense you've got? You'll just be in the way. Let the authorities handle it."

He opened his truck door. "I'm going." Kelsey scurried

around to the passenger's side. "If it was Levi, you'd do the same thing."

"Mmm. But you don't need to take the kid."

Kelsey frowned as she opened the door. "He's my daddy and I'm going. You can't tell me what to do."

Henry leaned over and whispered, "That kid has a mouth on her."

"Then don't tell my granddaughter what to do." He climbed into the truck. "I'll see you later."

"Oh, sh—"

Walt's dark look stopped him midcurse. "Shih Tzu. Are you satisfied?"

Walt nodded.

"I better go with you." Henry climbed into the backseat.

"Suit yourself." Walt backed out of the driveway. "You're my navigator, Kel. When we reach the highway, tell me where to turn."

Henry mumbled something under his breath, but Walt ignored him. He had other things on his mind. Kelsey had called Ethan *Daddy* for the first time. He wondered if she even realized she'd done it. It didn't matter. She'd said it. That was a big step.

He might be doing the wrong thing in joining the search, but he couldn't sit around waiting any longer. His son needed him and he had to be there. His only hope was that Ethan was alive.

CHAPTER NINE

By MIDAFTERNOON THEY were out of water, and Ethan's strength was waning. Abby lagged behind and he waited for her. Her dirty hair was matted to her skull. Her sweaty clothes stuck to her slim body. Defeat was evident in the slump of her shoulders. Where in the hell were the rescue people? With each passing minute, he grew more frustrated.

"Time to rest," he told her as she reached him. "It's too hot to keep walking and it's difficult to breathe." She followed him to a clump of trees and they sat in the shade. After a moment, she stretched out, her head on his thigh.

"I'm so hot, Ethan."

"Me, too." He stroked her hair from her face, feeling as close to her as he had to anyone in his life. Their circumstances had bound them in a way he hadn't expected. "Try to rest."

She went to sleep and soon he drifted off, too. Something woke him. He stirred restlessly and opened his eyes. The wind was blowing, whipping the heat around them. It whistled through the trees and stirred the leaves on the ground. Leaves gathered in piles and then scattered to other resting places. He noticed a group of leaves near some rocks that didn't move. Something glistened on them and drew his attention. Was it just the sun? Or...

He eased away from Abby and went to check. When he stepped on the leaves, it was squishy. Water! Where was it coming from? He squatted and raked away the leaves. Water pooled in a muddy puddle. He trailed it to the rocks and then he saw it. Water oozed from between the rocks. A spring. A natural spring.

"Abby," he called.

"What?"

"Come quick."

"What…" She paused when she saw the water. "Is it a mirage?"

"No. It's a natural spring. Come. Drink."

She stepped through the leaves and knelt by him. "How?"

He bent over and caught the water with his mouth. "It's like a water fountain."

She followed his lead, licking her lips. "Oh, it tastes so fresh."

They drank their fill and then sat back. "This is a godsend."

"I couldn't go much farther without water," she said, placing a hand on her stomach. "I'm so hungry."

"Me, too. Take a deep breath. It will pass." He studied the ground. "There are a lot of animal tracks around the puddle. This must be a watering hole, but because of the drought it's low."

"We haven't seen any animals, though."

"I was wondering about that." He scratched his beard. It was driving him crazy.

She touched it, her hand lingering on his skin. "Sexy."

"It itches," he replied, wanting to remove her hand, but it felt so good.

"I thought you were sexy from the first moment you glared at me."

"I didn't glare," he refuted. "I was pissed off."

"Oh, excuse me." She removed her hand and he wanted to catch it, to keep it close against him. "I stand corrected. From the first moment you were pissed off at me."

He didn't say anything. He felt it best if he didn't.

"And you thought I was annoying."

"Yeah, but I noticed how beautiful you were." He hadn't meant to say that. It had just slipped out.

She fanned herself. "Oh, I do declare I'm going to swoon from sheer delight."

"Abby."

"I'm sorry if my honesty makes you uncomfortable."

"I'm not uncomfortable. It's complicated."

"I know."

"And you're still fixing my bumper."

"Oh." She cocked her head. "I don't think so. It needs to be left as a reminder of everything we've been through."

He pressed the heel of his shoe into the dirt. She was right. He'd never repair that bumper.

They were silent for a while as they came to grips with the change in their relationship.

Once again their dire situation pressed upon him. "We need to go over our options."

"Like what?"

"We have water. We could stay here and wait to be rescued or we could walk on risking our lives without water in this heat. Or you could stay here and I could go on ahead and bring back help."

"No, Ethan, please don't leave me here. I'll walk faster. I'll keep up."

Unable to resist, he touched her arm in reassurance. "Don't worry. I won't leave you if you don't want me to."

"I don't."

"Then let's stay here for the night. We have water and we can rest. In the morning, if there's no sign of a rescue chopper, we'll start walking again."

"Okay."

A foul stench drifted to his nostrils. "What's that?"

"I don't know. I smell it, too, sort of like a cigarette scent."

He got to his feet. "I'm going over to that clearing to see if I can see anything. It might be rescuers with a diesel engine."

Out in the clearing he didn't see anything, but dirt and brittle grass. Then he looked up and froze. In the distance dark plumes of smoke billowed toward the sky. Above the treetops orange flames leaped.

Oh, my God!

A wildfire. And it was headed straight for them.

Abby!

"IT'S GOOD NEWS, Gayle," Everett told his wife. "The robbers told the detectives they didn't kill Abby or Mr. James. They left them on a ranch south of Bastrop. Rescue crews will be on the ground and choppers in the air. My daughter's alive. They'll find her."

"Everett, calm down. I'll get you a glass of tea and your medicine. The doctor said to take a half of a pill when you're upset."

"I'm not upset. I have hope now."

"I'm getting the pill anyway."

He sat in his chair, cell in his hand, waiting. Gayle handed him the tea and pill. He took it. He had to stay calm and strong.

"It's a big ranch, but with choppers it shouldn't take long to find them."

"I wonder if Doug knows?" Gayle asked.

"I'm not calling him. He can find out on his own since he seems to have so many contacts. I'm glad Chloe's with him. I don't want her to see how worried I am."

His cell buzzed and he reached for it. "It's Detective Logan," he said, clicking on.

"Mr. Baines, I'm sorry…"

"No," he moaned and dropped the phone. Gayle immediately picked it up.

"What is it?" she asked the detective.

He collected himself, forcing bad thoughts from his mind. He had to hear what the man had to say.

He grabbed the phone.

"Everett, no. Let me talk."

"No, she's my daughter. I can handle it."

"Mr. Baines, are you okay?"

"Is my daughter dead?"

"I don't know."

"What do you mean you don't know?"

"Rescues crews were set to go in, but the search was called off."

"Why?"

"A wildfire is raging across the ranch and we can't get in until the fire is contained."

"Oh, no!" A pain shot through his chest and he took a deep breath.

"I'll stay in touch and give you updates, but right now things aren't looking good."

"Thank you."

"Mr. Baines, reporters and TV crews are out here. Please don't turn on the TV unless you can take it."

Without another word he clicked off.

"Everett, what did he say?"

He told her the bad news. "Abby can't survive a wildfire. She will die a horrific death." He buried his face in his hands.

"Listen to me. We are not going to believe that. We will keep hoping until they bring her body in. Anything can happen and we're staying positive. Lie back and I'll get you a pillow."

As she left the room, he stared at his remote control. Against every objection in his head, he picked it up and turned on the TV. A wildfire scene immediately flashed onto the screen. A reporter talked into a microphone. The fire raged in the distance.

The reporter's voice finally penetrated. "As you can see the fire is blazing behind me. The entire area has been evacuated. The fire is burning west to east across Old Mill Ranch. We've been told no one lives there and the main focus now is to contain the fire."

"Phil," a newscaster at the station butted in. "We have reports that the two hostages taken from an early-morning bank robbery yesterday in Austin might be on that property. Have you heard anything to confirm that?"

"There are a lot of rescue teams here along with emergency vehicles. We're on the south side, away from the fire. The rumor is that they were ready to go in to search for—" he looked down at the iPad in his hand "—Ethan James and Abby Bauman, the two people taken from the bank. As of now, no one is allowed in. It will be a game of wait and see. But the fire is the top priority."

"Everett, what are you doing? Turn that off. You'll have a heart attack." Gayle clicked off the TV.

"It doesn't matter, Gayle. Nothing matters anymore."

WALT TURNED DOWN the country dirt road and stopped the truck. Emergency vehicles, trucks and people were everywhere.

"There's a lot of searchers here," he commented.

"Walt, look." Henry pointed out the window.

Thick, heavy smoke rolled toward the sky. "What the…?"

A man wearing an orange vest came to his window. "Sir, you'll have to turn around. This road is closed."

"I'm Walton James and I'm here to help in the search for my son, Ethan."

"Sorry, Mr. James, the search has been called off for now."

"Why?"

The man waved toward the smoke. "Firefighters have to control the fire first."

"You mean…?"

"Mr. James, turn the truck around and go home."

"I'm not going anywhere until I talk to Ross Logan or Levi Coyote."

"I don't know where they are."

"I do." Walt reached for his cell and called Levi. He picked up immediately.

"Walt, what's up?"

"You didn't tell me about the fire."

There was a slight pause. "I haven't had time. Just sit tight."

"I came to help, but no one is searching for my boy."

"What do you mean?"

"I'm here, but they won't let us in."

"Us?"

"Yeah, me, Henry and Kelsey."

"Oh, shit."

"Watch your language."

"I'll be right there."

"Told you, Walt, this ain't a good idea." Henry, as usual, had to put in his two cents.

Walt looked at his granddaughter and saw her big eyes and frightened face. For once, Henry was right. This wasn't a place for Kelsey. They had to go home.

Levi ran through the group and came around to the driver's side. "Walt." He rubbed Walt's shoulder. "Please go home. Only professional firefighters, officers and volunteer firemen are allowed in. It's too dangerous."

"I just wanted to help my boy."

"I know, Walt." Levi glanced in the backseat. "Pop, stop encouraging him."

"Well, son, it's kind of like stopping a train. When you realize that's impossible, you jump on for the ride."

Levi just shook his head. Sometimes it was hard to understand Henry.

"Carson and I are going in as soon as we can. The moment we know anything, I'll call."

Walt nodded. "I brought water and Gatorade. The firefighters might need it."

"Thanks, Walt." Levi motioned to two guys. They came running and unloaded the bed of the truck quickly. "Try not to worry." Levi looked over at Kelsey. "We'll find your dad."

Kelsey didn't say anything. Walt backed the truck into a

bar ditch and turned around. They headed home, somber and quiet. Kelsey kept looking back at the smoke.

ABBY RAN TO Ethan's side and stared at the sky in horror. A fire! Flames leaped ferociously over the treetops. Clouds of dark smoke billowed straight toward them. The wind kept whipping it closer and closer. The stench of burning grew stronger. There was no way to outrun it. "Ethan, what do we do?"

"We have to find some sort of shelter." He looked around and they both knew the fire would devour anywhere they could hide. Her heart drummed in her ears and fear snaked up her spine in vivid clarity. This time they would not survive.

Ethan grabbed her hand. "We have to get back to the water. Do exactly as I tell you. Run."

She didn't plan on doing anything else.

They ran until they could barely breathe. Ethan fell down by the puddle. "Start digging with your hands as fast as you can. We have to make a hole big enough to lie in."

She dug on one side, he on the other. Her arms grew tired, but she kept slinging mud until they had an indentation big enough for both of them. She had mud up to her shoulders and all over her.

Once Ethan was satisfied with the depth and length, he said, "Remove your panties. Nylon will melt to your skin. Your slacks and top are cotton, right?"

"Yes."

"And remove your shoes."

She kicked off her shoes and jerked off her slacks. Her hands and body were wet and muddy, but she managed. Ethan removed his underwear because of the elastic. His shoes he threw into the woods.

With their clothes back on, Ethan pulled her into the trough. "Lie facedown."

She did as instructed and Ethan began to cover her with the mud. He smeared it on her face and hair until not a spot of her skin was showing. Ethan then lay beside her and pulled more mud around them. He shifted covering most of her body with his. She knew what he was doing. That way he would take the brunt of the fire.

"Ethan."

"Shh." He rested his face in the curve of her neck. "Keep your face down. Breathe only when you have to."

The burning scent became intense and then the roaring, cracking, popping and hissing followed. The fire was seconds away. Waves of unimaginable heat rolled toward them. She thought of Chloe and bit back a sob.

"Ethan."

"Shh."

If they were going to die, there was something she had to tell him. "Ethan, I love you."

His arm tightened around her and they seem to sink farther into the mud. It wasn't important that he answer her. She knew he wouldn't. It was just important that she say the words she might never get to say again.

The roar of the fire drowned out her thoughts and then the smoke blanketed them as flames leaped around them with searing, scorching heat. Pain stung her shoulder, her neck. Smoke filled her lungs and she fought to breathe. Fire and brimstone rained around them and a hell like she'd never known devoured them. She gasped, fighting for air, and then everything went black.

ETHAN FLOATED IN and out of consciousness. His legs and back burned and smoke filled his lungs. He couldn't breathe and he fought to stay awake. He wasn't sure how long the fire raged. It felt like hours, but it could have been minutes. Then he realized the roar, hissing and cracking had stopped. And the intense heat had passed. The smoke, ash and soot lingered, coating them.

He lifted his head. "Abby."

She didn't respond. Her body was so still.

"No! Abby!" He pulled her face from the mud. She wasn't breathing. "No!" His hand shook as he wiped mud from her nose and mouth and then he placed his mouth over them and blew air into her lungs. "C'mon, Abby."

She sputtered and coughed. Soon she lifted her mud-coated lashes and looked at him with her gorgeous baby blues. He'd never seen a more beautiful sight.

"E…"

"I'm right here."

"Are we dead?"

"No."

"Are you sure? This feels like hell."

He hoped this was as close as either of them would ever get. "Let's get you out of the mud." He raked away clumps with his hands and helped her to sit up. They sat there looking at the total devastation around them.

The monster fire had burned everything. The trees were tall black charred sticks, smoldering and smoking. Ash and soot continued to rain around them. The ground was black as coal, and hot. Sparks glowed from the bigger trees and the wind circulated the smoke.

"Oh, my God!" Abby cried.

"Shh." He gently rocked her. "As soon as the ground cools we have to walk out of here."

"We don't have shoes," she pointed out. "It will be like walking on ashes."

"We'll wait until it cools. The wind will help with that."

She coughed and couldn't seem to stop. He had a smoke taste in his mouth he couldn't shake. His back and legs burned, but he had to stay focused to get them to safety.

"Firefighters will be coming in and they'll find us. We had to get out of the mud so they can see us."

"I don't have any strength left, Ethan. I can't move."

"Rest while the ground cools."

She laid her head on his chest and he prayed for strength.

After some time, he noticed the ground had stopped smoking. He eased away from her. "I'll check it out." He stood and the horrible scene swayed. He felt as if he was standing on quicksand, but he quickly regained his balance and tested the ground. It wasn't as hot as he'd thought it would be and there were patches of dried dirt untouched by the fire. They could make it out of here.

He went back to Abby. "Let's go. We can make it."

She had a coughing fit and he gave her time. "I—I can't."

"By now Chloe's missing her mommy." He hated to do that, but she needed incentive.

Tears rolled from her eyes down her muddy cheeks. His heart took a hit. "Hey, remember what I told you about crying? You haven't cried during this whole ordeal and now isn't the time to start."

"My baby," she moaned.

"I know. C'mon, I'll help you up." With his arm around her waist, he lifted her out of the mud. She staggered, but he held on. "Take a step." Holding on to each other they started to walk.

They made it to the clearing and there were no rescuers in sight. Where in the hell was everyone? Had the whole world forgotten them?

They kept walking. The smoke was heavy at times and breathing even more difficult. Abby continued to cough, as did he. Suddenly, she went limp and he swung her into his arms and kept walking. His legs cramped, his back burned but he took long strides willing his body to keep going. *He had to keep going.* He stumbled, but he caught himself in time. Then he heard a chopper. Voices. Shouting. Rescuers? Or was it his imagination?

The sounds grew louder. Help had arrived. He sank to his knees and then fell to the ground, still holding on to Abby.

Finally, she could go home to her family.

And so could he.

But their lives would never be the same again.

CHAPTER TEN

To PASS TIME, Walt, Henry and Kelsey played dominoes at the kitchen table. He and Henry started and then Kelsey wanted to play. Walt didn't see any harm in that. They weren't at the Rusty Spur where they played with murder in their eyes and beer on their breath. The game was for fun and to keep their minds on something else besides the fire and Ethan's dire situation.

Kelsey slapped her last domino on the table. "Domino. I win. Yay!"

"Shazam," Walt said.

"Shih Tzu!" Henry shouted and Walt wanted to laugh, but he wasn't in a laughing mood. "Walt, your granddaughter is cheating."

Kelsey made a face. "I'm just very good. My grandma taught me." She shuffled the dominoes. "Let's go again."

Walt looked at his five dominoes. "Son of a beady-eyed bitty."

Henry peered at his. "Shih Tzu."

Kelsey placed a double-five on the table. "Ten points for me." She scribbled the score on a pad.

"Are you Shih Tzuing me?" Henry frowned at her.

"You sorry baboon," Walt said to Henry. "Don't talk to her like that."

"Shih Tzu on you," Henry came back at him.

"Stop it." Kelsey held up her hands. "You're driving me crazy with those stupid words. Shih Tzu is a dog."

Walt just stared at his granddaughter.

"Grandpa, I've heard bad words before. My mom said them and so did my grandma. You don't have to make up words."

"Now, I promised your dad and I'm not going back on my word."

"Bull Shih Tzu," she said with a smile.

"Listen, young lady…"

"Oh." Kelsey jumped to her feet. "There's an update on the fire." She ran into the living room where they had the TV on. A reporter was on the screen with a microphone in his hand. Smoke swirled behind him.

"Just a warning—what you are about to see is gruesome. You might not want your kids to watch or if you have a weak stomach you might want to turn away. One of our cameramen caught this a few minutes ago."

Thick smoke hung in the air and suddenly out of it emerged a figure. Actually, two figures. One was carrying the other. The camera zoomed in and the two were charred from head to toe. Ethan fell to the ground and emergency personnel surrounded them. The whirl of a chopper pierced Walt's numb composure.

"Oh, my God!" Walt cried. "That's Ethan." Realizing Kelsey was staring at the screen, he grabbed her and held her face against his chest. "Don't look, Kel. Don't look."

"Grandpa, is he…is he burned?" she muttered into his shirt.

"Shh, child." His hand shook as he stroked her hair.

Henry turned off the TV. "Let's go. I'll drive y'all to the hospital. On the way I'll call Levi to find out where they're taking Ethan."

Walt couldn't move his feet. All he could do was hold on to Kelsey. He'd been waiting for news of Ethan, but he never thought it would be like this. What kind of horror had his son gone through? And how much pain was he in? It was too horrible to think about. He had to be there for his son, but his damn feet wouldn't move.

"C'mon, Walt," Henry called.

Kelsey took his hand. "C'mon, Grandpa, we have to go help Daddy."

Besides her brown eyes, Walt never saw much of Ethan in his granddaughter. Until now. She had Ethan's strong spirit.

"He'll be okay," she said, and led him out of the room.

When did she get to be so confident? He was shaking like a baby.

EVERETT SAT IN his chair, resting and waiting. He'd lost all hope, but he would never stop waiting until Abby came home. He should be stronger, he told himself, but he didn't know how to handle the loss of his only child. Disgusted with himself, he sat up. Abby would not want him sinking into this self-pitying crap. She was strong and he would emulate her.

He was never quite sure where his daughter got her strength. He and Anna were both quiet, gentle people who stayed close to home and minded their own business. Yet their daughter was the neighborhood poster child for helping everyone. When she was nine, she started babysitting neighbor's dogs and cats when they were out of town. Mrs. Wilkins, who lived down the street, had been diagnosed with cancer and soon became so weak she could no long get in and out of her house or her bathtub. Abby wrote a letter to the paper telling Mrs. Wilkins' story. People volunteered to build a ramp and a walk-in shower. Abby then had a lemonade stand and earned enough money to decorate the new bathroom. His daughter had been an amazing kid, and she was an even more amazing woman. Abby would never give up and neither would he.

He reached for the remote control and clicked on the TV.

"Everett, turn that off," Gayle called from the kitchen.

He paid her no mind as a reporter appeared on the screen. Smoke lingered in the background.

"I have an update on the two people rescued here a few minutes ago," the reporter said. "As we suspected they are Ethan

James and Abby Bauman, the two people taken from an Austin bank robbery yesterday morning."

A video came on. A figure trudged out of the smoke carrying someone. Everett caught his breath. The two were badly burned.

"Oh, no," Gayle cried, wrapping her arms around him.

"Be quiet. I can't hear."

"We were informed that Mr. James is awake, but Ms. Bauman remains unconscious. It's a miracle they survived that inferno. We will keep you updated on the extent of their injuries. The fire has moved off to the east and firefighters are still fighting it. We'll have a full report at ten."

Everett clicked it off, refusing to think bad thoughts. They'd found his daughter. The wait was over. Everything else he could handle. "We need to go to the hospital."

"I'll get my purse. I'm driving."

"I'll call Detective Logan on the way. And I have to let Holly know."

One hour and thirty minutes later they were directed to a waiting area of the burn unit at Brooke Army Medical Center in San Antonio. It was one of the best in the country, treating severely burned soldiers from Iraq and Afghanistan. The best burn doctors were here, and they would help his daughter.

Two elderly gentlemen and a girl were at the information desk. The girl's long black hair was in a ponytail and had a purple streak in it. He glimpsed it for a second, glad Chloe wasn't a rebellious teenager—yet.

"I'm Walton James, Ethan James's father. I want to see my son." One of the men told the lady sitting at the desk.

"Sorry, Mr. James, the burn team is working on your son. No one can see him."

"How badly burned is he?"

"I can't give you that kind of information. A doctor will come out and speak with the family once he's made an assessment."

"Thank you." The threesome took a seat in the waiting area.

Everett approached the lady. "I'd like to check on my daughter, Abby Bauman."

"It's the same as I told Mr. James. You'll have to wait. Your daughter is in very good hands."

"Thank you."

He and Gayle walked to the waiting area. Instead of sitting in a padded wooden chair, he stepped over to Mr. James and held out his hand. "Everett Baines. Abby Bauman is my daughter."

The man stood in worn jeans, cowboy boots and a hat in one hand. With the other, he shook Everett's hand vigorously. "Walton James, nice to meet you. This is my granddaughter, Kelsey, and my friend Henry."

He acknowledged them and then said, "I'm glad your son was with my daughter."

"Ethan's tough. He can handle any situation."

Detective Logan and Levi came around the corner. Everyone shook hands.

"Have you heard anything?" Walton asked.

"Not yet. We just have to be patient," the detective told them.

"So what happened?" Everett asked.

"Everett." Doug walked into the waiting room, carrying Chloe. She was asleep on his shoulder.

He was stunned for a moment. "Doug, what are you doing? And with Chloe? She shouldn't be here."

"I saw the story and that awful video on the news and I had to come to be here for Abby. My parents are out with friends, the maid doesn't work on Sunday and the nanny is unavailable. I stopped by your house and you weren't there so I had no choice but to bring her. How's Abby?"

"We don't know anything yet."

"That's absurd. They have to tell us something."

"No, they don't," Detective Logan said. "Ethan and Abby

are alive and the burn team is working to ensure they stay that way without family barging in demanding answers."

Doug stared at the tall detective with the gun on his hip and backed down like the weasel he was. "Yes, of course. I'm just very worried."

Everett had no choice but to make the introduction. Chloe stirred and Gayle gathered the baby from Doug's arms and sat with her in a chair.

"I rode with Ethan in the helicopter," Levi said. "Since he was burned so badly, the paramedic had a hard time starting an IV. They put him on oxygen and gave him something for pain, but he wanted to say something so the paramedic let him. First, he asked what the hell took so damn long."

"That's my boy." Walton nodded.

"Then he wanted to know how Ms. Bauman was. I told him she was being treated and he relaxed. The paramedic gave him more oxygen and he closed his eyes. Then he opened them, and I could see he wanted to talk again. He said to tell Kelsey he was sorry. He was on his way home to take her horseback riding when Ms. Bauman suddenly stopped in front of him on the highway. He rear-ended her and he was steamed."

"Why would Abby do that?" Everett asked.

"She said she'd missed her turn and slammed on the brakes without thinking because she was upset with her ex for pulling a no-show when he was supposed to have their daughter for the weekend. She had to interrupt her dad's Saturday once again to keep the baby."

Everett was so angry he couldn't speak and was glad when Detective Logan spoke up. "As we suspected, Ethan followed her to the bank to exchange insurance information. As he walked to the door of the bank to meet her and Mr. Harmon, the robbers showed up and pushed them inside. After that, he didn't say anything else and I didn't press him. I just told him he'd be okay and that Kelsey was fine."

Everett couldn't hold his anger in any longer. He pointed

a finger at Doug. "This is all your fault. If you had been man enough, responsible enough, to care for your daughter the way the divorce decree stipulates, Abby would have been safe inside that bank before the robbers showed up. Since it was Saturday, only the drive-through was open. The doors to the bank would have been locked. I'll never forgive you for this. Never."

Doug walked off down the hall.

Everett was shaking so much he had to sit down. Gayle rubbed his forearm and he tried to calm down. Chloe stirred again and then raised her head, her eyes sleepy.

"Grandpa." She held out her arms and he took her, holding on for dear life.

The James family didn't say anything. They looked bewildered at his outburst, but then maybe they understood. Walton's son was suffering because of Doug's thoughtlessness.

Walton turned to Levi. "Was Ethan in pain?"

"I'm not gonna lie, Walt." Levi shifted uneasily and Everett thought that was probably something the man rarely did. "Yes, he was in pain, but they gave him something immediately."

"How bad is he burned?"

"I don't know. There was so much soot, ashes and mud on him I couldn't tell."

"Mud?" Walt frowned. "Where did the mud come from?"

Levi shook his head. "I don't have a clue. We'll have to wait for answers."

The detective glanced at his watch. "I hope the doctor comes out soon. I have to get back to Austin, but I'm not going anywhere until I know Ethan's condition."

The two lawmen took seats and the room became quiet. Doug came back, but he didn't say anything either. Finally, a man in a white coat came out. Everett handed a sleeping Chloe to Gayle.

"I'm Doctor Giles Grayson," he said.

Walton stepped forward. "I'm Ethan James's father and—" he pointed to the girl "—this is his daughter, Kelsey."

They shook hands and Everett introduced himself. "I'm Abby's father and—" he waved toward his family "—that's Abby's daughter, Chloe, my wife, Gayle, and Abby's ex, Douglas Bauman."

The doctor nodded. "Nice to meet everyone."

"How are our kids?" Everett asked.

"Right now they're in critical condition. Ms. Bauman more so than Mr. James. She slipped into a coma, but we were able to bring her out of it. She's stabilized for now."

"Oh, no," Everett moaned.

Gayle jumped up, handed Chloe to Doug and was by his side. "Stay calm."

"Our main goal is to keep them stabilized," the doctor went on. "They're both severely dehydrated and suffering from smoke inhalation."

"And the burns?" Walton asked.

"Their bodies are covered with so much mud and crude it's hard to tell. We'll work through the night removing it as gently as possible. Our main objective is to remove the mud without removing skin so we can establish the degree of damage to the tissues of the body. It will be a long and painstaking process. By morning we should know the extent and depth of their burns and we will treat them accordingly."

"Thank you, Doc," Walton said. "I know you're doing your best. If Ethan wakes up, you tell him I'm taking care of his daughter and she's fine. Tell him not to worry."

"I will."

Levi moved closer to the doctor. "Did Ethan say how they got the mud on them?"

"I had to ask Mr. James that to be sure of what we were dealing with. He said they happened upon a natural spring that was drying up, but it was still trickling with water. They were able to drink from it by lying on the ground. It ran down some rocks and had made a small muddy pool. When they became aware of the fire, they ran back to the mud and dug a big hole with their hands. They lay facedown in the hole, and he covered Ms. Bauman with the mud and then he covered himself. It probably saved them from being burned alive."

No one said anything as once again they grappled with what Abby and Ethan had been through. And how they still had a long road ahead of them.

"It would be best if everyone got some rest. There are a lot of motels on I-35. In the morning we'll have more news."

"Which motel is the closest?" Walton wanted to know.

"Quality Inn is about a half a mile away and they have a small restaurant."

"That'll work." Walton nodded. "We'll be back first thing in the morning."

"Good deal. Leave your phone numbers at the desk in case anything changes during the night." The doctor walked away.

Walton held out his hand and Everett shook it. He felt the calluses that denoted a life of hard work. "Keep positive thoughts and we'll see y'all in the morning."

"You, too, Walton."

"Call me Walt. Everyone does."

"Good night, Walt."

Levi gave cell numbers at the nurse's desk and the James family left. Everett couldn't help but think they were good, hardworking people, the kind you'd want as your neighbors and your friends.

"Everett, I'll check and see if I can find a hotel." Gayle browsed the internet on her phone.

"I'm going to the Quality Inn. If it's good enough for the James family, it's good enough for me."

"You can't be serious."

"I am."

"Everett…"

She stopped complaining as Doug walked up. "Do you mind taking Chloe? I'd like to stay here in case Abby needs me during the night."

"Well, Doug, that would be a first."

"I'm sorry, Everett. I know I screwed up. I screwed up bad."

His remorseful tone got to Everett. "Yes, you did, and I don't have the energy to keep blaming you. My top priority is Abby and Chloe."

"Mine, too."

"Of course I'll take Chloe." He scooped the child out of Doug's arms.

"I have her suitcase in my car."

"I'll follow you out."

They started down the hall and Everett remembered his wife. "Are you coming with us or you getting a hotel room?"

"I'm coming with you." Her heels made an angry tapping sound on the floor. "I have your medication."

"Oh, I'd forgotten about that."

"You forget a lot of things, Everett."

"But I never forget you're my wife."

She fell in step beside him. "Sometimes it feels like it."

Same old problem. Same old complaint. But Everett wasn't stressing about it. That was the difference. He'd asked for a miracle and he'd gotten one. His daughter was alive.

WALT AND KELSEY walked behind Levi and Henry to the truck. The night was dark now except for the moon that hung high in the sky. It had been a long day, and it wasn't over yet. But he knew where his son was, and that would make sleeping a little easier tonight, if he slept at all.

"He was worried about me," Kelsey said beside him.

"You mean Ethan?"

"Mmm-hmm."

"He's been worried since he found out about you two years ago."

"I didn't know. I didn't think he cared."

"Well, now." He held one hand high in the air as they

walked. "To Ethan, you're way up here." He put his other hand down low. "The rest of the world is down here."

"Really?"

"You bet." If anything good came out of this tragedy, it was that Kelsey was seeing her father in a whole new light.

"Grandpa."

"Hmm?"

"I didn't bring my stuff."

"What stuff?"

"You know…my pads."

"Oh…oh, we'll stop and pick up some."

"But I don't want them to know." She flung a hand toward Levi and Henry. "It's embarrassing."

"Don't worry. Grandpa will take care of it." He felt sure he should have said something about how her developing feminine body wasn't something to be embarrassed about, but his grandparenting skills only went so far. He'd leave the rest up to Ethan.

Levi found a Walmart and Walt and Kelsey went in to shop. Henry complained, but that was Henry and no one paid him much attention.

They found the pads and then Kelsey wanted to know if she could buy some jeans. Being a new grandpa, he couldn't refuse. Once she got started shopping, she picked out jeans, a sparkly top, panties and shorty pajamas. Then they bought toothbrushes, toothpaste and deodorant for everyone.

Walt wound up getting a shirt, underwear and pajamas for himself. He felt Kelsey wasn't going to want to sleep in a room by herself, and he was right. She didn't want to leave his side so he got a room with double beds, as did Levi and Henry.

He let her have the bathroom first and he thought she'd be asleep when he came out, but she was wide-awake, sitting on her bed.

He pulled back the sheet. "Time for some shut-eye."

She crawled into bed and he turned out the light. So much

had happened today and sleep would not come easy. Tomorrow would be stressful as they'd learn how badly Ethan and Ms. Bauman were burned. But Ethan was strong and they'd get through it no matter what.

Kelsey twisted and turned in her bed. She was worried just like he was. "What's wrong, Kel?"

"I can't sleep. I keep seeing him burned…"

He reached to flick on the lamp. "Do you know how to pray?"

"No."

He sat on the side of the bed and patted the spot beside him. "Come here."

She scrambled to sit beside him.

"Fold your hands."

She did as he requested.

"I'm not much of a praying man, but your grandma, God rest her soul, was. Since your dad went missing, though, I've been praying a lot. Repeat after me."

"Okay."

He folded his hands. "Dear Lord, thank You for saving my boy."

"Dear Lord—" she repeated "—thank You for saving… my dad."

Thank You, Lord, he said to himself.

"Please watch over him and help his wounds to heal. Please grant me strength for tomorrow. Your faithful servant, Walton James."

She repeated every word until the end where she added Kelsey James. Up until now, she'd gone by her mother's maiden name even though James was on her birth certificate. Another step forward.

"Does prayer work, Grandpa?"

"Your grandma said it did and I believe."

"Then I believe, too."

"Good. Do you think you can sleep now?"

"Yeah." She stood, but didn't move. She looked at him. "Can I hug you?"

He swallowed. "You betcha." He enfolded her in his arms and felt as if he was hugging the most precious thing on earth. And he was—his granddaughter.

She hopped into her bed. "Good night, Grandpa."

"Good night, child."

Walt stared up at the dark ceiling. Lordy, Lord. What a lesson. A man was never too old to learn, to accept and to love. He was beginning to like black-and-purple hair.

Now Ethan had to see his child as Walt was seeing her. And Walt prayed it wasn't too late.

CHAPTER ELEVEN

WALT AND THE crew arrived back at the burn unit before seven. Kelsey got up when he called her though she was a little sleepy-eyed.

Levi let the lady at the desk know they were back and then went to get everyone coffee. They'd already had some with breakfast, but they needed more to get through the morning.

Everett and his family soon came in and he and Everett shook hands. "Hope y'all had a good night's rest," Walt said.

"We rested. That's about all I can say." Everett took a seat, the little girl in his lap. She was wide-awake, clutching a doll and peering at everyone cautiously. She was a cutie—big blue eyes and blond curls. Probably favored her mom, but her dad was a blond, too.

Almost on cue, the man strolled in looking as fresh as a daisy. Everett frowned at him.

"Did you go to a hotel, Doug?"

"I left about one. The nurse said Abby would be out for the rest of the night."

"We were told that earlier."

"I wanted to be sure."

"Mmm." There was a lot more simmering under Everett's cool demeanor, but being a gentleman he kept it to himself.

Walt sensed a lot of tension in that family. The wife, he'd forgotten her name, was frosty as the north wind, in control and about as friendly as a rattlesnake. But Everett was a nice enough fella and he wouldn't mind having a beer with him one day.

The little girl slid off Everett's lap and walked to Kelsey. "My name's Chloe. What's yours?"

"Go away, twerp."

Walt almost choked on his coffee. Good heavens, that child was going to be the death of him. He leaned forward. "Her name is Kelsey and she's glad to meet you."

"What's a twerp?" Chloe wanted to know.

"An annoying kid," Kelsey spat at her.

"Chloe, come back to Grandpa."

Chloe trailed back to Everett, her eyes on Kelsey.

"That was a big disappointment," Walt said to Kelsey.

"I didn't want to talk to her."

"Now no one wants to talk to you, including me."

Kelsey hung her head. Walt wanted to wrap his arms around her and tell her everything would be okay and she didn't need to be defiant to hide her pain. But that was one of those things his granddaughter had to learn on her own.

Walt noticed Chloe didn't go to her father, but stayed with Everett. He found that odd, but then Everett had said his daughter was divorced so maybe Chloe didn't see her father much. Before Everett could stop her, Chloe dashed over to Kelsey again.

"My mommy is sick and Grandpa said your daddy is sick, too."

"Yeah," Kelsey mumbled, not raising her head.

"Wanna hold my dolly?" Chloe persisted. "That makes me feel better."

"No," Kelsey mumbled again, but this time with much more force.

"Can I hold your dolly?" Walt asked. "I'd like to feel better."

"'Kay." Chloe handed him the doll and he cradled it in his arms. Kelsey shot him a sharp glance.

"Give it to her." Chloe pointed to Kelsey and Walt placed the doll in her lap.

After a moment Kelsey thrust the doll back at Chloe. "I don't play with dolls."

"Why not?"

"I'm too old."

"How old are you?"

"Twelve."

"Oh."

"Go away, twerp."

Chloe's eye narrowed. "You're a twerp."

The feisty response startled his granddaughter and Walt thought Chloe probably got her spunk from her mother. The dad seemed rather self-absorbed, texting on his phone and unaware of what his daughter was doing.

"You're a baby," Kelsey came back.

"That's my doll's name." Chloe smiled. "Wanna hold her?"

Kelsey groaned and buried her face in her hands.

Before anyone could intervene, Dr. Grayson entered the room with a nurse by his side. Everyone immediately got to their feet. He signed something in a chart for the nurse and put his pen in his pocket.

"Good morning," he said. "I hope everyone got some rest."

"We tried," Walt replied. "How's my son and Ms. Bauman?"

"I'm happy to say they're much better this morning. If anyone was praying for a miracle they got one."

"What do you mean?" Everett asked.

Kelsey moved closer to Walt and he patted her shoulder.

"We treat a lot of burns here, mostly soldiers, and when we see someone who appears to be as charred as Mr. James and Ms. Bauman, we know the outcome is not good. I fully expected that when we removed the mud, soot and ash from their bodies their skin would come off with it, leaving third-degree burns or worse."

"But it didn't." Walt was holding his breath.

"No. Once the debris was removed the epidermis was red

and intact. What your son and daughter have now is pretty much a bad sunburn."

A collective gasp sounded around the room.

The doctor looked at Everett. "In your daughter's case, it's first-degree and she should heal in a few days."

"Oh, thank you. Thank God!" Everett and his wife hugged.

"What about my son?" Walt asked.

"Mr. James has first- and second-degree burns and will be in some pain for a few days. His back and calves received the worst burns. Seems he didn't tell me the whole story. Ms. Bauman said he covered her body with his and received the brunt of the fire."

Walt shook his head. "That's my crazy boy."

"In my opinion, the ground was wet and the fire jumped over them or we would be dealing with something entirely different. The severe heat caused the burns, not the actual fire. As I said, they got a miracle."

"Do you mean I can take my daughter home?" Everett seemed almost afraid to ask the question.

"Not for a few days. I'm still concerned about the loss of oxygen and Ms. Bauman will be undergoing tests as well as taking breathing treatments and more lung X-rays because of the smoke inhalation. She's very weak and asking for her daughter and her father. I will allow a short visit to reassure her. Don't ask questions or pressure her. I would advise, though, that afterward you go home and let her recuperate. Someone constantly in her room will only be stressful for her."

"My daughter is alive and not burned. I'm so grateful I'll do anything you say." Everett shook the man's hand vigorously.

The doctor turned to Walt. "Mr. James is asking for his daughter so I'll allow you and the girl to see him for a few minutes. Same thing I told Mr. Baines—just reassure him. I've only known your son a few hours, but I have a feeling we won't be able to keep him here long."

"Yeah," Walt mused. "He's kind of stubborn. Don't know where he gets that from."

Henry coughed behind him and Walt decided not to respond.

Doug walked up to the doctor. "I'm Abby's husband. Could I see her, please?"

Dr. Grayson frowned. "Husband? She didn't mention a husband."

"They're divorced," Everett told him.

"But we're reconciling."

"That's news to me," Everett fired back.

The doctor held up a hand. "I'll ask her. If she agrees, you can see her for five minutes."

"Thanks." The man preened like a satisfied cat.

They thanked the doctor and he walked out of the room. Walt and Everett shook hands and then hugged.

Everett wiped away a tear. "I thought I'd lost my daughter. This is a great day."

"Yep," Walt agreed. "I've been doing a lot of praying. Something I hadn't done in a long time."

"I prayed, too," Kelsey said beside him.

Walt put his arm around her shoulder. "Yes, you did."

Chloe handed Kelsey the doll once again. "Wanna hold my dolly?"

"Okay, okay." Kelsey jerked the doll from her.

Chloe's bottom lip trembled. "I want my doll back. You're mean."

Kelsey shoved it at her.

Walt shook his head. "Everett, we have a little tension between our families."

"Don't worry about it, Walt. Kids will be kids."

Walt caught a glimpse of Everett's wife sitting by herself, looking lonely. He knew without anyone telling him that the woman wasn't Abby's mother. If she were, she'd be jumping for joy.

Everett followed his gaze and went to his wife. "Honey, did you hear? Abby's going to be okay."

"I heard, Everett."

Oh, yeah. Lots of tension.

ETHAN LAY ON his stomach, his head turned to the left. He lay on a mat with a lighter one draped over his backside. It felt cool and comfortable and it took away the burning sting. Of course, the stuff they put in his IV had something to do with that, too.

Everything seemed surreal, but he knew with certainty they'd made it out of that inferno without being burned or scarred for life. And the doctor had assured him Abby was okay—only had first-degree burns. That was unbelievable and more than he'd hoped for. He'd done everything to protect her and now she could get on with her life. That was important to him.

The door opened and he waited for a nurse to come in. Then someone kissed his head. The scent of sweat, Old Spice and coffee reached him.

"Hey, Dad. You haven't done that since I was about ten." His throat was sore from the smoke.

"Thought it was about time." His dad's voice was husky.

"I'm fine, Dad."

"You gave this old heart a scare."

"Sorry." He tried to see beyond his dad, but couldn't. "Where's Kelsey?"

Walt made a motion with his hand and Kelsey came into his line of vision. "I'm here."

"Hi, Kel. I'm sorry about Saturday morning. We'll do it real soon."

"It's okay," she mumbled.

Was she crying? He hadn't seen her cry. Maybe it was his imagination. He wished he could turn over and see her properly, but he was anchored to the bed and moving would be painful. But he did see new jeans and white T-shirt with all kinds of sparkly stuff on the front. No black. No earrings.

"Where did you get the new clothes?"

"Grandpa bought them for me."

"Grandpa, huh?"

Where was the defiant attitude? His daughter seemed to be a completely different person than the one he'd last seen on Friday.

"We're getting along just fine, son. You don't have to worry about Kelsey."

"Thanks, Dad."

"Are you in pain?" Kelsey asked.

"Nah." For now he wasn't lying, but other times his body felt on fire. But he would never tell her that.

"Son, the doctor said for us to go home and let you recuperate."

"That's good. I don't want you sitting up here. There's nothing you can do and I'll be home in a few days."

"Now you listen to those doctors and stay as long as they want you to."

"Dad."

"I can stay and hand you stuff when you need it. I can take care of you, Daddy."

Daddy.

At the sound, his heart pitter-pattered all the way to heaven and back. Had he heard correctly? She usually called him Hey. What had happened since he'd been gone?

He reached for her hand and she clasped it. "I appreciate the thought, Kel, but I want you to go home with Grandpa and clean my room. Have him buy some really soft sheets. My skin's gonna be a little sensitive for a while." He had no idea why he was telling her that. He just wanted her to feel needed.

"I will, Daddy. I'll clean it real good."

"Thank you, sweetie." He'd been waiting for two years to

call her that and it seemed ironic that he had to go through hell to accomplish it.

"Bye, son." His dad kissed his head again. "I'll check with the hospital for updates and call home if you can."

"Bye, Daddy."

"Bye." He let go of Kelsey's hand even though he didn't want to, but they'd taken a big step forward in their relationship, and he had an even bigger reason to get out of this place as fast as he could.

The nurse came in and put an injection into his IV and he grew drowsy. The last thing he heard as he drifted off to sleep was *Daddy*.

Then the nightmare started. Fire blazed all around them, hot and ferocious. He covered Abby's body with mud, making sure no skin was vulnerable. Afterward, he quickly pulled mud on top of him. The soaring heat was intense and he buried his face against Abby's to protect her face from the fire.

"Ethan."

"Shh."

"I love you."

He twisted his head, trying to shake the memory from his mind. She didn't love him. It was only gratitude.

And he had to remember that.

Even in his dreams.

ABBY LAY IN a hospital bed with the head raised slightly, feeling weak and disoriented, but she was alive and she was grateful for that. Ethan had saved them. Unbelievable. If she closed her eyes, she could still feel those moments of terror, the heat and the smoke. Her hand went to her cheek. She could also feel Ethan's muddy cheek pressed against hers, trying to protect her. He had risked his life to save hers and they'd been spared. They would survive the burns, but she didn't know if she'd survive knowing a man like Ethan. He'd changed her way of thinking, of looking at life, and she knew she would never be the same again.

Oxygen tubing was fitted into her nostrils and she lay on a cooling pad with a topical burn ointment covering her body. The pain wasn't bad. The doctor had said Ethan's burns were more severe and she wondered if he was in a lot of pain. She wanted to go to him, but she didn't have the strength to move. Tomorrow she would be better and she'd see for herself.

The door opened and her father came in carrying Chloe. She tried to smile, but even her face hurt. Chloe eyed her suspiciously.

"It's Mommy," she said to reassure her child, realizing she looked a mess with her red skin covered in gook and her hair plastered against her head.

Even though Abby's voice was hoarse from the smoke, it did the trick. Chloe held out her arms. "Mommy."

Her dad gently sat her on the bed. "Be careful," he told her. "Mommy's skin hurts."

Everett kissed Abby's hair. "Thank God, you're alive, my precious."

"Thanks to Ethan. He's an amazing man."

"I've heard."

"Mommy got boo-boos?"

"Yes, baby."

Chloe laid her head on Abby's chest and Abby stroked her hair. It felt so good to touch her child.

"We can't stay long," her dad said.

"I know. I'm so tired."

"Then we better go."

Abby couldn't help but notice her stepmom's absence. "Gayle didn't come?"

"Yes. She's outside, but the doctor said only Chloe and me."

"That's ridiculous. I said my family. Go get her." Ethan had said she needed to make an effort and she needed to start to include Gayle in her life. Strange how surviving a bank robbery and a fire could change one's attitude. Three days ago she wouldn't have cared that Gayle was left out because Gayle had made her feel left out so many times. The battle ended today.

"I'll get her." Her dad's eyes lit up. Why couldn't she have seen years ago that her defiance only hurt her father? "Do you want me to take Chloe?"

"No, she's fine right here."

"Mommy?"

"Hmm?"

Chloe lifted her head, her face scrunched up. "That girl was mean to me."

"What girl?"

Chloe pointed toward the door. "Out there. She had funny hair."

Abby put two and two together. There could only be one girl in the waiting area with funny hair.

"Was her name Kelsey?"

"Yeah, and she called me a twerp."

"Why would she do that?"

Chloe shrugged.

"You know Kelsey's dad is hurt, too, and she was probably worried."

"That's why I wanted her to hold Baby. It would make her feel better, but she was mean."

"You remember how we talked about being nice to people."

"Yeah, but I'm not talking to her anymore."

"Oh, baby." She gave her daughter a hug, trying not to get gook on her. "I'm so glad to see your pretty face."

Chloe picked at the hem of her shorts. "Can you come home?"

Abby's heart lurched. All this had disrupted Chloe's life and she wanted reassurance her little life was the same.

"Soon, baby." She kissed her cheek with dry, cracked lips. "Mommy's boo-boos have to heal first."

The door opened and her father came in again followed by

Gayle, who was holding Chloe's doll. Abby wanted to laugh because that seemed so out of character for the stern straight-laced woman she knew.

"I'm sorry, Gayle, the doctor must have misunderstood me. I said my family, and you are part of my family."

Gayle looked as if someone had hit her in the face with a dead chicken. Ethan was right. A lot of the tension was Abby's fault.

"Don't worry about it, dear," Gayle replied in her usual stiff tone. Then her stiff demeanor changed drastically. Gayle's eyes watered and filled with concern. "Oh, Abby, look at you. Are you in pain?"

"Discomfort mostly."

"We better go," her dad said. "Abby needs to rest."

"I'm staying with Mommy," Chloe declared.

"No, baby." Abby stroked her child's cheek. "You have to go with Grandpa and Grandma." As soon as the word left her mouth, she wanted to jerk it back. Why had she said that? And how did she take it back without appearing like an utter ass?

"Is Gayle my grandma?" Chloe asked with curiosity.

Abby took a deep breath, trying to figure out how to handle her faux pas. She had no idea how Gayle felt about being called Grandma. Doug's mother didn't like it so her grandkids called her CeCe because her name was Celeste.

She swallowed, her throat as dry as ash, and went with her gut instinct. "Yes, Gayle is your grandma."

Chloe smiled as if she'd discovered something neat.

"We have to go," Everett said and reached for Chloe, but Chloe held out her arms for Gayle.

Abby held her breath. Gayle lifted Chloe into her embrace as if she'd been doing it forever, which Abby knew she hadn't.

Chloe took her doll from Gayle. "Grandma and me played Barbies."

"Did you?"

Chloe bobbed her head.

"Do you mind if we pick up some of her toys from your apartment?" Gayle asked.

"No, of course not."

"And we might buy more."

"Oh, boy." Chloe was all for that.

Abby wanted to say Chloe didn't need any more toys and that Gayle didn't need to buy Chloe's love. But suddenly it was obvious. Gayle had somehow earned it in the two days Abby had been in hell.

"Tell Mommy bye," Gayle instructed.

"Bye, Mommy." Chloe held up a hand, her face sad. "I love you."

"Love you, too, baby."

Gayle and Chloe walked out and Abby grew misty-eyed.

Her dad kissed her hair. "Thank you, my precious. Thank you. I'll check on you every day and come and get you as soon as the doctor says you're ready to come home."

"Thanks, Dad."

He walked out with a spring in his step. It was amazing how a little kindness went a long way. How she wished she'd made the effort sooner. How she wished she'd met Ethan sooner.

She closed her eyes, and in her mind his face was so close she could breathe his scent. *Ethan.*

She wanted to see him so badly that tears welled in her eyes.

Maybe tomorrow.

CHAPTER TWELVE

THE CREAK OF a chair woke Ethan. He lay on his stomach, sore, tired and hot. He wanted to turn over, but his back was too tender. Opening one eye, he saw Levi sitting and watching him.

"Hey, buddy," Levi said. "You look a lot better than the last time I saw you. You got a nice red going there."

"It feels as bad as it looks."

"Man—" Levi scooted forward "—when I saw you walk out of that smoke, charred beyond recognition, I almost lost it."

"You? Big, tough Levi?"

"Yeah. It's not easy seeing a friend like that. I thought no way in hell could you survive."

"Me, neither. It looked worse than it was. The ash and soot falling from the trees stuck to the wet mud."

"Thank God. You should be resting, but the doc said you wanted to see me."

"Yeah. Is Ross here?"

"He had to go back to Austin."

"In the chopper you said y'all caught the robbers."

"Don't worry. They're locked up tight."

"What about the third person?"

"What third person?" Levi looked confused.

"They talked about how the boss was going to be pissed that they didn't follow the plan. Rudy said to screw the plan. He was taking over. He intended to take Abby with him wherever they were going. They stashed us in a rat-infested deer cabin. I could hear them talking and I knew I had to get her out of there as fast as possible."

"How'd you do that?"

"The windows were broken out and even though our hands were duct-taped, we managed to crawl out and run into the woods. They followed. We hid under a fallen tree. Devon said he was leaving and taking the money. Rudy changed his mind then, but he fired a few rounds into the woods. Luckily none of the shots hit us."

Levi stood. "They just keep lying to us. To avoid a murder charge being tacked onto their other crimes, they finally cracked and admitted…"

"Murder?"

"Mr. Harmon died from a massive heart attack."

"Oh, no. The man was scared to death and white as a sheet. I'd thought he'd fainted."

"It was much more serious. They operated, but he didn't last long."

"Does Abby know?" He hoped they hadn't told her. It would be too much right now.

"I don't think so. The doctor's orders were to be brief, which means I have to go."

"I just wanted Ross to know about the third person."

"I'll let Ross know and he'll be on it ASAP. And since the good ol' boys lied, I'm sure the D.A. will upgrade their charges again. As soon as you're better you can give Ross and the boys in Robbery a full statement."

"Good deal. My throat's dry and…"

"And you need to rest."

"Yeah."

"I'll catch you later."

"Okay." Ethan closed his eyes, welcoming much-needed sleep. But the door didn't open and he still sensed Levi's presence. Lifting an eyelid, he saw Levi standing there as if he didn't know what to do, which seemed at odds with his confident can-do personality. "You're not going to hug me, are you?"

"Nah. Not today, but when you're better, I might hug the crap out of you."

"Now that would destroy our macho images."

"It's just good to see you alive, man."

"Yep. I know the feeling," he murmured.

"Get better, buddy." Levi walked out and Ethan heard the door quietly close.

He, Levi and Carson had been friends since they were boys growing up in Willow Creek. They'd suffered through each other's hardships and he knew they were hurting for him now. He'd truly been through the fires of hell. No one could say he didn't know what hell felt like. But then, he always knew what heaven felt like.

Abby.

He slowly drifted into sleep with her name on his lips.

ABBY WAS HALF-ASLEEP when Doug walked into the room. He rushed to her bedside. "Abby, honey, I'm so sorry."

"It's okay." Three days ago she'd have torn into him like a wolverine. Today she just wanted peace.

"It was an emergency, Abs. Dad called early and wanted to go over some details about the bank before he and Mother went on vacation. You know how he is. He expects me to drop everything when he calls and if I don't, he'll call Robert."

"And your brother will take over your job."

"Yes."

"Doug, ever since I've known you he's held that threat over your head."

"I can't let my younger brother take over. I'm the oldest and next in line for my dad's job."

"When you don't show up to collect Chloe, have you ever thought about how it affects her? She's all packed and has her doll and books ready to visit Daddy. Then I have to tell her you're not coming and scramble around to find someone to keep her. Her little world is turned upside down once again."

"I'm sorry." He winced. "Dad keeps me wound up."

"Maybe it's time to grow up and tell your father that it's your weekend with your daughter. Your responsibility for Chloe should come first."

"I…"

"Please," she said as she sighed, "I'm tired and I don't have the energy to have this conversation. But as soon as I'm better I'm hiring another lawyer, and if you miss your times with Chloe, I will be filing for full custody."

"Abby." He ran a hand through his professionally high-lighted blond hair. "I will do better. I promise."

"You will do it or you will lose custody of your child. I promise you that." She didn't know if she could fight and win against the Baumans' powerful attorneys, but she would do her best. If the horror she'd lived through had taught her anything, it was that she was strong. And she wasn't putting up with any more crap from Doug.

"All I want is for us to be a family again. If only you'd give me a second chance."

She closed her eyes and felt her strength draining away. "I can't do this now."

"I know, honey. Just get some rest. We'll talk when you're better."

Through her exhaustion her talks with Ethan surfaced and she had to tell Doug one important thing. Her emotional health depended on it. "Doug, I'm not angry with you anymore for destroying our marriage."

Hope brightened his eyes and she hated that.

"I was at fault, too, and I don't know if there is a way for us to go back to the way we were in the beginning." She didn't even know if reconciliation was what she wanted now, especially after knowing Ethan. But she'd promised Ethan she'd sort out her defunct marriage. It was the only way to move forward.

"No, Abby, it was all me." Doug tried to take all the blame. "You were the perfect wife."

She wanted to laugh. She was nowhere near perfect in their marriage bed. For some reason unknown to her she'd never allowed herself to experience a kaleidoscope of sensual pleasures as she had with Ethan. There was no holding back. Just giving and taking until there was nothing left but two people needing each other the way lovers should. The way married couples should.

"We'll talk later" was all she could manage.

"Don't worry about Chloe. I'll hire a nanny for her."

"No, please, I'd rather she stayed with Dad and Gayle. She's comfortable around them and a stranger would be unsettling for her."

"Whatever you think, honey."

Don't call me honey. Resentment flashed inside her at his audacity, but she let it pass.

He leaned over to kiss her and she drew away. "Don't kiss me. We're not even close to that point yet." Even a robbery and a fire hadn't changed her mind-set.

"But we will be," he said with confidence, and walked out the door.

Her hand went to her dry lips covered in ointment. She couldn't imagine anyone's lips touching hers but Ethan's. She was clinging to Ethan with everything in her. He was safe, secure; no one and nothing could harm her as long as he was around. But her emotions went deeper than that—all the way to her heart.

Those feelings wouldn't last, though. She was aware of that. When she was stronger, they would fade away. If she told herself that long enough, she would soon believe it.

Almost.

ON THE SECOND day, the redness and pain on Ethan's back and calves became severe. Blisters popped out across his shoulders. The doctor said it was to be expected. Ethan said curse words that he told his dad not to use around Kelsey, but it was the only way to get the frustration out of his system. Instead of going home to help nail the third person involved in the robbery, he had to stay in the hospital a few more days. At least until he could get clothes on his body. All he could wear were hospital-issued loose-fitting boxers, and he didn't think his lieutenant would allow him in the station that way.

He was still on an IV and taking liquids by mouth. He had soft foods for lunch, but he didn't have much of an appetite. In the late afternoon a male therapist got him up, and he walked around the room. At first he felt dizzy, but soon he had the hang of it again. Every muscle in his body screamed. He ignored the pain and soreness and kept walking.

By the end of the week, he was off the IV and eating solid foods. He refused more pain injections and would rely on pills if he needed anything. He had to tough it out so he could get back to work and to his daughter.

He was able to sit now, but it hurt to put any pressure on his back or calves. Abby was doing fine and going home, he was told. He wanted to see her one last time, but he resisted the urge to reach out to her. It was better to make a clean break. The two days they'd spent together was a time out of time they would remember forever.

Conflicting thoughts warred inside him, though. He'd protected her just as he was sworn to do. But he'd also crossed so far over the ethics line he couldn't even see it anymore. He now realized there were two Ethan Jameses—the man and the cop. The night on the porch of the deer cabin, the man had been in complete control. And Ethan the cop was feeling all the guilt.

He sat on the side of the bed, careful not to let his calves touch it. He had thought Abby would come to say goodbye. But what would that accomplish? He'd just told himself they needed to make a clean break. *What was happening to him?* He wasn't a sentimental guy, clinging to fairy tales like Abby. He was a hard-nosed, badass cop and a night with Abby wasn't going to change that.

He would miss her, though—this was all the sentiment he'd allow himself.

Something caught his attention and he glanced toward the door. Abby stood there. His heart took off like a thoroughbred racehorse galloping at full speed. She wore white shorts, a blue tank top and flip-flops. Her blond hair was clipped back, clean and inviting, as was her face. He hardly noticed her red, peeling skin. She was beautiful.

"May I come in?" she asked.

"Sure."

"How are you?"

"Better."

"They said you have second-degree burns, but you're red like me, except for the beard."

He gingerly rubbed it. "I can't shave until the burn clears up. It would irritate the skin more."

She shifted from one foot to the other. "Uh...you seem like a stranger."

"I am a stranger."

She stepped closer to him and the scent of honeysuckle reached him. "You'll never be a stranger to me, Ethan."

For a moment there was an awkward silence as they grappled with the aftereffects of what they'd been through. And all the heartfelt emotions they'd shared.

He watched the hand of the big clock on the wall tick off seconds. What could he say to her that wouldn't hurt her feelings?

She cleared her throat. "Why did they say you were severely burned?"

"It's my back and my calves. They received the force of the heat."

She leaned over to look and gasped. "Oh, Ethan. Is it painful?"

"Not too much." Of course, he lied.

She waved toward the bed. "Do you mind if I sit?"

"No." *Yes.* She was fresh and inviting like a new spring

day with the sun shining and flowers blooming. *Was it him thinking that?*

She sat next to him and he wanted to scoot over. She was too close for his guilty cop conscience.

"I didn't know you were going to cover my body like that."

"There wasn't time to consult. I'm much tougher than you."

"Oh, really?" She glanced at him with a lifted eyebrow and he glimpsed the spunkiness he'd first witnessed in her. From her calm demeanor he'd feared the robbery and the fire had altered her personality. He was glad to see it hadn't.

"Yes, really," he countered.

"I should be mad at you."

"But you're not?"

"No. It's hard to be mad at someone who risked his life for mine."

"I was trained to protect—in the Marines and as a cop. It's just a natural instinct."

"Well, you'll pardon me if I see it as heroic."

"I'm not a hero."

"You are to me."

"Abby…"

The hurt in her baby blues stopped him. That look could stop a Mack truck.

"I know what you're thinking."

He sighed. "You don't know what I'm thinking."

She cocked her head. "How's this? She's getting personal and I don't do personal or clingy or needy. I was doing my job and I wished she'd understand that." An eyebrow arched high, daring him to refute it.

And he couldn't. Maybe she *could* read his mind. Nah. She'd be blushing now if she could. She was just a damn good guesser.

"Close," he admitted to the gleam in her eyes.

She coughed and couldn't seem to stop. "I'm…sorry." She took a deep breath. "I'm still coughing a lot, but the doctor said my lungs are much better. I'm taking breathing treatments and have to continue those for a while. How about you?"

"Twice a day and sometimes more."

"It's not too bad, is it? Considering we escaped with our lives."

"We were incredibly lucky."

She picked at a piece of peeled skin on her forearm. "When I heard the roar and felt the intense heat, I knew we were as good as dead." She drew in deeply. "That's why I wanted you to know how I felt."

"Abby…"

She looked into his eyes and smiled. "I can see a big ol' traffic light in your eyes. It's red and blinking a warning."

"It's a caution sign."

"Oh."

"What you were feeling was gratitude, Abby."

"I know, but the emotions were very real at the time."

There was an awkward pause for a second and he thought it best not to dwell on what they'd felt at that moment.

"Do you know our daughters met?" she asked rather hurriedly.

"No."

"Chloe said she's not talking to Kelsey again."

"Why?"

"Kelsey called her a twerp."

"I'm sorry. Kelsey's not people-friendly."

"Mmm. With the big age difference I thought it was odd for them not to get along. Usually a twelve-year-old likes to mother a three-year-old."

"Kelsey's not the mothering type."

"So I gather. I guess they had the same negative reaction we did when we first met. And for the record, I'm still not fixing your bumper."

"Noted." No one was touching that bumper now. It would stand as a reminder of the time he'd known Abby Bauman—

intimately. He coughed and cleared his throat. "Did you talk to the detectives?"

"Yes. I told them everything that had happened and signed a statement. They were very inquisitive about the third person, but I didn't have any answers."

"They'll get to the bottom of it. Rudy and Devon will eventually talk, especially to avoid a murder charge."

She frowned. "Murder?"

No one had told her about Mr. Harmon. Damn! He couldn't keep it from her. She'd find out eventually. There was no easy way to say it. "Um…Mr. Harmon died."

"Oh, no." Her eyes filled with tears. "He was such a sweet man. He could have fired me at least ten times for being late, but he never did. He was considerate of my situation." She hiccupped.

He did the only thing he could. He put his arm around her shoulders. She laid her soft, warm cheek against his hot, bare chest, which generated heat of another kind and reminded him of touching her soft supple skin in the dark of night.

"He was retiring and couldn't wait to move closer to his daughter, who lives in Florida. He'd found a nice retirement villa about a mile from her house and he'd be there for the birth of his oldest granddaughter's first child. Those hoods took that away from him." She raised her head, her watery eyes flashing. "I hope they put them away for life."

"They'll get the max," he assured her.

She brushed away tears with the back of her hand. "I better go. My friend Holly is waiting to drive me to my dad's. I agreed to stay there for a few days until I'm stronger."

"That's probably wise."

"I did what you suggested."

"What was that?"

She ran the palm of her hands down her thighs. "I made an effort to be nice to Gayle and it was amazing. It was like watering a wilted flower. Gayle perked up immediately. I wish

I had reached out to her sooner. Life is too short to live with hostility."

"And it will make your dad's life so much easier."

"Yes. I never thought of that before. All I could see was my own selfish feelings." She glanced at him. "You could be a therapist."

"As I recall, when I mentioned those things you weren't too happy."

"No one likes to see their faults pointed out by a big ol' tough guy." She held up a hand as he started to answer. "I even talked to Doug without all the anger."

"You did?" That didn't make him happy but it should. He'd told her to sort out her marriage.

"I don't know if there's anything left of my marriage or if I can truly ever forgive him, but we're talking. I'm not filled with rage anymore at what he did to our lives. Surviving death, I somehow lost all that righteous indignation and I have to admit I was partly to blame, too. But I know with certainty that I'm not the cold mannequin he called me. I can respond passionately and without inhibitions."

He wasn't sure how to respond to that so he didn't.

"I have so much to thank you for, but a thank-you just doesn't seem enough."

"It is. Be happy, Abby. You deserve it."

"I better go."

But she didn't move. "Something wrong?"

"Yes." She clenched her hands. "I'm scared to death of leaving this hospital. If I close my eyes, I can feel the cold steel of the gun pressed against my temple, the suffocating heat and the intensity of the fire. In here it's safe. Out there, it's a brutal world."

"As you grow stronger, you'll overcome that feeling. We would never have survived if you were a weak person. Feel the fear and let it go. Promise me you won't let it get you down."

She stood. "I won't." Leaning over, she kissed his cheek

and rubbed gently across his bearded skin with her thumb. His breath stalled in his throat and he wanted to catch her hand and never let go. "Goodbye, Ethan." She stared into his eyes for an eternity and then walked out.

Goodbye, Abby.

CHAPTER THIRTEEN

HOLLY TALKED ALL the way to Austin and Abby listened with half a mind. With each mile away from Ethan, she felt more alone and afraid. She had the same debilitating feeling she'd had when her mom had died. Her mother had been her security blanket and Abby didn't know what to do without her but cry. With the help of her father she'd gotten through it and moved on.

But now…how did she get over Ethan? And the safety and security she felt with him? How did she stop being afraid?

"You're very quiet," Holly said.

"I'm just tired."

"I can't even imagine what you've been through. All your friends have been praying and thinking about you."

"Thanks."

"And, thank God, you had Ethan James with you."

She turned to look at her friend. "You know Ethan?"

"I know of him. He, Ross Logan and Levi Coyote are well-known cops for getting the job done—their way. Of course, Levi is no longer a cop, but he has connections to the department."

"I would be dead if it hadn't been for Ethan. He saved my life more than once."

"I can believe that. And it didn't hurt that he's a hunk, did it?"

"I didn't notice," she replied and felt herself smile for the first time in days. "At first I thought he was an arrogant jerk."

Holly laughed. "Now, that I can imagine."

Normally she would tell Holly everything that had happened with Ethan. But the subject wasn't up for discussion—it was personal, intimate and private.

Holly shot her a glance. "Maybe when you feel better we can hit the town. Trish, Lori, Marcie, Vicky and several other friends have called to check on you. We can have a big girls' night out to celebrate your recovery."

"Maybe later." Right now the thought didn't appeal to her. She just wanted to be left alone.

Holly whizzed into the Baineses' driveway. "Are you sure about staying here with the evil stepmom?"

"Yes. It's time to let go of all the hostility."

"Wow. That's a big step for you."

"Yeah."

Holly switched off the engine. "Are you okay?"

"I don't know, Holly. I really don't know."

"Oh, Abby."

"But I'll be fine." She brushed off a sense of doom that seemed to weigh her down. She had to overcome it. Opening the door, she heard Chloe screaming.

"Mommy! Mommy! Mommy!"

Chloe ran down the sidewalk and into her arms. Abby hung on to her until her arms ached. It was so good to hold her child. Chloe wiggled to get down, and then she took Abby's hand. The trio made their way to the front door where her dad and Gayle were waiting.

Her dad put his arms around her. "Welcome home, my girl."

Abby turned to Gayle and did something she wouldn't ordinarily do. She hugged her, too. To Abby's surprise, the hug was returned fiercely.

"Let's go inside," her dad said.

Abby stopped short in the den. A "Welcome Home" banner hung across the French doors with balloons of every color attached to it. She wanted to cry and didn't know why. Maybe because she'd never been this welcome in her father's house.

"Come, Mommy." Chloe tugged on her hand and pulled her into the breakfast room. More balloons were tied to the chairs and a bouquet of yellow irises sat in the center of the table. A cake and punch were also on the table.

"See?" Chloe pointed. "Grandma and me made you a cake."

"That was so sweet," she replied and couldn't find another word to say. She was that shocked.

"Sit," Gayle said. "And we'll all have a piece."

Chloe scooted her chair with a booster seat closer to Abby. "I'm sitting by Mommy."

Gayle served the cake and poured punch for everyone.

Chloe stared at the slice of coconut cake—Abby's favorite. Gayle remembered, and Abby was touched.

"I don't like white cake," Chloe announced with a frown.

Gayle got to her feet. "Don't you worry, sweetie. Grandma has your favorite." She went into the kitchen and came back with a chocolate cupcake on a dessert dish.

"Yay!" Chloe clapped her hands.

Abby had a feeling her daughter was being spoiled here, but she didn't have the energy to do anything about it at the moment. That would change, though.

Holly laid her napkin on the table. "I have a late shift, so I better go."

"Bye," Chloe called, her mouth full of chocolate cupcake.

Abby walked her to the door.

"You seem so down it's breaking my heart," Holly said.

"I'm just trying to adjust to everything that's happened."

"I know. If you need me, just call. Anytime. Night or day."

"I will."

Holly nodded over her shoulder. "It's a little weird in there. Did Gayle have an out-of-body experience or something?"

"No. It's just amazing what a kind gesture can do."

"Oh." Holly lifted an eyebrow.

"I'll explain later."

"Okay, friend." Holly hugged her. "Take care of yourself."

"I will."

"And call."

"I will."

There was an awkwardness between them now, and it had nothing to do with Holly. The tragedy had changed Abby. She was struggling to find herself, the woman she used to be. The woman who had the courage to get out of a bad marriage. The woman who was unafraid to step out on her own and raise her daughter. The woman who could handle anything life threw at her.

But now she felt like a child needing someone to hold her hand. And that was the biggest tragedy of all.

She went back into the breakfast room. "I'm a little tired. Do you mind if I lie down for a while?"

Gayle was immediately on her feet. "Of course not, I have your room ready."

Chloe jumped out of her chair and grabbed Abby's hand again. "Come look, Mommy."

She followed her down the hall and into a bedroom. Abby stared in awe. Pink-and-white candy-striped furniture met her eyes. The bed had a rail on one side and a canopy of white lace trimmed in pink, which matched the white lace curtains. A large Barbie dollhouse sat in a corner. It was a room for a princess. Her dad and Gayle were spoiling her daughter royally.

"I prepared the bedroom next door for you," Gayle was saying. "It shares a bath with Chloe's room, but the other bedroom has a private bath if you'd rather have it."

"No. I prefer to be close to Chloe."

"That's what I thought."

They walked through a lavish bathroom with granite vanities into a lavender-and-ecru room. Gayle folded the comforter neatly and placed it in a chair.

Abby sat on the bed, feeling a little out of it. "I'll rest for a while."

Her dad came into the room. "Rest all you want." He pointed

to a desk. "Your breathing machine is hooked up and your medication and ointments are there, too."

"Thanks, Dad." She stretched out and Chloe crawled up beside her. "I'm resting with Mommy."

Gayle flicked off the light as they walked out. Abby wrapped her arms around Chloe. "I missed you, baby."

"Me, too, Mommy. Are you hurt?"

"No, baby." She kissed her cheek. "Mommy's fine." But she knew she was far from fine. She prayed for strength to handle the days ahead.

Soon Chloe fell asleep, as did Abby. When she woke up, Chloe was gone and it was dark out. Knowing Chloe was with her dad and Gayle, she turned over and went back to sleep. The next time she awoke it was light out. She glanced at the bedside clock—7:00 a.m. She'd slept all night. Easing out of bed, she felt her muscles ache. She wondered how long it would take for her body to recover.

She went through the bathroom to check on Chloe. The bed was empty. Abby used the bathroom and washed her face. She hardly recognized the somber woman staring back at her. There was no light in her eyes or smile on her face. She looked tired and defeated. Where would she find the energy to change that?

Her skin was still red and peeling, but how she looked was a minor thing compared to her emotional state. She began to cough and she trailed back into the room for a breathing treatment. After putting the medication into the machine as the nurse had showed her, she sat in a chair to breathe it into her lungs. She had an appointment with a doctor in Austin tomorrow. He would monitor her recovery.

Afterward, she stared at the phone on the desk. On impulse she picked up the receiver and called information. She got the number for the burn unit in San Antonio and punched in the number. She told the nurse who she was and asked about Ethan's condition.

Her response was that he was progressing very well, although he was a little grouchy about his confinement. She could just imagine that. Ethan was a man of action. Resisting the urge to talk to him, she thanked the nurse and hung up.

She had to let him go.

But how did she do that without losing the most important part of herself—her heart?

ABBY'S DAYS FELL into a routine. She rested, played with her daughter, had long talks with her father and spent her afternoons by the pool, watching Chloe swim. She sat on the patio in the shade. Her skin was too tender to endure the sun. She might never enjoy the sun again.

Every day she felt a little stronger, and soon she'd have to do something about her life. Doug came by every afternoon and they were able to talk without the anger and resentment. He wanted her to move back in with him, but she wasn't ready for such a drastic step. Her emotions were still strongly attached to Ethan. She intended to take things slowly.

Detective Logan and Detective Beecher had come by with more questions. She had nothing else to tell them, but she definitely had heard Rudy mention a boss. They were still investigating. Devon's appendix had burst and he was in the hospital for now. The case seemed to be at a standstill.

The bank had given her a month off with pay to aid her recovery. That eased her worries about money.

She'd gotten Mr. Harmon's daughter's address and written her a long letter, conveying her condolences. The image of his body lying so pale and still on the floor of the bank would always be with her, as would the horror of those two days. At night in her sleep, a hot suffocating feeling would come over her and she'd call for Ethan. But he was never there.

That hurt more than the memories that tortured her.

She called often about Ethan to keep tabs on his recovery.

She learned he was going home at the end of the week, and she was excited for him. He could now return to his daughter.

She wondered if he ever thought about her. The night they shared. His touch was branded on her skin, her fingertips. All she had to do was close her eyes and he was there holding kissing her, making her aware of the passion that had missing in her life.

How did she forget that when it was all she thought about?

The answer was easy: by leaving the cocoon and safety of her father's house. She had to start living again.

Without Ethan.

"GRANDPA."

Walt took a sip of his morning coffee. Lordy, if that child thought of one more thing they needed to do for Ethan's homecoming, he might have to escape to the barn.

She breezed in with a sheet of paper in her hand. "I was looking on the internet for soft sheets for Dad's sensitive skin. It said Egyptian cotton is the softest."

"What's wrong with American cotton?"

"I don't know. I'm just telling you what I found."

"Your dad is tough as an old boot and he's not gonna want some sissified sheets."

Her eyes narrowed just like Ethan's when Walt said something he didn't like. "They're not sissified. They're soft."

"Same thing."

She rolled her eyes.

Walt tried another tactic. "We ordered those cooling pads and he'll sleep on those."

"You can't just put cooling pads on a mattress. He needs soft sheets. I'll check online to see if Macy's or Dillard's has them."

"Who's paying for this?"

She glanced at him. "You are."

"You're very free with my money."

"It's just money, Grandpa."

"Says someone who doesn't have any."

She made a face and went back to the computer in Ethan's room.

"Your dad is not going to use any of the stuff the doctor ordered. He's stubborn," he shouted after her.

"Like someone else I know," she shouted back.

"Aw, I'm going to check on my cows."

"Don't stay too long. We have to go to the mall."

"The mall! I don't do malls."

"We have to get the sheets."

"Shih Tzu."

"Shih Tzu to you, too." She giggled and Walt smiled.

He didn't know what he was so grouchy about. He was happy his son was coming home. The good Lord had answered all his prayers, but all of Kelsey's preparations were for naught. Ethan wasn't a mollycoddling kind. He'd go back to work as soon as he could and no one would ever know his pain, especially his daughter.

Walt headed for the back door. Kelsey had to find that out on her own. Having a granddaughter was great, but sometimes she was a pain in his keister.

AN HOUR LATER they were at the Barton Creek Mall in Austin.

Kelsey undid her seat belt. "I can go get the stuff so you don't have to walk so far."

"You're not going into a mall alone," he told her, glancing at all the parked cars and people trailing inside. "Too many people."

A grueling hour later Walt was revising his decision. His feet ached and his head hurt. They'd gotten items on Ethan's list like boxers, baggy shorts, big T-shirts and a pair of brown Croc shoes. But they still hadn't gotten the sheets. Kelsey didn't like the color at Macy's so they had to traipse all the way to Dillard's. A sheet was a sheet to him. He didn't understand all the fuss.

Finally, she found something that caught her fancy. She held up two sheets. "Camel or brown, Grandpa?"

"Camel. Let's go."

"I don't know," she wavered.

"Ethan loves camel. Let's go." He had no idea which was which. They both looked brown to him. He just wanted to get out of the busy place. Everywhere he stood, some woman was trying to push past him. Women were like cows at a feed trough, anxious to get all the good stuff before it was gone.

He almost lost his breakfast when the lady rang up the items, but he paid for them. Good thing he'd brought his checkbook. Shopping bags in hand they headed for the truck, which was clear across the mall now.

Suddenly, Kelsey stopped. "Grandpa..."

"No. We're not buying one more thing."

"This is important," she said in a low, tearful sound. Damn. He was dead meat.

"What?"

She waved a hand to his right and he noticed some sort of beauty salon. "Can we see how much it costs to get my hair turned brown again?"

"Oh, no. That's something for your dad to handle."

"Please, Grandpa. I want it brown like it is in the photo on his nightstand when he comes home. Please."

"Oh, Lordy, child." He walked into the place and a scent like ammonia hit him in the face like a dead fish. Hair spray and other foul smells clogged his sinuses. Brightly colored bottles decorated a shelf. Women sat in chairs while stylists did their hair. A reception area was to the left and he spoke to the young woman who sat at the desk.

"My granddaughter would like—" He glanced at Kelsey. "You tell the lady what you want done."

"I want my hair to be brown again."

"Oh." The woman was chewing gum about ninety miles an hour. In between chews, she shouted, "Janine, up front, please."

A girl in black boots, a short skirt and a skimpy top sashayed over. "What is it?"

Walt was mesmerized by her hair. It was spiky and dyed a bright red. The tips were green.

"This girl would like her hair returned to its natural color," the chewing gum lady said. "Can you do it?"

"Mmm." Janine felt Kelsey's hair. "Was it colored in a salon or did you do it at home?"

"My mom did it at home, but she bought the products at a beauty supply place."

"How many times has it been colored?"

"Just once."

"Mmm." She studied Kelsey's hair. "The purple is dark and might be a problem, but, sure, I'll give it a try. Just realize it might turn orange."

"Orange!" Walt had heard enough. "No. We better wait and let your dad handle this."

"Grandpa, please." Her sad, soulful eyes begged him.

"Aw, all right. What is this gonna cost?"

"About two hundred dollars," the girl replied.

"Are you Shih Tzuing me?"

"W-hat?"

Kelsey took his arm and pulled him aside. "I'll do the dishes, the laundry and anything else to help pay for it. Grandpa, please."

And quicker than he could swat a mosquito, he found himself sitting in a beauty salon waiting for his granddaughter.

"Would you like something to drink?" the lady at the desk asked.

"No, thanks."

After thirty minutes of flipping through women's magazines and seeing more skin than he ought to, he took a Coke. Then he had to go to the bathroom. He left his packages with the lady and set out to find one. After that, he sat again.

Getting tired, he went outside the shop to call Henry, and

then he stretched his legs. Walking back in he had to go around
a girl to find his seat.

"You didn't recognize me."

Walt whirled around and stared. She looked so much like
Ethan it was eerie. Her brown hair hung down her back in
bouncy curls.

"What do you think?"

"No orange. Good."

"Yeah. Now you have to pay her."

He pulled out his checkbook and wrote a check.

"You have to tip her, too," Kelsey whispered.

"Two hundred dollars is enough."

"Grandpa."

"Humph." He found a five in his pocket and placed it with
the check.

As they walked through the mall to the truck, Kelsey kept
looking at herself in the glass store windows. She was happy.

That was worth every penny.

CHAPTER FOURTEEN

HE WAS GOING HOME.

And it wasn't soon enough.

Ethan paced his hospital room in his boxers. Carson and Levi were on the way to pick him up, to save his dad the long trip. His release papers were signed and he was more than ready to bust out of this place. Not that Ethan wasn't appreciative of the medical care he'd received. He was. He'd just been confined too long.

The doctor said he was a fast healer. Once the blisters dried up his pain lessened, and now he had a lot of red peeling skin. The good part was he could tolerate pressure on his back and calves. He just needed clothes. He glanced at the clock on the wall. Where were Carson and Levi?

He sat on the side of the bed and wondered how Abby was doing. He couldn't seem to stop thinking about her—which was probably normal under the circumstances. They'd been bonded by horrific circumstances. He had no doubt she'd put her life back together. She was strong, resilient. She'd make it.

Feeling restless, he got up. He hoped she wasn't too lenient with the ex. She deserved better than a guy who'd cheat on her. *Whoa.* He was the one who'd encouraged her to forgive. So what was his problem?

The vivid memory of her hands touching his skin tentatively, and then aggressively, rolled through his mind. He took a deep breath. He had to stop thinking of that night.

Forcing the memory away, he saw his daughter's face. *His*

daughter. When he thought those words, life felt surreal. He had a daughter, and now he'd get the chance to know her.

Glancing at the clock he said, "Damn." He wanted to leave this place where all he could do was think. It was driving him crazy.

"Do I hear cursing?" Levi asked as he and Carson walked in. Levi placed a carryall on the bed.

"You're damn right. I'm ready to get out of here." He unzipped the bag and pulled out khaki shorts.

"Did your boys get scorched in the fire, too?" Levi asked.

Ethan paused over a button, frowning. "No, my boys didn't get scorched. They were well protected."

Carson pushed back his Stetson. "Why would you ask a question like that?"

"Did you see all those pretty nurses out there?" Levi thumbed over his shoulder. "After all he's been through, I thought it would be a just reward if one of them rubbed ointment onto his balls or other sensitive areas."

Carson laughed and Ethan stared at his friend. Levi had a dry wit, but it was unlike him to be so outspoken and crude.

"What's wrong with you?"

"He's punch drunk—" Carson replied "—from investigating the robbery along with his other cases. He hasn't had much sleep."

"Oh, well, if it will make you feel better, a pretty nurse shaved my beard off with an electric razor this morning." He rubbed his smooth jaw. "And she did rub ointment over it."

"Now we're talking."

Ethan searched for a T-shirt in the bag. "So the lieutenant's letting you investigate the case?" Ethan tugged the shirt over his head.

"Hell, no. I'm doing it undercover and finding squat. Devon and Rudy both had cell phones and we've checked out everyone they called. No one they contacted is involved. They were just looking for a place to hide. The third person has hidden his or her tracks very well. We can't find a trace, and most of the money has been recovered. We're trying to figure out what a third person's involvement would be besides money. And to really get your juices flowing Beecher has been ordered to focus on the evidence he has. The higher-ups are pressuring the lieutenant to take Ross off the case because he's too closely involved. He's bucking that."

"More procedure bullshit."

"Yep."

"Those hoods talked about a boss. I didn't make that up."

"Why do you think I'm busting my ass on this?"

Ethan reached for the Crocs in his bag. "Let's go. The quicker we start comparing notes the quicker we can figure this out."

Levi shook his head. "Sorry. No can do. You're going home." He glanced at Carson. "That's why I brought extra muscle, in case you had other ideas."

"Of course I'm going home. I have to see my kid. But then…"

Levi sighed. "No *but then*. You're on paid leave until otherwise notified. Lieutenant's orders."

"Like hell."

"I brought a rope just in case we need it," Carson quipped.

"Funny." Ethan picked up the bag. "Let's go."

Within minutes they were on the road headed home. They talked more about the robbery case, but Levi soon fell asleep in the backseat. Carson caught Ethan up on what was going on in Willow Creek, which was pretty much nothing. Rarely did anything happen in the small town, except the double murders that had happened years ago. Carson's brother had been shot by his girlfriend's father. Lamar Brooks was killed later that night. People said Asa Corbett avenged his son's death, but it was never proven. As the constable, Carson did his best to keep Willow Creek crime-free.

Of the three friends, Carson was the go-by-the-book lawman. Ethan admired his friend's integrity and his dedication to the law. Ethan and Levi had the same dedication, but they were lacking the wait-and-see tactic. Even when they were rowdy boys, Carson was always the one reining them in.

Carson's life had sorely been tested. His wife had died after giving birth to their daughter. He became a single parent with two kids to raise. Last year his father, Asa, the man who owned most of Willow Creek, had a stroke and was now in a wheelchair. Dealing with the old reprobate took all of Carson's patience.

"Are you still in pain?" Carson asked as they crossed the cattle guard to the James property.

"Mostly discomfort."

"I guess you know your story and photo has been in every newspaper and on every newscast in the country."

"Yeah. A couple of reporters tried to get into my room. Security was very alert. Hopefully, the excitement has died down."

"Don't count on it."

Carson drove into the yard of the brick house his dad had built for his mom. Her dream house. A double detached garage was to the right. His truck was parked inside.

"Hot damn. My truck beat me home."

"Levi and I brought it back. Thought you might need it."

"You bet."

"Your dad has your wallet, keys and cell phone."

"Thanks." He turned his head, taking in the familiar scene. Barn, sheds and cow pens stood to the far right. Cows milled around a water trough. Others stood beneath a huge oak to get out of the hot August sun. Horses lazed in a pasture on the right side of the barn, where an old John Deere tractor was parked in front. Home. A part of small-town America. No matter where he went in the world, he was always happy to return here.

When Carson stopped the truck, Levi woke up and crawled from the backseat. Ethan got out, too, and grabbed the carryall.

From the inside of the house they could hear Kelsey screeching, "He's home. He's home!"

Levi slid into the passenger's seat. "Someone's excited. I'll talk to you later—and I mean later."

He waved as his friends drove away. Opening the gate on the chain-link fence that enclosed the house and yard, he stopped short. Kelsey stood on the porch, his dad behind her. Long hair flowed down her back. It was brown—not black and purple. Gone were the black jeans and T-shirt. She wore denim shorts and a white tank top with a peace sign on it. What had happened while he'd been gone?

She tentatively shifted from one leg to the other as if she wasn't sure what to do. He did what any father would do. He dropped the carryall and held out his arms. Clearing the step with one long jump, she practically flew to him. He held his child for the first time and he didn't want to let go. Anger bubbled inside him that he'd been kept away from her for so long.

"Come inside," Walt called. "You're supposed to stay out of the sun for a while."

Arm in arm they walked inside. He hugged his dad and Kelsey ran back for his bag. Back in the living room, she spun around, flipping back her hair.

"What do you think?"

"It's beautiful," he replied. "You're beautiful."

"Grandpa paid for it and now I have to do the dishes, the laundry, clean the house and help with the cooking."

"Wait a minute." Walt was quick to object. "Don't make me out to be the big bad wolf. It was your idea."

"I know, Grandpa." She gave him a quick hug.

This was as surreal as it could get. When he'd left Friday night for a stakeout, his dad was in the kitchen muttering that the aliens had landed. Kelsey was mumbling about a crazy old man and had locked herself in her room. He'd planned to get back early to defuse the situation. But, obviously, it had defused on its own.

"Daddy, I have your room all ready." He followed her to his room as she talked. "We bought really soft sheets so they wouldn't irritate your skin. I put the Chillow pads on the bed in case you want to lie down." She pointed to his dresser. "Your breathing machine is there with the medication, and there's ointment, too, if you need it. I'm making sandwiches for lunch and we have Blue Bell ice cream. Tonight I'm making spaghetti. I used to make it for my grandma and her sister all the time. I can get you anything you want. You don't have to get up or anything. I…"

He held up a hand. "Whoa. Take a breath."

"Yeah. Your head is about to explode," his dad told her.

"It is not. I'm just excited."

"We know." Walt grinned.

"I'd like a glass of iced tea," he said, just to give her something to do. But if she thought she was going to wait on him, they'd have to have a talk. He planned to go back to work in a couple of days. He couldn't rest until the robbery case was solved.

Kelsey dashed out the door.

"Lordy. Lordy." His dad shook his head.

"I take it a lot has happened since I've been gone."

"You wouldn't believe. I'll fill you in later." He patted Ethan's shoulder. "Glad to have you home, son, and glad you've lost that tomato color."

"Me, too. Now I'm just getting browner." They followed Kelsey into the kitchen. She had a glass of iced tea on the table with a napkin.

"You want tea, Grandpa?"

"Nah. I'm going to feed the cows."

As Walt went out the back door, Ethan sat down and pulled another chair close to his. "Have a seat. We need to talk."

"Okay." Kelsey plopped into the chair.

He leaned forward. "You didn't have to change the color of

your hair to please me. I'm your dad and I will love you whether your hair is black, blue, green or whatever."

"But you like it, don't you?" Her voice wavered a little.

"Yes."

"Good." She let out a long breath. "I got tired of it the other way and people looked at me funny."

"And that bothered you?"

"Sometimes. Grandpa really didn't like it."

"Grandpa has an older mind-set."

"But he's cool. Maybe grouchy, but still cool."

"When I left for work on Friday night you thought he was a crazy old man. What happened to change your mind?"

"Well." She twisted her fingers together. "You went missing and Grandpa was upset and I tried not to care. I came into the kitchen to ask if he'd heard anything and I said *hey* and he lost it. He said—" she dropped her voice to sound like her grandfather "—'You will not call me Hey. My name is Grandpa, Pa, Pop or whatever you're comfortable with, but you will not call me Hey.'"

"What did you say to that?" He tried not to smile but feared he was failing.

"I said, 'You will not call me alien. My name is Kelsey or Kel and that's what you will call me.' He apologized for saying that and we made a deal to be more respectful."

"I'm glad."

"Then I got my...you know...period and I was scared."

His mouth fell open and he quickly closed it. Tough-ass cops weren't supposed to be surprised or shocked. They'd seen just about everything, but for the first time in a long time he didn't know what to do or say. He went with what was in his heart.

"I'm sorry I wasn't here."

"That's okay. Grandpa handled it."

Grandpa handled it. That was like saying Grandpa found a cure for cancer. It didn't fit. He was almost positive his dad knew nothing about young girl's menstrual cycles. Nor did he.

"But you knew what to do?"

She shifted nervously in the chair. "Sheryl said it would happen and we had classes on it in school, but I didn't pay much attention. I thought I'd be older before it happened. Stupid, huh?"

"Maybe a little." It irked him that Sheryl hadn't talked to Kelsey about this. That was a mother's job. Now it was his. "How did Grandpa handle it?"

"I was scared and crying and he wanted to know what was wrong. He kept on until I told him. We went to Walmart and got some stuff I needed and Grandpa almost got slapped by a woman."

On and on she talked, the light in her eyes blinding as she talked about everything she and Grandpa had done. "When the lady told him what it would cost to strip my hair, he said, 'Are you Shih Tzuing me?' She thought he was nuts. Dad, we have to do something about the crazy words he uses. I've heard curse words before. Please tell him it's okay to use them."

"I'll think about it." He didn't want his daughter hit with a barrage of obscenities every day and his dad was doing very well with his made-up words. The fun part for Walt was it irritated the hell out of Henry. Besides, they had more pressing matters to discuss.

He reached for her hand. "There's a Dr. Morrow who does a lot of work for the department on abuse cases. She's a pediatrician. I'll make you an appointment for a checkup and she can explain what's going on with your body."

She frowned. "Pediatrician? That's a baby doctor."

"A pediatrician sees kids up to eighteen years of age."

"Oh. Will you go with me?"

"Of course. I wouldn't let you go alone." Evidently Kelsey had been pretty much on her own since the day she was born. Thank God she'd had her grandmother in her life. At least she'd had someone. He would make sure he would always be there for her. "Do you have any questions? I'll try my best to answer them."

Her hand squeezed his. "I can get pregnant now, right?"

His heart stopped on a dime and he strove to be nonchalant and fatherly without breaking into sweat. "Yes."

"My friend's sister was fifteen and got pregnant. Her whole family freaked out."

"That's definitely a freaking-out moment." He paused for a second, trying to push the next words through his throat. "Have you and your mom had the sex talk?"

"Oh, no. That's gross." She covered her face in embarrassment.

"But you know about it?"

"Yeah. We had it in school when we had the class about our cycles. It was gross. I'm never letting a boy touch me."

He hoped she held on to that thought until she was about thirty, but he knew that time would come faster than he wanted.

"I'll remind you of that," he said with a smile. "Dr. Morrow will go into detail and don't be afraid to ask her anything."

"Okay. Oh, oh." She jumped up. "I have something to show you." She ran to her room and came back with a tattered photo album. "I saw the photo on your nightstand and thought you might like to see this. My grandma made it. It has my baby pictures and my school pictures. She told me never to lose it and I haven't. I have more in a box. She died before we could make another album."

Time flew as he devoured the photos of his daughter from the day she was born until she was about nine. There were very few after that. Evidently, unlike her mother, Sheryl wasn't into taking pictures.

There was one thing painfully missing in all of them. Him. He wasn't there. He could blame Sheryl until the sky turned black, but it took two to create Kelsey and two to mess up her life. To the day he died, he would regret walking away so easily and not demanding a DNA test, not doing anything. As a young man, freedom was all he'd wanted. Freedom from a woman he didn't know. Freedom from the enormous responsibility.

He would pay for it now in unimaginable and painful ways as he watched his daughter grow into a woman. He would never have the memories of the years she'd grown into a feisty little girl. There was no way to get those years back, and they would weigh heavily on his heart forever.

She followed him around the rest of the day, talking and talking. He never knew she was a talker. Around him she was usually sullen and quiet. But now he had a feeling he was seeing the real Kelsey. But he knew once something didn't go her way the attitude would return. That was okay. He could deal with it now. They'd bonded in the most unusual way.

After supper, she fell asleep on the sofa. He woke her up to take a bath. She went like a dutiful daughter. In ten minutes she was back in shorty pajamas. She kissed his dad's cheek.

"Night, Grandpa."

"Night, child."

She hugged Ethan around the waist. He was standing because his back was aching a little, but no one needed to know that. "I'm glad you're home, Daddy."

"So this feels like home now?" When Sheryl had finally arrived with her, Kelsey had said she wasn't living in this dump.

"Yeah." She flashed a big smile and ran to her room.

"What do you think, Dad?"

Walt paused in flipping the TV channels. "I think we got a keeper."

"Yep. She's something." He squeezed his dad's shoulder. "Thanks for taking care of her while I was gone."

"That what grandpas do."

"Mmm."

"And you owe me a wad of money. I'm keeping a tab."

"Tell me what I owe and I'll write you a check."

"Aw, I'm watching TV. I'll tell you later."

Which meant his dad would never tell him. "I'm going to work at my computer for a while."

"You haven't lay down all day. Don't you think you should rest?"

"I will. I just want to check on the progress of the murder cases Ross and I were working."

"That can't wait until tomorrow?"

"Night, Dad."

His dad was worried about his health, but he was fine. His hot back said otherwise. It would only take a few minutes and then he'd lie down.

He signed on to the police database. There was no progress on the cases. Out of curiosity, he switched to the robbery. Nothing new. But he noticed information about Abby. Without a second thought he jotted down her cell number and her address, as well as her father's. What was he doing? He didn't need the information.

He turned off the computer and paced the floor. He couldn't call her. Everything he'd told her, he'd meant. That brought up another question. Why was he sneaking her number off the police database?

He couldn't call her. He couldn't.

It would only encourage a relationship fueled by gratitude. Even he realized he needed to question his feelings for her. But tough, badass cops didn't go that deep. At the moment, though, he wasn't feeling tough or badass. He was feeling like a man.

He picked up his cell from the desk where his dad had it charging.

And quickly laid it down again.

CHAPTER FIFTEEN

CHLOE CRIED AND CRIED, not wanting to go to bed. Gayle had let her stay up as long as she'd wanted or until she'd conked out. Abby lay with her until she fell asleep, which she'd never had to do before. When it was bedtime, Chloe went to bed. Abby would read to her for a few minutes before she drifted off. Now it was a battle to get her down.

She was clingy, too, and she hadn't been before. If Abby was out of her sight, she'd start to cry. And she threw temper tantrums if she couldn't get her way. Her daughter was becoming a spoiled brat. All of this gave Abby added motivation to leave the safe cocoon of her dad's home. She had to take Chloe back to their apartment and their normal routine. She needed discipline and structure.

So did Abby.

Chloe asleep, she went into the den to speak to her dad and Gayle. They were having a glass of wine and watching a movie.

"Did you get her down?" her dad asked.

"Finally." She sank onto the sofa. "She's getting so spoiled."

"I'm sorry, dear," Gayle said. "I can't say no to her."

"It's not just you, Gayle. The robbery and the fire have affected her, too. We need to get back to our lives and our routine so she'll feel secure again. I need that, as well."

"Oh, no, dear. You're too weak. You need more rest."

Abby let that pass. "Doug's picking up Chloe in the morning so she can spend some time with his parents."

"But it's the middle of the week. He doesn't get her until the weekend."

"I've agreed to it, Gayle." She refrained from gritting her teeth and screaming.

"This is Abby's business, not ours," her father put in.

Gayle took a gulp of wine.

"While Chloe is with her father, I'm going to my apartment to clean out the refrigerator and give the whole place a good cleaning."

"You don't have to do that," Gayle said. "I'll do it."

"Gayle," her dad snapped. "Let it go."

Abby scooted closer to her stepmom. "I really appreciate everything you've done for me and Chloe. I couldn't have gotten through this without your help. You've waited on me hand and foot, and taken care of Chloe. You must be exhausted."

"I've enjoyed every minute."

"And I've enjoyed getting to know you, but please understand that I have to go."

"Fine." Gayle placed her glass on a coaster and stood. "If that's the way you feel." She quickly disappeared into the kitchen.

"Dad?"

He got up and sat by her. "Don't worry about your stepmom. She's a little nutty at the moment. I'll talk to her."

She hugged him. "I'm sorry I've caused you so much stress. Gayle told me about your panic attacks."

"I'm so grateful you're alive." He squeezed her. "Now go live your life."

"Thanks." Her dad always understood. He was that type of person. Hopefully, she'd inherited some of that.

She took a quick shower and slipped on a big T-shirt. She'd gotten into the habit of having frozen bottled water on her nightstand. Sometimes she woke up and her skin would feel on fire. The ice water melted during the night and she'd drink several sips to cool off. Then she could go back to sleep.

After a breathing treatment, she headed for the kitchen. As she neared the den, she heard her dad and Gayle arguing.

"You're her father. You can make her stay."

"Abby's a grown, independent woman and makes her own decisions. That's the way I raised her and even if I could I wouldn't lay a guilt trip on her and beg her to stay."

"Don't you care about her and Chloe?"

"I'm not answering a stupid question like that. You're losing your mind, Gayle. One minute you don't want them around and the next you want them to live with us. That's crazy."

"I hate to see them go back to that tiny apartment."

"It's a nice apartment. What's wrong with you?"

"I feel so guilty."

"Why?"

"Um...you know...for the wasted years."

"You and Abby are both to blame for that so there's no reason to feel guilty. Abby's going back to her life and we're continuing with ours. We haven't played bridge, tennis or golf lately. Tomorrow we're going to the club for lunch and maybe get a bridge game going. And we have a cruise in September, so we'll be busy."

"I canceled it."

"What?"

"We need to be here for Abby."

"Gayle, you've tested my patience many times in our marriage, but this is the last straw..."

Abby crept back to her room. She'd get the water after the fireworks had died down. Her dad was right. Gayle was losing her mind.

ETHAN WAS UP early and took a breathing treatment, and then he had his coffee on the deck watching the sun peep over the distant treetops, heralding another day. It was relaxing, comforting. He needed to do this more often instead of rushing off to work. His dad joined him and they talked for a few minutes.

Kelsey wouldn't be up for a couple of hours or so. The first thing he'd learned about her was that she was a late sleeper. She'd had a busy day yesterday so he'd just let her sleep.

It seemed strange not having a schedule. He pulled his phone out of his pocket to see what he had on his calendar.

"Damn."

"What?" his dad asked, sipping coffee.

"Kelsey and I have to meet the principal and tonight there's an open house. She'll get to meet her teachers. Damn. School starts on Monday. I have to get her up. The appointment's at nine."

The rest of the morning was a rush as they scrambled around to make it on time. While he waited for her to get dressed, he called Dr. Morrow's private line and left a message. In minutes she called him back and agreed to see Kelsey at 8:30 a.m. tomorrow morning before her other patients arrived. He was happy to get it done so quickly.

By ten o'clock Kelsey was enrolled at Willow Creek Junior High School. It was just a formality. He'd known Miles Chapman, the principal, for years, and Ethan had already talked to him and faxed Kelsey's school records.

When they returned to the house, his cell buzzed. It was Ross. He went into his bedroom to talk.

"Devon Williams is back in jail," Ross said.

"About time."

"Can you come in about nine in the morning for a witness ID?"

"You bet. Oh, wait. Kelsey has a doctor's appointment at 8:30, but I'll be there after that."

"That should work. Ms. Bauman is coming in, too. She said she didn't actually see their faces so we're doing a voice take to see if she can recognize their voices."

Abby would be there. His heart rate increased just by hearing her name.

"Before you walk in here, I better warn you. The lieutenant's on the warpath. He found out Levi's been nosing around about the robbery and he knows Levi's a friend of yours."

"So? It's a free country and Levi can investigate who he wants as long as he's not breaking any laws."

"I'll stand right behind you when you say that to the lieutenant."

"Chicken."

"Come on back to work, partner, and we'll take on the lieutenant like we always do, and the bureaucrats upstairs, too. They're not taking me off this case."

Ethan laughed. They were known for being the lieutenant's number-one headache.

"Hell, I guess I should ask how you are first."

"I'd rather you didn't. I'm tired of answering that question. I'll see you in the morning."

The rest of the day passed quickly and soon they were back at the school for the open house. Kelsey was quiet and nervous and stuck to his side. He was overwhelmed by how many people wanted to shake his hand and tell him how glad they were he was alive. This time wasn't about him. It was about Kelsey and her fitting in to a new school.

He was glad when Carson showed up with his kids, Trey and Claire. Carson suggested that Trey introduce Kelsey to the kids. Kelsey was hesitant at first, but went. Trey was a little younger, but it didn't matter. Willow Creek was a small school and the kids all knew each other.

"How it's going?" Carson asked.

"Unbelievably good."

"Her hair looks better."

"Yep. She did that all on her own. My kid is something."

Claire tugged on Carson's arm. "Daddy, can I go play?"

"Sure, baby, but don't leave this room."

Claire ran off to join some little girls who were drinking punch and eating cookies.

Ethan searched for Kelsey and saw her with a group of girls.

She was talking and the girls were laughing, not at her but with her. If he had a guess, he'd say she was telling them about her grandpa. She was fitting in and he couldn't be prouder.

Like his friend Carson, Ethan was a father. And it felt good.

THE NEXT MORNING was rush, rush, rush. He had a hard time getting Kelsey out of bed. She'd talked on the phone to her new friends until about eleven. He would have to set a time for her to go to bed or she'd never be able to get up for school and stay awake in class.

They arrived at the doctor's office at eight and he filled out paperwork. Kelsey was a little nervous, but once she met Dr. Morrow she relaxed. Tina was in her fifties and had a soft voice that kids responded to.

When the exam was over, the nurse took him back to the doctor's office. Kelsey was all smiles and had a handful of pamphlets.

"You have a healthy twelve-year-old daughter, detective."

"So, everything's okay?"

"Yes. The exam went well. Everything is normal. Kelsey's a real trooper. We discussed everything from mood swings to boys to babies, and Kelsey has a better understanding of how her body is changing and how to take care of it."

"Yeah, Dad. I know all kinds of stuff now."

"I highly suggest you get her fitted for a bra."

"A bra? She's twelve."

Dr. Morrow leaned back in her chair with a smile. "Oh, detective, your world is fixing to be turned upside down."

He winked. "Too late. It already is."

After that, he stopped and bought Kelsey a phone. He wanted her to be able to call him whenever she needed. She was so excited she jumped up and down with excitement. It took a while to calm her down so they could go into the police station.

"You can sit at my desk while I'm busy," he told her.

"Okay. Cool."

As soon as he entered the building, he was swamped with officers shaking his hand and offering words of support.

Finally, he was able to guide Kelsey to his desk. She was busy with her phone and didn't notice much. Removing his wallet from his back pocket, he took out his desk key and opened the left drawer where he kept his badge and gun. Seemed like a long time since he'd put them there on that Saturday morning. A lot had happened since then. He'd met Abby.

Taking a long breath, he clipped the badge onto his shorts and then locked the drawer again. He headed down the hall to find Ross.

"Hey, Ethan."

He turned to see Ross coming out of the lineup room.

"You're just in time," Ross said. "The guys are still in the lineup."

"Has Ms. Bauman been in?" he asked out of curiosity.

"Yes. She just left. She did a great job identifying the voices."

Damn. He was hoping to see her, but it was better if he didn't. He walked in, looked through the glass at the six guys standing in jail-issued jumpsuits. "Two and four."

"Could you take a little more time to be sure?"

"I don't need time. I saw their faces in bright sunshine and it's two and four. Rudy is number two and Devon is number four."

Ross pushed a button on the wall. "Take 'em back."

Hal Beecher from Robbery came in. "Hey, Ethan." They shook hands. "Good to see you."

"Thanks."

Beecher glanced at Ross. "Ready?"

"Yeah. We're interrogating Rudy and Devon again, hoping they'll trip up or get tired of this bullshit and give us the third person," he told Ethan.

"I'd like to listen."

"Ethan." Ross sighed. "Okay, the lieutenant is out. His daughter is having a baby and his wife insisted he be there. Just listen."

Ethan walked into a room that had a view of the interrogation room. Rudy sat at a table, his hands and feet shackled. Ross and Beecher fired questions at him. Rudy shifted nervously, but he never wavered in his answers. There was no third person. He and Devon acted alone. It was their idea. They needed drug money. On and on it went until Ethan's temper got the best of him.

He shoved past Ross and Beecher as they came out of the room.

"Ethan. Wait. No. Ethan!"

But he wasn't listening to Ross. He went in and closed the door. Ross didn't follow.

Ethan pulled out a chair and sat close to Rudy. A look of disbelief flashed across the man's face. There was no doubt he recognized Ethan.

"What are you doing here?" Rudy asked.

"I'm here to talk to you."

"I don't have to say nothing. You're not a cop."

Ethan lifted his T-shirt and hooked it over the badge attached to his waistband. "Think again."

Fear joined the disbelief on his face, and Ethan was going to work that in his favor. "You kidnapped a cop, Rudy."

"You forced us to, man. You wouldn't stay out of it."

He leaned slightly back. "You must have missed Robbery 101."

"What are talking about?"

"Every bank robber's goal is to get in, get the money and get out as fast as possible. You took a civilian and a cop. That's like holding a loaded gun to your head, Rudy."

"I'm not talking to you anymore."

"I'll do the talking then." He scooted the chair closer. "You said the boss was going to be pissed that you didn't follow the plan. You told Devon it was your plan now. Does that ring a bell?"

"You're making that up, man."

"Stick to that story, Rudy, and you'll be an old man before you walk out of Huntsville prison."

"My lawyer says I'll only have to do a few years."

"Your lawyer's an idiot. Armed robbery, Rudy. One man dies. You kidnap two people and leave them on an abandoned ranch in a hundred and two degrees with no water. You left us there to die."

"No, man, I…"

"Shut up and stop lying. If you have two active brain cells, you better use them."

"My lawyer…"

"Your court-appointed lawyer is fresh out of law school and knows squat. The D.A. will tear into him like a pit bull tears into a Chihuahua."

"I got my own lawyer."

That threw Ethan for a split second. "Where did you get money for an attorney?"

"My mom's paying for it."

"You lying piece of crap. The other person paid for a lawyer for you and whoever he or she is has you bamboozled. You'll do the time while this person enjoys freedom."

Rudy sat stone-faced.

"Keep your secret, Rudy. We don't need a name anymore. Do you know why?"

No response.

"Your friend just made a big mistake. Lawyers don't do anything without money on the table first, and money can be traced, especially big chunks, and I'm betting you got a large sum."

No response again, but a nerve begin to jerk in his neck.

"I'm on paid medical leave." He leaned into Rudy's breathing space. "What do you think of my tan? I'm going to get you for that, too. I'm going to nail your hide to a wall for what you did to Ms. Bauman and me. And I got the time to do it. By Monday I'll know everything about you. So send a message to your friend. I'm coming. And when I'm through you're going to wish you never took a gun and walked into a bank." He slapped his hand on the table. Rudy jumped. "You're going to wish you'd never been born."

Ross was waiting when he walked into the hall. "You just had to do that, didn't you?"

He ignored the question. "What's the deal with the lawyer?"

"We just heard about it this morning."

"Who is it?"

"Bryce Grundy."

"Grundy? The last I heard his retainer was about twenty-five grand."

"Yeah."

"Someone is shoveling out big bucks."

"Yes, and I'm on it as soon as I get you out of the station before the lieutenant shows up."

"I'm gone. I have to take my kid shopping for school clothes." He stopped at his desk as something caught his eye. The reception desk was at the front and he glimpsed blond hair. Could it be?

"Come on, Kel." He called his daughter, still occupied with her phone, and strolled to the front, his pulse racing. It was Abby. She stood looking out the window in a yellow-and-white sundress. She now had a gorgeous tan.

"Abby."

She swung around and smiled. "Ethan. Oh, Ethan." She ran to him, threw her arms around his neck and hugged. It didn't take him long to return it. She smelled great and felt even better.

She touched his face. "You look wonderful." His face felt warmer than it had after the fire.

"So do you." He'd forgotten how beautiful she was, or

maybe he'd chosen not to remember. It was better for his peace of mind. "Ross said you'd left."

"Doug has Chloe and he's bringing her to me. He's running late, but he just texted he's on the way."

Kelsey moved closer to him and for a moment he'd forgotten his child was standing there. "Abby, this is my daughter, Kelsey."

"It's nice to meet you, Kelsey. Your dad has told me so much about you."

"Whatever," she mumbled, to Ethan's surprise. The old Kelsey was back. Before he could scold her, a tall blond guy came through the door carrying a little girl with blond pigtails.

"Mommy," the girl cried and held out her arms for her mother. As Abby took her, Doug kissed Abby's cheek.

"Sorry I'm late, honey."

Honey. His stomach clenched at the word.

"Doug, this is Detective Ethan James and his daughter, Kelsey." Abby made the introductions. "Ethan, this is Douglas Bauman."

Doug shook his hand vigorously. "I'm so glad I got this chance to meet you. I wanted to thank you for what you did for my wife."

Wife? Abby didn't correct him so maybe they were back together. The thought caused a bitter taste in his mouth.

"No need to thank me," he managed.

"I've got to run." He kissed Abby's cheek again. "I'll call you later."

Ethan wasn't sure what to say. *Congratulations* stuck to the roof of his mouth like old peanut butter. Chloe saved him from saying anything. She wiggled down from Abby and went straight to Kelsey.

"What happened to your hair?"

"Go away, twerp."

"Kelsey," he scolded.

His daughter hung her head.

"Come to mommy, Chloe," Abby urged the child.

Ethan didn't want to discipline Kelsey in front of Abby. It would embarrass her. He would handle it later. Right now he had a desperate need to know the situation between Abby and her ex. Without thinking it through, he said, "Kelsey and I are going shopping for school clothes. We could use some help. Are you game?"

"I'd love to help." She smiled and every resistance he ever thought he possessed vanished.

"Why does she have to come? I can pick out my own clothes."

Ethan stared into the resentful eyes of his daughter and realized that being a father required a lot more patience than he possessed. "Kel…"

"Ethan, no." Abby stopped him. "It's okay. It was nice seeing you."

She took her daughter's hand and moved toward the door. As she walked away, he had that same hollow feeling in his gut that he'd had when his dad had called to say his mom passed away. He had that sense that he'd just lost something precious and he hadn't even known he'd had it. Or that he'd wanted it. But the ache around his heart told him Abby meant a great deal to him. All his talk meant nothing. He wanted her. A single word clung in his mind and he didn't push it away.

He wanted her forever.

CHAPTER SIXTEEN

ETHAN TOOK KELSEY'S arm and led her into an interrogation room. "Sit," he said in his sternest no-nonsense voice.

She scrambled into a chair and he pulled up one next to her. "I'm a new father and I have to admit I'm a soft touch where you're concerned. I'll let you get away with just about anything, but I will not tolerate rudeness. You were very rude to Abby and Chloe for no reason."

"I don't like them," she said with vigor. "They're like big Barbie and little Barbie." She waved her hands and rolled her eyes. "They make me want to barf."

"Why? Because you're not a Barbie?"

"What? No. I don't want to be a stupid Barbie."

But she did. He could see it in her sad eyes. He cupped her face. "When you're happy and smiling, your beautiful eyes are blinding. No one can touch that."

"Really?"

"Yes, really." He gave her a minute. "You're afraid I'll like a blue-eyed blonde better than my brown-eyed daughter?"

"No." She denied it, but he knew she was trying to save face.

He sat back in his chair. "You're my daughter and you're my top priority. Nothing will ever interfere with that. I know your mother had many men friends and left you alone a lot and…"

"She left me in a motel one time for four days with nothing to eat but candy. I was scared and hungry. The motel lady called someone and they put me in a foster home, but then Sheryl came and got me."

His heart took a hit and for a moment it was hard to find

words. He cleared his throat. "That's not going to happen here. That's why I bought you a phone. I want a way to be in contact with you at all times. You'll never be alone or hungry again. You'll either be with me, Grandpa or at school."

"Okay," she murmured.

"I want to be clear about one thing. No one is ever going to take me away from you. But we do not live in a bubble. People will come and go in our lives, your friends, my friends, Grandpa's friends, neighbors and a host of others. None of them will affect our relationship. That's solid. Do you understand what I'm saying?"

"I guess."

He wasn't sure she did. All she could see was Abby as a threat to her happiness. He had to go a little further. "Abby and I went through a horrific ordeal and we have a bond. That's it. But I'm thirty-three years old and I always thought I'd get married one day."

Her eyes grew wide in distress.

He hastened to reassure her. "I would never get involved with anyone my kid didn't like, but I hope my kid would love me enough to make an effort to get to know the woman." He didn't know why he brought up marriage, except he was trying to make a point and was relying on some things he'd read in a couple of parenting books. "The same holds for when you start dating. I'll do my best to be objective about the boys you bring home."

She frowned and he realized he was really getting offtrack. "Bottom line, sweetie, is that it breaks my heart when you're rude and defiant."

"I'm sorry," she blubbered, fat tears rolling down her cheeks.

He pulled her onto his lap and stroked her hair. "It's okay." After a few more pitiful hiccups, he asked, "Ready to go shopping?" He was not good at this parenting stuff, but he was doing his best.

"Uh-huh." She brightened immediately and jumped off his lap.

He was a little disappointed as they made their way to the truck. He thought she would offer to apologize to Abby, but she didn't. One of the books he'd read said never to force a child unless it was a last resort. If he asked her to do it, she would, but he wanted her to think of it on her own.

Buckling her seat belt, Kelsey said, "Daddy?"

"Hmm?"

"If we call that lady, will she still go shopping with us?"

"Who?" He wanted her to say the name.

"You know."

"She has a name."

"Abby."

He was so proud of his daughter. He didn't push or force her and she'd come through with flying colors.

"Let's see." He reached for his phone.

ABBY APPLAUDED HERSELF on her performance. She was cool and friendly. She'd kept all her feelings inside, except for that one spontaneous moment when she'd hugged him. She couldn't stop herself, and she hadn't wanted to let go. But she did.

At his touch, so many memories swirled through her head and they all made her weak and limp. He may think what she felt was gratitude, and she even harbored the idea herself, but she now knew it wasn't. It went deeper. Convincing him of that might take time and she was willing to wait.

Kelsey was a handful. Poor Ethan. How she wished Kelsey hadn't objected to the shopping trip. She would have loved to spend some time with them.

But she had her own problems. Gayle was on a rant this morning about Chloe spending the night with Doug. Abby escaped as soon as she could to go to the police station. Hearing the robber's voices again unnerved her for a moment, bringing back all the suffering she and Ethan had endured because of them. Luckily, they would be locked up for a very long time.

She kept stalling and waiting for Ethan, but he'd never showed. Doug called and she had to leave. For once she was glad Doug was late.

She got to see Ethan and she felt fifteen again. Giggly and unnerved.

Negotiating traffic, she wondered if Ethan thought about that night. Did men even do that? Keep thinking about someone they couldn't forget? Probably not. Men were wired differently. And Ethan's thoughts were on his daughter and solving crimes.

Her cell beeped, alerting her she had a text message. If it was Gayle, she was turning off her phone.

It was from Ethan. She pulled into the parking lot of a church. Driving, reading and texting at the same time was not her forte. She wasn't that good of a driver. She might have to tell Ethan that one of these days—although he probably had already figured it out.

Her heart raced as she opened the text. How about a second chance? Have to have K fitted for bra. In big trouble. Need help. Please.

She quickly replied. Where r u?

Mall not far from station. Front of Dillards.

On my way.

She sped back onto the highway, feeling happy for a change. And it felt good. She'd see Ethan again and get a chance to know his daughter. She only hoped it went well.

Turning into the mall parking lot, she noticed Ethan's truck immediately. She zoomed into the spot next to it. Ethan and Kelsey got out and she unstrapped Chloe.

"Need any help?" Ethan asked.

"No. Thanks." She set Chloe on the payment and locked the

car. "Her stroller is in my stepmom's car so I don't know how long this will last. We can probably rent one inside."

"Don't worry. We'll wing it." He glanced at the back of her car. "You had your trunk fixed."

"My dad and Gayle picked up my car when the police released it and had it repaired," she explained on their way into the mall.

With his longish hair, dark glasses and bronze skin, Ethan looked roguish, handsome and tempting. It made her think of the two of them alone in the darkness with nothing but hot sweat between them. The thought spiked her blood pressure and she turned her thoughts to shopping.

It started out slow. Kelsey was reluctant and hesitant about voicing her opinion. Fifteen minutes later she was warmed up and in the throes of shopping. Ethan and Chloe trailed behind them. She glanced up to see Ethan holding Chloe and she paused and stared. He looked so comfortable with a child in his arms. Her child.

Kelsey called her and she went back to shopping. The bra fitting went well. A woman in her thirties measured Kelsey and Kelsey was very comfortable with her. Abby gave Ethan a thumbs-up when they came out of the dressing room. He mouthed, "Thank you."

After all he'd done for her, she was elated she'd been able to do something for him.

At the fifth store, Ethan said, "I want to remind you ladies that my credit card has a limit."

"Okay, Dad." Kelsey giggled.

Ethan looked at his watch. "It's almost two o'clock. Let's have lunch."

"Pizza!" Kelsey shouted.

"Yeah!" Chloe wriggled down from Ethan's arms and ran after Kelsey. "Wait for me." She tripped and fell.

Abby started toward her daughter, but Ethan caught her arm. "Let them work it out."

"Kelsey," Chloe cried.

Kelsey walked back. "Get up, twerp."

"Think of that as a term of endearment," Ethan whispered and she poked him in the ribs with a bag.

"I fall down," Chloe said.

People walked by, glanced at the kids and then at them. Very clearly they were thinking the adults needed to do something.

"Good grief." Kelsey reached down with one arm and picked up Chloe. Settling her on her hip, she took off again.

"She's not going to hurt my baby, is she?"

"Nah," Ethan replied. "But we better catch up."

Kelsey had Chloe sitting in a booster seat at a table in the food court when they arrived. Ethan went to order the pizza and drinks. Lunch was a lively affair with the girls trying to outtalk each other. Afterward, Chloe wanted to go to the play area and surprisingly Kelsey took her.

"Stay where we can see you," Ethan called.

"Okay, Dad."

Then it was just the two of them sitting alone, or as alone as they could be in a crowded mall.

"So, how are you?" he asked, taking a sip of his drink.

"Much better. I'm moving back to my apartment tomorrow. Things are getting a little crazy at my dad's place." And before she knew it she was telling him everything. That's what she loved about him. He was so easy to talk to.

"That does sound a little strange."

"Gayle's never had children and never allowed herself to get too close to us emotionally. But with Chloe there during the robbery and the fire they made a connection. And now she doesn't want us to leave."

"Are you ready to go back to your apartment? You were afraid when you left the hospital."

"I'm much stronger now, and I have to get Chloe back into her regular routine. Gayle is spoiling her terribly."

"Daddy." Kelsey came running. Chloe trailed behind her. "Can we have some money to ride the horse?"

Ethan dug in his pocket and pulled out two dollars. "See if you can get some change and remember Chloe's right behind you."

"Come on, twerp."

"See, I told you. It's a form of endearment."

Abby lifted an eyebrow. "Yeah, right, but since Chloe seems to think it is, I'm not saying anything. And I know it's a tenuous time for you and Kelsey. I won't do anything to cause you more stress."

"I appreciate that."

"How did you get her to change her hair?"

"She did that on her own while I was in the hospital. The first time I saw her I took a photo with my phone. I have it framed on my nightstand. Dad said she wanted to look like that when I came home from the hospital."

"That's so sweet."

"She has a good heart. She's just had a very rough life and she's protects herself every way she can. Mostly with her attitude. I'm sorry she was rude to you and Chloe."

"You don't have to apologize. About twelve years ago I was Kelsey, doing everything I could to keep Gayle away from my father. The only thing my bad behavior accomplished was to hurt my dad. I understand Kelsey completely."

"Mommy," Chloe called. Chloe was on the slow bucking horse. Kelsey had one hand on her to keep her from falling off.

"I told you my kid was awesome," Ethan remarked.

"My kid's pretty awesome, too." She glanced at him and had a hard time keeping a smile from spreading across her face.

"We could probably have a good argument about that."

"Yes. But we won't."

"Mmm." He twisted a disposable cup on the table. "So, you and the ex getting back together?"

"No. Why do you ask that?"

"He's kissing you and calling you 'honey' and 'wife.'" He gripped the cup and she thought it was going to break into tiny pieces in his grasp.

"Are you jealous?"

"No, of course not." He brushed that off quickly. "I thought you'd given him a second chance."

"No. He wants me to move back into our house and quit my job. In light of everything that's happened, he says it's too dangerous. He'd rather I stay at home and take care of Chloe."

"You didn't agree?"

"The first couple of days I was home I was weak and thought maybe he was right. Maybe I needed to work on my broken marriage. I mean I could actually talk to Doug without wanting to slap him. But once something is broken I've found you can't put it back together the way it was. I don't love Doug anymore. The feelings I had for him in the beginning are gone."

"How do you know that?"

She looked into his dark eyes. "I'd tell you, but you'd freak out."

"I'm not a freaking-out type guy."

"Not when it comes to robberies, fires or murders. But when it comes to real emotions you freak out."

"Try me." He scooted his chair closer and she felt breathless.

She swallowed hard. "I know you think what I feel for you is gratitude, and I was inclined to believe that. I'm not sure. All I know is that I have strong feelings for you. I think about you all the time. I can feel your lips on my skin, touching me, kissing me in ways I've never been kissed before. And it's not only the sensual, the sex or the passion. It's much more. During the robbery and the grueling heat I felt safe with you. Even when we knew the fire was coming and we were going to suffer a horrible death, I felt a peace inside because I was with you."

"Abby…"

"Let me finish." She stopped him. "I know in here—" she placed her hand beneath her breast "—that I can trust you. You will never betray me, lie to me or disillusion me. You will always be honest and straightforward and treat me as an equal. I know that with all my heart. That's not gratitude. It's something much deeper."

He reached for her hand on the table and linked his strong fingers with hers. Staring into her eyes, he asked, "What are we doing in a mall?"

"Your daughter needs clothes."

"Oh, yeah." He squeezed her hand. "Here's the thing. We're both dealing with a lot of emotions right now. We need to take it slow."

"Could we meet for coffee one day or go out for a drink?" She rubbed her thumb over the back of his hand.

"I don't see why not." At the gleam in his eyes she wanted to wrap herself around him, uncaring of where they were.

"Mommy. Mommy." Chloe's little voice quickly brought her to her senses. "Did you see me?"

"Oh, yes." She reached for a bag on the floor to still her excitement. "It's time to go home."

They made their way through the mall to their vehicles. Halfway there Chloe grew tired and Ethan had to carry her. When they reached the truck, Kelsey gathered the shopping bags from them.

"I'll put these in the truck, Dad."

He reached in his pocket and threw her the keys.

"Abby," Kelsey called as they turned to Abby's car. "Thank you. I'm sorry I was…you know…rude earlier."

"Thanks, sweetie."

"Isn't she awesome?" Ethan said with pride, buckling Chloe into her seat.

"Her dad's pretty awesome, too."

They were both leaned over Chloe in the door opening. Chloe impulsively kissed Ethan's cheek. "Bye, E-tan," she said.

Impulsive as her daughter, Abby kissed his cheek, too. "Bye, E-tan." He smelled of pizza, sunshine and tough, badass maleness. She wasn't sure that had a scent, it was more of a sense of who Ethan was—enormously strong, honorable characteristics and raw masculinity bundled into one hell of a man.

He stared into her eyes and her heart spun with exhilaration at what she saw in his dark, warm depths. One long finger lightly touched her bottom lip and she trembled. "Thanks for the help, lady. I'll call."

She didn't mind him calling her "lady." Not when it was said with so much feeling.

HE WASN'T FREAKING OUT. Ethan silently repeated the words several times on the drive home. He was just accepting that something was happening between them. Not only for her, but for him, too.

The moment he saw her ex kiss her and call her "honey" was a defining moment for him. It bothered him that she'd given Doug a second chance. And he was jealous. There, he'd admitted it.

They had a connection and it might be gratitude on her part. On his it might be a desire to protect her. Whatever it was, he was willing to take a chance and find out.

Then there was his daughter, who was talking nonstop about school and clothes. An occasional "uh-huh" was all that was required of him. It might be too early to bring someone else into their lives. But he would take it slow and hope for the best.

He had no idea where his relationship with Abby was going. He just needed to be with her and to admit that he knew his emotions were involved. The days ahead would test those emotions.

That rest of the day was chaos as Kelsey showed all her new clothes to her grandpa and then modeled them. Walt tried to be excited but all the girly stuff was out of his range of excitability. It was a little out of Ethan's, too. Having a young girl in the house was changing their lives and keeping them on their toes.

He made her go to bed at ten o'clock—her new curfew time

to be in bed so she could get up for school. With no complaints she took a bath and went to bed.

His dad was asleep in front of the TV. Ethan took a shower and went to his room. He would spend the weekend with his daughter, the one he'd planned weeks ago. His back burned a little so he crawled into bed to rest. Kelsey had put a cooling pad in the bed and it felt good. She was determined to take care of him.

Stuffing a pillow under his head, he wanted to tell Abby about his daughter. He reached for his cell on the nightstand.

"Are you busy?" he asked as she answered.

"No. I'm in bed. I'm avoiding my stepmom."

"Don't be too hard on her. I'm sure she means well."

"I know. Let's please talk about something else."

He told her about Kelsey.

"I'm glad you're getting along so well."

"If anything good came out of the robbery or fire, it's my relationship with my daughter. When I left that Friday night, she told me she didn't care if I came back or not."

"She was just trying to protect herself."

"Mmm."

"Is your room dark?" she asked.

"Um...yes."

"Mine, too. I feel like we're in the woods talking. I can almost hear the crickets and your voice. 'Lady, haven't you ever been in the woods before?' You were very grouchy."

"And you were very frustrating. I don't know how you managed to be so beautiful in dirt and sweat."

"Ethan..."

"Hmm?"

"I feel like I'm part of you."

He sat up and jammed a hand through his hair, unsure of what to say. Unsure of emotions that were new to him.

"Are you freaking out?"

"A little."

"Big, tough Ethan is admitting that?"

"Yep."

She laughed and he felt something unfold inside him. It was the lock he had on his heart.

"Are you yepping me?"

"Yep."

"Oh, I love it."

They talked on and on about any and everything. And a lot about the robbery.

"Do you think they'll find the third person?" she asked.

"Yes." He told her about the lawyer. "There's a paper trail somewhere and we'll find it. I'm going back to work on Monday."

"Ethan, is that wise?"

"I won't rest until this case is closed."

"Please be careful."

"I'm always careful."

"You're not. You're a daredevil."

"Let's change the subject." He thought that might be best. "I'm spending the weekend with Kelsey—the one I promised her. If I get any free time, I'll call."

While they'd talked, the time had flown. It was late, but it was hard to end the call. "Good luck tomorrow."

"I may have to sneak out."

"You'll do fine. Good night, Abby."

"Night, Ethan."

His hand gripped his cell and three little words hung in his throat. Words he'd never said to anyone but his parents and Kelsey.

I love you.

And they scared the hell out of him.

CHAPTER SEVENTEEN

THE MOVE WENT smoothly. Abby had breakfast with her dad and Gayle, and there was no pleading or begging her to stay. Her dad had obviously had a long talk with his wife. Gayle teared up when Chloe hugged her goodbye.

Feeling wretched, but to show she had no hard feelings, Abby hugged her, too. "Thank you for everything. We will visit often."

"Call if you need anything." Gayle wiped away a tear.

Her dad embraced her in a big bear hug. "I'm so glad you survived everything. Now I just want you to be happy."

"Me, too." One last hug and she and Chloe walked to her car in the driveway. As she drove away, she felt as if it was the first day of the rest of her life.

It was an uplifting feeling.

When they entered the apartment, Chloe ran from room to room. "We're home, Mommy." Then she dashed into her room, pulling out toys. Even if you were three, you needed a place to call home.

She unpacked their clothes and put them away and then went into the living room and looked out the French doors to the pool. Her apartment was upstairs and she had a small balcony. Children played in the pool, enjoying their last free weekend before school started.

Wrapping her arms around her waist, she stared up at the bright blue sky. The heat of August was fading into September and milder temperatures. But this August was a month she'd never forget.

She'd met Ethan.

She wanted to call him, but she knew he was busy with Kelsey. Sinking onto her comfy cream-colored sofa, she relaxed and enjoyed the feeling of being in her own space once again. She'd decorated the place on a dime, not wanting to spend more than she had to. After the divorce she'd been very careful with her money.

She'd purchased most things at thrift shops or used-furniture stores. One wall she'd painted a goldenrod color, the others were an off-white. She'd found a large area rug with a cream center and a border of tan and an orangy goldenrod. It looked great on the dark hardwood floors. Orange throw pillows pulled everything together. That, and her glass-and-stainless-steel coffee and end tables. She was home. But things were different. *She* was different. At times, if she closed her eyes, she could feel that intense heat rolling over her and Ethan. The sense of knowing she'd escaped death was something she'd never forget. Time would dull the awful memories, but Ethan would always be a part of her. She was sure of that.

Her cell buzzed and she jumped up to get it out of her purse in the kitchen. It might be Ethan. It wasn't.

"Abs, I have a big favor to ask," Doug said.

Asking for favors was his specialty. "What?"

"My sister flew in from New York and we're meeting at my parents for a family weekend. I'd like Chloe to be a part of it."

"We just moved back to the apartment. It's too much going back and forth for her."

"Abs, please. It would mean a lot to my parents'. I know they just saw her, but other than that they rarely see her."

Whose fault was that? She'd patted herself on the back for not saying the words out loud. "Okay, but after this I want her back into her normal routine."

"You didn't tell me you were moving back to the apartment."

"We're divorced. I tell you very little."

"Abs, please…"

"What time are you picking her up?"

"About three."

"I'll have her packed and ready to spend the night. And, Doug, put her to bed yourself. Chloe's not familiar with the housekeeper or the nanny your parents hire to watch the grand-kids. She'll get scared and cry."

"I'm not insensitive. I'll take care of my daughter."

She laid her cell on the counter calmly and resisted the urge to throw it across the room. Taking a deep breath, she picked it up again and touched a name in her contacts.

"Hey, Hol. What are you doing tonight?"

"Laundry."

"How about a girl's night out?"

"You're on. I'll call…"

"No. Just us. I'm not in a mood to go out."

"Okay. Where's Chloe?"

"Doug's picking her up at three."

"Didn't he just have her?"

"I'll explain later. Bring wine or anything to get me in a better mood."

"You got it. See you at three."

"Oh, Hol, I'm at the apartment."

"I talked to your dad earlier and he said you were home. I was giving you time to get settled in before I called."

"Sorry. I should have phoned you."

"Don't worry about it."

She spent the next thirty minutes talking Chloe into going. "I not going," she said as if it was her decision. "I staying home."

She started to call Doug, but she didn't want Chloe to feel as if she could make the decision of whether to see her father or not. In the end, the Bauman's two poodles changed Chloe's mind. She loved playing with them. And it was sad that she cared more for the dogs than her grandparents. But the Baumans had never made any attempt to spend quality time with Chloe. She barely knew them.

Doug arrived promptly at three. She kissed Chloe. "Have a good time."

"Okay," Chloe said and took her father's hand.

"Wait," Abby called. "You forgot Baby."

Chloe ran back to get her doll.

"Dad said she's too old to cling to a toy. It's time to wean her away from it."

Something about the way he kowtowed to his father rubbed her the wrong way. "Tell your father he can kiss my ass. I will raise my daughter my way."

"Our daughter. I have a say in her raising, too."

"You do. Your father doesn't."

"Abs, what's wrong? You're not acting like yourself."

This was so typical of their marriage. Whenever she voiced her opinion she "wasn't acting like herself."

He slid his hand around her neck, his thumb caressing her cheek. "Come with us. Mom and Dad would love to see you. It will be like old times and it will show them that we're working on putting our marriage back together."

She stepped back, breaking all contact with him. "We are not getting back together so please stop touching me, kissing me, calling me 'honey' and your wife."

"But you said you were partly to blame for the breakup of our marriage and…"

"Yes. I meant that. I didn't say we were getting back together, though. I would like for us to remain friends so that we can raise Chloe without all the resentment and bitterness."

"Okay." He raised both hands. "I'm not going to push you. I know you're still dealing with the aftereffects of the robbery and the fire. I can wait."

"Doug…"

"I ready." Chloe came running back and they left.

Abby wanted to beat her head against the door, but she decided to wait for Holly to bring liquor. She needed something numbing.

MONDAY MORNING WAS chaotic at the James house. Kelsey ran into the kitchen three times in three different outfits asking, "How does this look?" Before they could answer she was off to try on something else.

"Son." Walt took a sip of his coffee. "If you have another child, could we get it as a baby so we can get used to all the craziness first?"

Ethan shook his head and got up from the table. He knocked on Kelsey's door. "Kel, the last outfit was fine. Don't change again."

"You sure?"

"Yes. I'm coming in." He paused at the clothes strewn all over the room. Taking her arm, he led her to the bed. "Take a deep breath and calm down."

"I can't," she cried. "It's the first day of school and I'm nervous. I don't know anybody."

"You met everyone the other day. Just be friendly and you shouldn't have a problem."

"Okay."

He glanced around the room. "Hang up all these clothes and come eat. Grandpa's fixed a big breakfast."

After that things went smoothly until he stopped at the school. She seemed petrified. "Everything will be fine," he told her. "If not, you can always call me. I'll be in Austin, about thirty minutes away. But I'll come."

"Okay, Dad. I'm going in."

Smiling, he reached over and gave her a hug. She grabbed the backpack at her feet and got out. Joining other students as they walked into the school, she turned and waved one more time before disappearing into the building.

He waited a moment and drove away. She would be fine, he

told himself, but he'd keep his phone handy. From US-290 he took the TX-1-Loop Mo-Pac Expressway into Austin. Levi's office was off Congress Avenue and soon he was pulling into the parking area of Coyote Investigations.

"I'm in here," Levi called as Ethan opened the door. Levi had acute hearing, something he credited to his Indian ancestors on his grandmother's side.

The office consisted of a tiny reception area and, to the right, a room with a refrigerator, a microwave and a cot where Levi spent many nights when he was working a case. To the left was a bathroom and Levi's big office, which contained every evidence-gathering electronic device known to man. Levi was a whiz at hacking into computers, but no one knew that except his closest friends.

Levi stood as he entered. "Hey, you have clothes on. Jeans, boots, white shirt. Back to being a detective, huh?"

"Almost." They shook hands.

"How you doing?" Levi asked as they took seats.

"Fine. I just dropped my kid off at school."

"It sounds weird when you say 'my kid.'"

"Sounds weird to me, too, but things are going good. She's finally settled in."

"I'm glad, man."

"Thanks. What do you have on the case?"

"A whole lot of nothing." Levi shuffled through some papers. Folders covered his desk and were stacked on the floor.

"How do you find anything in here?"

"Don't touch a thing. I know where everything is."

"If you say so."

"The money paid to Bryce was cash," Levi said, "And you'll hear the gist of that from Ross and Beecher. The last I heard they were meeting with Grundy. I've been ordered to stay out of it, so now you can take over. It's going to take a lot of digging to find that third person, but it begs the question—would why someone with twenty-five grand instigate a bank robbery?"

They tossed theories around for a bit and then Ethan left. When he got into his truck he saw it was only eight-thirty. He reached for his phone to call Abby. On Saturday night he'd talked to her for a few minutes and she'd been a little tipsy. She'd said she had a friend over and they were drinking wine. He wasn't sure who the friend was and he didn't ask. But he would today.

"Ethan." She answered quickly. "I'm sorry I was out of it on Saturday."

"You were having a good time. You giggled."

"I did not."

"Yeah, you did."

"Oh, good heavens, I must have had more wine than I thought."

"You said you had a friend over."

"My friend Holly was trying to cheer me up."

"Was there a reason you needed cheering up?"

"I had an encounter with Doug that left me grinding my teeth."

"How would you and Chloe like to meet me for coffee and you can tell me all about it?"

"I'd love that, but I took Chloe to day care to get her back into our normal routine. She was excited to see her little friends. She missed them."

"Then you and I can have coffee."

"Yes."

"You name the place."

"There's a coffee shop on Lamar Boulevard."

"I know it. I'll meet you there." He swerved into the next lane and took the exit. Coffee with her was more appealing than going head-to-head with his lieutenant. Anything with her was more appealing.

ABBY RAN TO her bedroom, brushed her hair and applied lip gloss. She had on a summery, sleeveless, V-neck lavender-and-white dress. She wasn't changing. It was good enough. In less than ten minutes she drove into the parking lot of the coffee shop. Ethan's truck wasn't there so she went inside and sat at a table in the corner, facing the door.

A man walked in dressed in jeans, boots and a white shirt. He headed straight for her. *Ethan.* Her heart knocked against her ribs in anticipation. He was handsome, sexy and for some reason *finger-licking good* came to mind. She swallowed nervously. She'd made love with him. His hands had touched her body as hers had touched his. And he'd made her feel things she'd never felt before. So why was she so nervous? Maybe because she was seeing him for the first time—as a man she wanted in her life.

"Hi." He smiled and her body flooded with warmth. "What would you like?" For a moment the question threw her because there was only one answer in her head. *You.* Then she realized orders had to be placed at the counter for coffee.

"Um…mocha latte."

"Anything else? Sweet roll? Muffin?"

"Ice water would be nice."

He looked confused, but said, "Coming up."

In a few minutes he was back carrying all three drinks effortlessly in his hands. He placed them on the table and slid into the chair across from her.

She took a gulp of the water.

"I drink a lot of water, too," he commented. "Can't seem to get enough. Must have something to do with our bodies being baked."

"I keep a bottle on my nightstand."

He took a sip of black coffee. "What's up with the ex?"

She told him about Doug. "He can't get it through his head that we're not getting back together. He says I need time. I'm back to wanting to slap him."

"If you keep saying no, he'll get the message."

"Let's talk about something else. How's Kelsey?"

"I dropped her off for her first day of school. She was real anxious."

"She'll do fine."

"That's what I'm hoping." He took another sip. "You planning to go back to work?"

She twisted her cup in her hands. "Soon. How about you?"

"I'm headed there now."

"The reason for the outfit?"

"Yep."

"Have they made any progress in the case?"

"Rudy and Devon have a lawyer now. A high-priced attorney."

"How can they afford that?"

"That's what we're going to find out." He glanced at his watch. "I better go. The lieutenant should be in his office by now."

They walked out together. His truck was parked next to her car. They stood between them in their own small alley. Turning to face him, she asked, "Do you think we could see each other one night—without kids?" The words came out rushed before she lost her nerve.

"That would be hard because of Kelsey. I have to be there for her."

Her heart sank. "I understand."

"Hey." He cupped her face. "This isn't a brush-off."

"It feels like it."

"I could probably come by during the day when I get a break."

"Okay." She could hardly think with his hands on her face.

"Please don't think it to death. We're both adults."

"Mmm."

His head dipped and he took her lips in a slow gentle kiss that melted every bone in her body. She leaned against him for support. Finally, he broke contact and stepped back. "I'll call."

Her palms were sweaty, her hands shook and her pulse

hummed in her ears. She'd never had this reaction to the opposite sex before. And it had never felt so good.

ETHAN WALKED INTO the homicide department at the police station feeling cocky and ready to take on the world. He and Abby would start a relationship—he was more than ready.

He slid into the chair at his desk. Ross's desk faced his and he looked up as Ethan attached his badge and gun to his leather belt.

"Glad to have you back, partner."

"Thanks."

Ross glanced over his shoulder to the lieutenant's closed door. "Let's see how long it takes him to notice you."

The words had barely left Ross's mouth when the lieutenant's door flew open. "James, in my office," he bellowed like a stuck bull.

"Showtime," Ethan murmured and marched into the office.

"Close the door," the lieutenant ordered.

Ethan closed the door and faced his superior. Craig Eagon was in his early fifties and balding, with a spare tire around his middle. He was a by-the-book cop all the way, which is why he and Ethan bumped heads on numerous occasions.

Craig sat in his oversize chair, and it creaked under his weight. "You look good, Ethan." His voice was calm but Ethan knew that wasn't going to last long.

"Thanks."

"What are you doing here?"

"I work here."

"You're on paid medical leave."

"I'm better, and I'm not the type of guy to sit at home."

The lieutenant eyeballed him. "Go home, Ethan. That's an order."

"Sorry, sir. I'm working the robbery case. I know what happened better than anyone."

Craig's eyebrows knotted together. "Are you disobeying a direct order?"

"I'm just saying I'm working the case."

Craig sighed. "I just got the call. The Feds are taking over completely next week."

"I'll have it solved by then."

"You just don't stop, do you, Ethan? Give me your damn badge!" Craig shouted.

Ethan removed his badge from his belt and laid it in front of the lieutenant.

"Now go home before I take it away permanently."

Ethan gritted his teeth, ready for battle.

Before words could leave his mouth, the lieutenant added, "Ross and Beecher are on top of things. They'll brief the FBI. You're too involved. I can't have you going off half-cocked and comprising this case."

"I won't."

"Yeah, you're saying you wouldn't confront Rudy Moss like you did the other day? Your judgment is off, Ethan. And, yes, I know everything that goes on in this squad room even when I'm not here."

Someone snitched, but Ethan wasn't concerned about that. It was probably Craig's secretary, who had eyes in the back of her head.

Craig scooted his chair forward. "Look, Ethan, I know how you feel…"

"No, you don't, sir," he shot back. "Not until you've lived through a bank robbery, kidnapping and being left in one-hundred-and-two-degree heat without any water can you tell me you know how I feel. And top that with a wildfire. Have you ever been trapped in a fire, lieutenant? Have you ever felt like your skin is being burned from your body?"

"Can't say that I have."

"Then don't tell me how I feel. I'm staying on this case,

with or without my badge, with or without the FBI, until every guilty person is behind bars."

"Don't push me, Ethan."

"I'm going to be there when we bring the third person in."

The lieutenant yanked opened his top drawer and grabbed a bottle of Tums. Dumping two into his palm, he slammed them into his mouth. He chewed, his eyes pinned on Ethan.

"Pick up your damn badge and get the hell out of my office. You have a week. As far as I'm concerned, you're working the Wallace murder. Anything other than that I don't want to know. Got it?"

"Yes, sir." He picked up his badge and walked out.

He sat at his desk and he could feel the eyes of everyone in the room on him. The lieutenant's voice carried right through the walls.

"One of these days he's going to keep that badge," Ross said.

"Yeah, but not before this case is closed." Ethan took a long breath to ease the tension inside him, but no way was he backing down. "So, what do we have?"

Ross threw two big folders on his desk. "Familiarize yourself with this. I have to be in court on the Sims murder. We'll talk when I get back."

Ethan opened a file and began to read. Rudy Moss and Devon Williams had been in trouble since they were teens. They were just two-bit crooks stealing to get by, and someone had used them to pull off a bank robbery. Who? And why?

CHAPTER EIGHTEEN

THREE HOURS LATER Ethan was absorbed in the case. Ross came back and Detective Beecher joined them. They moved to a conference room to spread out the files and talk.

Ethan leaned back. "We have two hoods robbing a bank with stolen Glocks. For their other crimes they were never armed."

"Criminals, especially drug-heads, get desperate and do stupid things," Beecher said.

"Nah." Ethan shook his head. "We got a puzzle here and several pieces are missing. Someone other than Rudy and Devon masterminded the robbery. Someone with money."

"Which makes no sense at all." Ross closed a file. "Why would someone with money rob a bank?"

"There's more to this than the robbery," Ethan said.

"Where do we even start on this?" Beecher asked. "I say let the Feds have it. They have the manpower."

"No way in hell," Ethan told him. "We have a week and I'm using every minute of it. By then I can figure this out."

Beecher grunted. "Yeah, you boys aren't so great with following the rule book. I have a wife and three kids I'm rather fond of, and I'm not getting involved in anything illegal. Remember, robbery has the lead on this and we're doing it by the book."

Ross slapped him on the back. "Don't worry. We'll keep you away from the wild side of life."

Ethan rummaged through a file and pulled out a piece of paper. "Good job, Hal, getting info out of Grundy so quickly."

"That dirtbag lawyer was ready for us. He had the deposit

slip handy and said we could search his records all we wanted, but everything was legit. He added he wasn't revealing his client and he didn't have to."

Ethan studied the copy of a deposit slip showing twenty-five thousand dollars cash going into Grundy's account. "Twenty-five grand is not something you carry in your pocket. An amount that big would be remembered. Just a minute."

"Take your time. I'm going to get coffee." Beecher walked out.

Ethan called Abby. Ross busied himself in the files.

"Hi, Ethan."

"I have a banking question," he said, his whole body relaxing at the sound of her voice.

"Okay."

"A banking deposit slip has a teller's number on it, right?"

"Yes, so that there's a record of who takes the cash or checks."

"Would twenty-five thousand in cash raise a flag?"

"Definitely."

"Do you report it?"

"Depends on who it is. A lot of gamblers deposit cash and so do people who have fund-raisers. With an amount that big I would alert my supervisor and he would take it from there."

"The teller who takes the money would have a number or code?"

"Yes."

"I'm looking at the slip. Where would it be?"

"All banks are different, but there should be a date and time the money was deposited. The account number and the amount will be on the slip. Somewhere above or below that will be the teller's ID."

"I see it. Thanks. I'll call you later."

"Let me know if you find anything."

"I will…in person."

She laughed and he looked up to see Ross frowning at him.

"What are you doing? You can't share..."

Ethan got up and ignored the question. "Let's go talk to the teller. She might remember something."

Fifteen minutes later he and Ross walked into the bank Grundy had used. Beecher and his partner had an appointment to interview a witness on another case. They planned to meet in the morning. Ethan glanced at his watch and realized he had to make this quick. He had to pick up Kelsey.

They spoke with the bank manager, Gene Carver, and told him they were investigating the robbery that had happened in early August off I-35. Mr. Carver was more than willing to help even though he didn't know what that had to do with his bank. But he was of the opinion that all bank robbers should be behind bars. Ethan didn't go into detail and just asked to speak with Teller 1335.

Mr. Carver allowed them to use his office. A young woman in her early thirties walked in. Her name was Ashley Holt.

She promptly sat in a leather chair, folding her shaking hands in her lap. Ross leaned against the desk and Ethan remained standing. He got right to the point.

"Ms. Holt, you took a deposit of twenty-five thousand dollars cash on Thursday at 10:10 a.m.?"

"Yes."

"How was it brought into the bank?"

"In a suitcase."

"Who brought it?"

"Mr. Grundy, the attorney."

"Was he alone?"

"Yes."

"Did he say anything?" Ross asked.

"It took time to count it. While he waited, he said he was taking on a new client and that he liked to be paid in cash since checks can be cancelled and traced. His large fee guaranteed no paper trails and anonymity for the person paying for his services. He added that he represented some shady characters and he deposited the money in the bank because he didn't want them breaking into his office or home to try to steal it back."

"So the person paying his fee met him at the bank?" Ethan asked.

"I suppose, but I didn't see anyone. He just came in with the suitcase."

"What types of bills were in the case?"

"All hundreds."

"What happened to the suitcase?"

"He left with it."

"Was Mr. Carver aware of what was going on?"

"Yes. It's not every day someone comes in with that much cash. Can I go back to work?"

"Yes, and thank you."

She quickly left.

Ross slid off the desk. "What do you think?"

Ethan glanced around the bank. "I think we need to look at some digital surveillance videos. If Grundy met someone in the parking lot, we might get lucky and see the encounter on tape."

Mr. Carver rushed back in. "Was Ashley helpful?"

"Yes. The bank has security cameras inside and out?"

"Of course."

"We'd like to see video from Thursday morning."

"Oh. I could have that ready about ten tomorrow."

Ross shook the man's hand. "I'll be here at ten."

Ethan did the same. "Thanks, Mr. Carver."

As they walked outside, Ross said, "We're not going to find anything. Grundy has been to this bank many times and he knows where every camera is located. He's not going to risk getting caught on one with someone paying him big bucks."

"Even slick bastards like Grundy slip up." Ethan glanced at his watch. "I've got to pick my kid up from school."

"Now? We usually work 'til midnight."

"It's her first day and I have to be there. Tomorrow I'll work something else out."

"We have a week before the case is handed over to the Feds. That means a lot of late hours if we're going to solve it."

"I know. I'll talk with Kelsey about the rest of the week. But if it's the last thing I do, I will bring the other person in for what he or she did to Abby." He strolled to his truck.

It was a vow he made to himself.

WHEN HE PICKED up Kelsey, she talked nonstop all the way home. He didn't catch half of what she was saying, but obviously she loved school and everyone was so cool. She repeated everything to her grandpa when they reached the house. Grandpa said a lot of "uh-huhs."

She darted off to her room to change clothes. Ethan turned to his dad. "I need your help for the next few days."

"Sure." Walt took a pan out of the oven. "I made a roast for supper. We can eat this for a few days. What'd you need?"

"I'll be spending a lot of hours on the robbery case. The FBI takes over next week, and by then I want to have it solved. Could you get Kel from school and make sure she does her homework?"

"No problem." His father turned the roast with a big fork and looked at him. "But I want to be clear. I'm not going to a mall again. That's your department."

"No mall visit required," Ethan said with a smile. "I'll tell Kel." He walked down the hall and knocked on her door.

"Yeah," she shouted.

He opened the door and went in. She lay on the bed, still in her school clothes, talking on the phone. "Get off the phone," he mouthed.

"Gotta go," she said, sitting up.

"We need to talk." He sat on the bed.

"Okay." She crawled to sit beside him. "Dad, there's all kinds of cool activities to do after school. See?" She handed him a sheet of paper. "I always wanted to play soccer and be a Girl Scout. And, oh, oh, this is so cool. There's a dance group at the school and Cathy's mom is the instructor. She said her mom would give me extra lessons so I could catch up. I really, really want to do this, Dad. I got the moves. Watch."

She jumped off the bed and wiggled her arms, hips and legs.

"You got something, all right."

She made a face and plopped down by him again. "Please, Dad."

"Have Cathy's mom call me."

She hugged him around the waist. "Thanks."

"Remember you have a tutor on Tuesdays and Thursdays to get your grades up."

"I know." Some of the enthusiasm left her voice. Living with her grandmother and mom she hadn't been able to join anything at school because there was little money and Sheryl was always moving. Behind the tough attitude was a little girl dying to be a normal girl with friends and activities.

"Pick two things on the list and we'll see how it goes."

"Oh, wow, gosh, thanks, Dad."

He caught her before she jumped up in excitement. "I want to talk to you about something."

"Okay."

"I'm going to be working a lot of late hours on the robbery case."

"Okay."

"Grandpa will pick you up from school."

"Okay. Grandpa's cool."

"You can call me about anything."

"I know." She patted him on the back. "Go catch the bad guys."

The conversation had gone better than he'd expected. She felt secure in her role in his life and knew he was always going to be there for her. That was a big accomplishment, and he was proud of his daughter.

Later, after everyone was asleep, he got comfy in bed and called Abby. He just needed to hear her voice and to tell her about Kelsey. They talked for a while and then she asked, "Are you in the dark?"

"Yeah."

"Me, too. I feel happy when I hear your voice."

"I feel horny."

"Ethan." She laughed.

"You weren't expecting that, were you?"

"No, Mr. Keep My Emotions Close to My Chest."

"I'm not anymore. I know what I want."

"Me, too."

"Do you have any free time in the morning?"

"I'll make time."

"I can be at your place a little after eight."

"Okay. My address is—"

"I'm a cop. I know where you live."

"Oh, should I be afraid?"

"Very afraid." It wasn't like him to be silly and flirty, but he was changing. She'd changed him—for the better. Maybe a normal life with a wife and kids was for him, too. And he couldn't see that happening with anyone else but Abby.

THE NEXT MORNING, Ethan drove into Abby's apartment complex right behind Abby after she'd dropped off Chloe at day care. They walked toward the stairway hand in hand. She didn't feel any nervousness, just jubilation that she'd get to spend some time alone with him.

"Did I tell you how much I like your lawman outfit? Men in tight jeans turn me on."

He lifted an eyebrow as they took the stairs. "All men?"

"No." She unlocked her door. "Just a dark-eyed badass detective."

"That's better."

She went in and laid her purse on the kitchen counter. "Would you like some cof…" At the look in his warm eyes, her voice trailed off.

"There's only one thing I want right now and she's about the sexiest thing I've ever seen." He walked to her and gathered her into his arms, his lips taking hers in a slow, drugging kiss. Her heart raced and she wrapped her arms around his neck, needing to be as close as possible. Her curves welded to his hard muscles and she felt weak with need. Before she crumpled to the floor, she took his hand and led him to her bedroom.

Once in the bedroom it was a frantic rush to shed their clothes. One long kiss and he sat on the bed to remove his boots. She knelt behind him, pulling his shirt from his shoulders. She paused.

"Oh, Ethan. Your shoulders are still slightly red."

"They're fine." He kicked off his boots.

She rained kisses along his shoulders, feeling the heat of his skin, the power of his muscles. "Are you in pain?"

"Only when you're not touching me." He twisted around, pushing her into the mattress and removing his jeans and briefs at the same time. Stroking her breast, he murmured, "Your breasts are beautiful. Sometimes at the oddest moment I can feel them in my hands."

At his first touch and hoarse voice she lost her train of thought. She just wanted to experience every inch of him. She didn't want to think so she didn't. Her hands and lips caressed every part of his hard, bronzed body. When he returned the favor and stroked her intimately, she cried out his name and begged for more, which shocked her at the same time. There was no holding back as their bodies began a dance that could only end one way. Had to end. If it didn't, she would scream.

"Ethan."

He caught his name with his mouth and entered her the same way he kissed—with power and control. With each thrust he drove deeper inside her until all she could feel was him. And her heart racing. She arched her hips, needing to be closer and closer until her body shuddered over and over into beautiful release. Without thinking, without reservation, she breathed,

"I love you." He joined her almost instantly and their sweat-bathed bodies lay entwined in perfect harmony.

He lifted his head from the hollow of her neck. His hair fell across his forehead and his eyes were as dark as she'd ever seen them. "You okay?" he whispered hoarsely.

She stroked his hair away from his forehead. "I'm as good as I can get."

"I'll say."

"Ethan." A bubble of laughter left her throat.

He kissed her lightly and his lips trailed to her breasts, lavishing them with attention. "I need to name these beauties."

"And what would that be?"

"I don't know." His tongue caressed a nipple. "Something no one else would call them."

"Not many people call my breasts by name."

"I got it. Wynken, Blynken and Nod."

She suppressed a laugh. "I only have two breasts. What's the third name for?"

His hand slid down her flat stomach to the triangle between her legs. "Here. The head of beautiful pleasure."

"Oh, Ethan."

Nothing was said for some time. Later, she lay in the crook of his arms, stroking his chest. "Your mother did read to you."

"Yeah. But tough cops don't admit that." He kissed her briefly. "Now, sweet lady, I have to go." He crawled from the bed, grabbed his briefs and jeans and jerked them on. "I'll be working long hours on the robbery case."

She felt bereft, needing his strength around her just a little longer. He sat on the bed to put on his boots and she noticed his red shoulders. Without another thought she reached for the sunburn ointment on her nightstand and knee-walked to his bare back. Squeezing a dollop into her hand, she massaged it across his shoulders.

"Ah, that feels good." He leaned his head back to rest on her shoulder. "I think I love you."

She tensed. "Think?"

"I'm almost certain. All I know is that my heart doesn't truly beat until I see you, until I'm with you. That has to be love because I've never felt it for anyone else." He turned his head and their lips met. "Oh, yeah. Lady, I have to go."

Not wanting to end this moment when Ethan James admitted he loved her, she ran her hands down his chest, stroking his hard abs and lower.

He caught her hands. "Abby, don't make this hard."

They both burst out laughing. He got up and reached for his shirt on the floor. "Bad choice of words."

"But appropriate," she teased.

"I'll call you later," he said, buttoning his shirt.

She sat back on her heels, her breasts in full view. "Aren't you going to say goodbye to Wynken and Blynken?"

"Not on your life. I'd never get out of here." He stared at her for an extra second and walked out.

She stretched out on the bed feeling wicked and very well loved. And there was nothing about gratitude involved. It was real and might even include a fairy tale.

ETHAN HAD TO take a moment, before walking into the squad room, to try to wipe the morning from his mind. Impossible. For years his job encompassed who he was. A cop—first and foremost. He'd dated. He'd had flings, but marriage was never on his mind. He didn't have that much time to spend on a relationship. Well, he finally had to admit that was a load of crap. He just hadn't found the right woman. Now the right woman was all he could think about. As soon as this case was wrapped up, he wanted his dad to meet Abby and he wanted Kelsey to know Abby better, too.

"Where the hell have you been?" Hal barked as soon as he walked into the room.

Having the best sex of my life.

"I have a kid to get off to school," he replied to keep Abby's name out of it.

"Oh, I forgot about your new fatherhood."

Ethan looked around. "Where's Ross?"

"Still at the bank waiting for the videos."

Ethan took a seat. "Want to throw this around a bit?"

"Sure." Hal opened a file. "Let's start with the crime scene. Everything we found is in the evidence boxes. Nothing of importance was found in the van. Fingerprints didn't reveal any secrets. A multitude of fingerprints were found on the front door of the bank, including Rudy's and Devon's. Idiots didn't even wear gloves."

"And they used Walmart bags," Ethan said. "We're not dealing with geniuses here."

"It sounds like it was an impromptu thing, and they used what they had in their van."

"Yeah." Ethan scooted his chair forward. "Maybe they were there for another reason and robbing the bank was an afterthought. Rudy mentioned changing the plan."

"Okay. I'll go along with that. If robbing the bank was a second thought, what was their main objective?"

Ethan picked up a pen and pulled a pad forward. "There were five people there that day—me, Ms. Bauman, Mr. Harmon, Rudy and Devon. We can scratch out me, Rudy and Devon. That leaves Ms. Bauman and Mr. Harmon." Ethan tapped the pen on the paper, remembering some of the things Abby had told him. "Mr. Harmon was the bank manager, yet he worked Saturdays. Why?"

"Could be kindhearted and not willing to flex his muscle."

"Maybe. Let's find out."

Hal stood. "I'll do a background check on Mr. Harmon while you and Ross look at the videos, if he ever returns."

Almost on cue Ross came in with a box.

"Damn, Ross, we just needed Thursday morning."

"This is Thursday morning from every angle."

"Have fun," Hal said as he left.

"Where's he going?"

Ethan explained as they went into the viewing room. For the better part of two hours they looked at the bank's front door and parking lot from every angle possible. They saw Grundy approach the door from the left, suitcase in hand. Two vehicles parked to the far left were fuzzy and unidentifiable. They looked from different cameras, but each time the cars were too far away.

Hal came back and threw a folder on the table. "Take a look at that."

Ethan opened it and could hardly believe what he was reading. "Mr. Harmon was a gambler and had two mortgages on his house and had applied for a third."

"I ran this by the guys in vice and they made a few phone calls," Hal went on. "A bookie named Bonner has been putting the screws to Mr. Harmon. He owes Bonner about fifty grand. He is now our number one suspect."

Ethan studied the file. "Except dead men don't deliver wads of cash to scumbag lawyers."

"That's the kicker." Hal leaned in to get a view of the computer. "Anything show up?"

"Not a damn thing that would give us a lead."

Ross joined in. "Let's look at what we have. A gambler who needs money. He could have been in cahoots with Rudy and Devon, promising not to push the alarm, but everything went very wrong. Then there's still the matter of the money after Mr. Harmon's death. It doesn't fit."

"That leaves Ms. Bauman," Hal remarked.

"Yeah." Ethan had a hollow feeling in his gut. The robbery had something to do with Abby.

CHAPTER NINETEEN

"I'LL START A background check on Ms. Bauman first thing in the morning," Hal said.

"Like hell." Ethan was immediately on his feet. "She's the victim."

Hal pointed a finger at him. "That's the reason the lieutenant doesn't want you on this case. You're too involved."

Ethan held up his hands. "Okay. Do what you have to do."

"We're looking for a clue. That's all. Someone might have a grudge against her and it might tie all this together."

"I know." He resumed his seat. "Just do it discreetly."

"I do everything discreetly," Hal quipped, walking out.

"Are you okay?" Ross asked Ethan.

"Yeah, but I need some air."

Before he could move, the lieutenant appeared in the doorway. "Ethan, you've been a detective for a long time and you know you can't share confidential information gathered on this case—not with anyone, and that includes Ms. Bauman. So you have a decision to make—Ms. Bauman or the case. Your choice."

The lieutenant walked out and Ethan glared at Ross. "Did you say something to him?"

"You know me better than that, but Hal is pissed and he's got big ears, if you know what I mean."

Without a word Ethan strolled from the room and out of the building. He hadn't eaten since breakfast so he stopped at Subway and got a sandwich. People came and went as he ate, but he didn't see them. His thoughts were turned inward.

Hal was right. He was emotionally involved, and because of that he could compromise the whole case. The lieutenant was right, too. He had to detach his personal life from his job. The only way to do that was to stop seeing Abby. At the thought, a pain pierced his chest.

ETHAN ARRIVED HOME at nine-forty-five that night, just in time to say good night to his daughter. After talking to his dad for a few minutes, he went into his room and called Abby.

She told him about her day and he wasn't sure how to bring up the difficult subject.

"You're very quiet." She picked up on his mood. "Is something wrong?"

"Yeah." He took a deep breath. "I've been told more than once that I'm too personally involved in this case."

"That's understandable. You went through hell and want this other person caught as much as I do."

"But I shouldn't have told you anything about the case and I have. I should never have mentioned the money. When I'm with you things slip out. That's a first for me. Until this case is closed I have to stop seeing you."

"You think I would tell someone what we share?"

"No, but something I mentioned could slip out without you being aware, like it did with me. It could compromise this case."

"I don't understand, Ethan, but I trust you."

She trusted him. He wanted to tell her that in the next few days the cops would investigate her and members of her family, and it would be invasive. She'd told him Gayle had money and he couldn't withhold that kind of information. The woman had a good motive to want Abby out of her life—he had to divulge that. But he couldn't tell Abby. He was a cop bound by ethics.

He hung up, stared down at his boots and felt like the scum of the earth. He hated himself and what he had to do. It did make him wonder, though, why a cop who was never afraid to break the rules wasn't breaking one now.

HOLLY HAD THE day off, so Abby talked her into going jogging on the University of Texas campus. They had lunch at Cheddar's, picked up Chloe and took her to the park to play. All the while Abby kept thinking about her conversation with Ethan. She didn't understand his reasoning. Since he was upset, she didn't push it. And she didn't want to jeopardize the case either. Waiting would be difficult, but she wanted this person caught. She just didn't know how she was going to get by without seeing Ethan. He'd become a big part of her life—and her heart.

It was after four when she arrived back at the apartment with her sleeping daughter. Holly went home and Abby rested on the sofa.

Before she could get comfortable, her doorbell rang. She hurried to get it before it woke Chloe. Two detectives stood outside. She recognized one of them.

"Ms. Bauman, we'd like to ask you a few more questions. Is that okay?" Detective Beecher asked.

"Sure. Come in."

They followed her into the living room and he made the introduction. "This is my partner, Steve Jannis."

"Nice to meet you," she replied. They sat on the sofa and she took the comfy chair facing them.

"We've interviewed you several times and we appreciate your help on this case."

"I want this person caught more than anyone."

"Then why did you fail to mention Bradley Cummins?"

"Excuse me?"

"We asked several times if anyone had a grudge against you and you said no. Yet Bradley Cummins stalked you in college. He was arrested. Spend a night in jail and said he'd get even."

"That was years ago and I haven't seen him since."

"Are you sure?"

"Yes, Detective Beecher, I'm sure." She took a controlled breath. "Are you implying I'm withholding information to protect someone?"

"No, ma'am. We're just hitting a brick wall on this third person."

"Well, I suggest you look elsewhere."

"Yes, ma'am." They soon left, which was good because she was about to explode from their sheer audacity.

Did the cops think she had something to do with the bank robbery? How absurd. Then it hit her. Ethan knew the detectives were coming when he'd called and he didn't warn her. Not that she had anything to hide, but loyalty to her would have been nice. Anger rose in her chest and she quickly quelled the feeling. It was an effort.

THE NEXT DAY Ethan didn't get home until after midnight, but he was up early to take Kelsey to school. Listening to her chatter brought him out of his foul mood—for a moment. It returned the second he walked into the squad room. He was beginning to hate this case. It was keeping him away from Abby, keeping him away from everything he wanted.

The men took seats at the table, as they did every day.

Hal started the conversation. "We didn't turn up anything on Ms. Bauman. There was a guy who stalked her in college, but that was another dead end."

Ethan gritted his teeth until his jaw hurt. "Did you check me out, Hal? I was there."

"Damn straight. There are a lot of guys you've arrested who would love to put the hurt on you, but no one desperate enough to plan a bank robbery."

"You bastard," he said with barely controlled contempt.

"Okay," Ross intervened quickly. "Hal, your people skills need some work, but until you're taken off this case we have to work with you."

"You boys know when you hit a brick wall on a case, you

start looking at it from every angle. That's all I'm doing. Ethan's the one with a problem."

"You have no idea," Ethan spat out, trying very hard not to jump across the table and belt the guy.

"Calm down," Ross suggested.

"I'm calm," Hal insisted. "Ethan's the one losing it."

"Remember that, Hal. Punching you might be the highlight of my day."

Hal's ruddy skin turned a blotchy pink.

"Back to work." Ross did his best to cool the temperature in the room.

"I'm all for that," Hal said. "I think we're avoiding looking at the elephant in the room."

"What are you talking about?" Ross asked.

"We're looking for someone with money. Douglas Bauman, Jr has access to a lot."

"What's his motive?" Ross pressed.

Hal glanced at Ethan. "What's your take?"

Ethan unclenched his jaw. "Bauman has money, but he's a banker. His family has been in banking for years. Setting up a bank robbery would be like a slap in the face to his family, especially his father. And Ms. Bauman said he wanted them to get back together. I can't see him harming her. We'd have to have a warrant to get anywhere near Bauman's records. Right now we have nothing to base a warrant on."

"I have to admit that Bauman is probably a dead end. He has too much to lose." Hal flipped through a file. "So where does that leave us?"

Ethan cleared his throat. "There's someone else who has money."

"Who?"

"Gayle Baines has money from her first husband. I don't know how much, but the relationship between Ms. Bauman and her stepmom isn't good."

Hal slammed the file shut. "You've known this for a while?"

"Yep."

"I'm talking to the lieutenant. You need to be off this case."

Ethan rose to his feet. "What Ms. Bauman told me in confidence while we were trying to stay alive is my business. I'm only bringing it up now because the money makes Gayle Baines a viable suspect."

"It made her a suspect a week ago!" Hal shouted. "You're not thinking straight."

"Lay off, Hal." Ross stood up, too.

Hal took a long breath. "I'll get the details on Mrs. Baines and you guys contact the people from the surveillance cameras whose cars were in the parking lot of the bank on Thursday morning." Without a backward glance, he stormed out.

Ross looked at Ethan. "You're involved with Ms. Bauman, aren't you?"

"Maybe."

Ross sighed. "Then take a step back. Your perspective is off."

Ethan ignored Ross's advice. "Let's check out the owners of cars we pulled from the videos. A Mr. Tarver was there. He might have noticed Grundy's black Porsche."

They drove to Lowe's, where Mr. Tarver was an assistant manager. He had noticed the Porsche, but other than that he wasn't much help. Neither were the next two people. They had one more to go—a waitress at Olive Garden. Before they reached the restaurant, they got a call to return to the station.

As they entered the squad room, Hal shoved papers at Ethan. "Mrs. Baines cashed in a twenty-five thousand dollar CD on Wednesday morning."

Shit. The bottom of his stomach churned with a sick feeling. "What do you want me to say?"

"Nothing," Hal retorted. "I've contacted Mrs. Baines and she's coming in for questioning. I don't want you in on it."

"I don't plan to be."

"Ross and I will handle it."

"Fine. I'll talk to the waitress whose car was parked near Grundy's." He walked out before Hal could protest. And if Hal made one more derogatory remark, Ethan would punch him. He stood outside and took a long breath, breathing in the warm September breeze. If Gayle Baines had hired those thugs, Abby was going to be devastated. At that moment, he thought of turning in his badge. He needed to be there for Abby.

But if Gayle denied everything, they would need evidence to tie her to Grundy and the thugs. And he'd never stopped in the middle of a case. He kept going because it was the only thing he could do.

He drove to Olive Garden and spoke with the waitress in the manager's office. The waitress was a college student, young and perky.

"Did I do something wrong?" she asked in a nervous voice.

He showed her a photo of her car in the parking lot. "You were at this bank on Thursday at 10:11 a.m.?"

"Yes. I stopped to deposit my tips. I don't like to keep them in my purse for too long."

"Did you notice a Porsche?"

"Yeah. A black one. It was gorgeous."

"Did you see anyone around the car?"

She shook her head. "No."

He showed her another photo. "From the security camera we can see the back of the Porsche. The rest of the car is out of range." He ran his finger along the side of the picture. "A lawyer's office is here. Did you see any cars parked between the two?"

"Oh. Yeah. An old tan Ford was parked there. I noticed it because my grandma has one just like it. It has twenty-four thousand miles on it. She literally only goes to the grocery store and church in it. My mom takes her everywhere else. I thought it was my gran's for a minute, then I noticed the back fender had a rusted dent in it. Not my gran's car. It's like brand-new."

Ethan waited for her to take a breath. "Did you notice any-one in the car or around it?"

"No. I didn't look that good. I was in a hurry to get to work."

"What year is your gran's car?"

"Gosh, I don't know. She's had it as long as I can remem-ber. I'll ask my mom."

He handed her his card. "Call me when you find out."

"Okay." She looked at the card. "Can I ask what this is about?"

"A bank robbery."

"Whoa, dude." Her eyes widened. "I don't know anything about a bank robbery."

"Sometimes you know more than you think." He shook her hand. "Thanks. I appreciate the information."

He walked into the station feeling much better. He had infor-mation that could lead to the identity of someone. At the sound of shouting, he stopped short. Loud sobs followed. He went to his desk to pull the jail visitation sheets on Rudy and Devon.

More sobs followed and he couldn't concentrate. The ques-tioning of Mrs. Baines wasn't going well. Suddenly a door banged opened and a man and woman hurried out. The man had his arm around the woman, who was sobbing into wadded-up tissues. It must be Mr. and Mrs. Baines, Abby's dad and step-mom. As they quickly left, Ethan had a bitter taste in his mouth.

Ross and Hal stopped at Ethan's desk. "She's not involved," Hal said. "She took the money out of her bank and opened an account at Abby Bauman's bank for Chloe Bauman's educa-tion. We verified it with the bank."

"That was brutal." Ross sank into his chair. "We should have done more checking before questioning her."

"Are you pointing a finger at me, Ross?" Hal wanted to know.

"I'm not pointing a finger. I'm saying we need to be sure of our facts."

"We don't have any facts!" Hal bellowed. "Everything's a damn dead end. We've got squat."

"I have a lead," Ethan interrupted before tempers took over.

"What?" Ross and Hal asked in unison.

Ethan told them what the waitress had said. "I was just checking the visitor log for Rudy and Devon to see if I can match a tan Ford to one of them."

Hal looked at his watch. "I have to be at the courthouse in fifteen minutes, but the last time I checked the log only three people had visited them. Rudy's mother, and Devon's father and sister. Rudy's mom visited Devon, as well. I did a background check on all three. It's in the file. I'll check back later." He turned and then swung around. "Abby Bauman was squeaky clean, just a couple of traffic tickets. Everyone likes her, especially the guys."

Ethan's gut clenched, but he didn't react. "I know, Hal. I read the file."

"Ethan, I…"

"Don't worry about it. This case is testing the patience of all of us."

"Then let's get it solved."

"You should have decked the blowhard," Ross whispered as Hal left.

"I'm not in a mood to punch anyone."

"Ethan, if you get any lower, I'll have to pick you up off the floor."

"I just keep thinking about what Abby and her family are going through because of us."

"Yeah. That sucks."

They ran the three names through the DMV database, and it didn't take long to get a match. Estelle Campbell, Rudy's mom, drove a 1996 Ford Taurus. As soon as the information came up, he got a call from the waitress. Her grandmother drove a 1996 Ford Taurus. They finally had a good lead.

"Rudy said his mother was paying for his attorney." Ethan

reached for a file. "Let's see what Hal has on Estelle Campbell. She lives in an apartment provided by the U.S. Department of Housing and Urban Development for low-income families. The HUD complex is off West North Loop. She's been married three times, but is now single. She works for a cleaning service at night and has twelve dollars and sixty-two cents in her bank account. Hmm. Wonder how she came up with twenty-five grand in—" he glanced down at the papers in front of him "—forty-eight hours. She visited Rudy and Devon on Tuesday and the money was deposited on Thursday."

"This whole cash money business is weird. What keeps Grundy from just keeping the money?"

"As the lady at the bank told us, he deals with shady characters. If he kept the money without doing his job, he's smart enough to know his days would be numbered. That's why he accepts the money at a bank so he can deposit it immediately. The person giving him the money sees this. Honorable bastard, isn't he?"

"Yeah." Ross chuckled. "So what do you want to do? Rattle Mrs. Campbell's cage?"

Ethan got to his feet. "Let's see if we can make her nervous."

ABBY KEPT WAITING for Ethan to call and explain why the detectives were questioning her again. When he didn't, she knew that whatever they had was gone, as if it had never been. She always chose the wrong guy—at least she should get points for still believing in love. She didn't know what that said about her, but she had to take control of her life.

She'd gone into banking because of her dad, but now she considered changing careers—to do something she really wanted. Since Chloe would start school next year, she'd like to be near her. She loved kids and the idea of teaching appealed to her. A visit to the university and she had a schedule of courses she needed to take to get her teaching degree.

Feeling better about her future, she spoke to the VP at the

bank. He agreed to let her work part-time so she could take classes in the afternoon and at night.

She would go forward—without Ethan. The thought caused her such heartache, but she couldn't dwell on it.

Abby picked Chloe up at three, and she was fussy so Abby put her down for a nap. As she flipped through the information she'd gotten at the university, her doorbell rang. She jumped up to get it. Gayle and her dad shot into the room. Gayle wiped at her eyes with a tissue.

"I feel like a criminal. A common criminal!" she wailed.

"What happened?" Abby asked, even as she felt a sinking feeling in her stomach.

Her dad guided Gayle to the sofa and they sat down. "We've just come from the police station. Detective Beecher called for Gayle to come in. He wanted to talk to her."

"About what?"

"They thought I paid those idiots to rob the bank and kidnap you." Gayle dabbed at her eyes, her voice quavering. "I would…never…hurt you."

Abby felt queasy. "Why…why would they think that?"

Her dad gripped Gayle's hand. "Evidently someone is paying for a very expensive attorney for the robbers. Gayle withdrew twenty-five thousand from her bank on Wednesday and they wanted to know what she did with the money."

Abby's breath hung in her throat as she waited for the answer.

"It was for Chloe's education. I put the money in your bank and you as a signee so you can have access to it. They wanted me to prove it. I felt like a criminal."

"Why would you do that? I put money away every month for Chloe's education, and I'm sure Doug will contribute, too."

"What am I going to do with my money? You, Everett and Chloe are all that I have. I just wanted to do something nice so you wouldn't have to worry. I was going to tell you. They just assumed…"

"Gayle." Abby sat by her stepmom and put an arm around her shoulders. It was kind of ironic she was comfortable doing that. "I know we've had a rocky relationship, but our situation is different now. You don't have to give us things for us to love you. You're her grandma and have a special place in Chloe's heart and in mine."

Gayle hiccupped. "Thank you, dear."

"I appreciate what you did, but I'd rather Chloe not know about it until she's older. I want her to earn the things she gets and not feel a sense of entitlement."

"If that's what you want."

"And you're not the only one the cops are investigating. They're looking at me, too."

"That's insane." Gayle snapped out of her woe-is-me mood. "Everett, you have to do something. They can't treat Abby like this."

"It sounds like they're marking people off a list so I feel it's best to leave things alone and maybe they'll find what they're looking for."

"Dad's right. They're looking at every little detail. Though I'm a little pissed, I'm putting it out of my mind and keeping my fingers crossed that they catch this person who made my life a living hell."

"Mommy," Chloe called.

Abby touched Gayle's hands. "Why don't you get Chloe. It will cheer you up and she'll be so excited to see Grandma."

"I'd love to." Gayle stood and headed for the hall. "Grandma's coming."

Abby turned to her father. "Dad, was Ethan at the questioning?"

"No, just two other detectives."

"I was so scared, Abby." Her dad leaned forward, rubbing his hands together in an agitated manner.

"Why?"

"When the detective spoke about the expensive attorney for

those hoods and brought up Gayle withdrawing a large sum from a CD, I was stunned. She hadn't mentioned a thing to me. She'd been acting so strange lately, saying over and over how guilty she felt about her relationship with you. For an agonizing five minutes I thought she might have done something stupid. My chest was tight, my hands clammy and I didn't know what I was going to do if she'd hired those hoodlums. If she'd hurt you…"

"Oh, Dad." She hugged him. "She didn't. Now we're going to have a nice family dinner here at my apartment and forget the whole mess."

Abby was trying very hard not to get angry about her family being interrogated. But an hour later she gave up and went into the bathroom to call Ethan. He answered immediately.

"Ethan, why are the cops investigating me and my family?"

"Abby, it's just routine. It's nothing personal."

"You knew this was going to happen on Tuesday when you called, didn't you?"

"Abby…"

"And you told them what I shared about Gayle? For so long I wrestled with my feelings for you, but now I see them for what they really are. Gratitude. You were right, but I went with my heart. You've hurt me more than Doug ever did. Please stay away from me. And that *is* personal."

Somewhere in her head, or maybe it was her heart, she'd thought Ethan would protect her at all costs. The thought shattered the rose-colored glasses she'd been looking through, and she saw Ethan for who he really was—a badass cop. He had never professed to be anything else. She'd put him on a pedestal, given him her heart and body and woven silly fairy tales once again. Did she never learn? There was no such thing as happy ever after. Not for her.

ETHAN STOOD WITH his cell in his hand, unable to move, unable to do anything except feel the hurt in her voice ripping through his chest.

"Ethan, are you okay?" Ross asked.

No, he'd never be the same again. He'd lost a part of himself and there was no way to get it back. He'd broken her trust, her love.

"Ethan?"

"What? Yeah. I'm fine." He got into the unmarked squad car, ignoring his aching heart. The only thing left was to nail the bastard who'd caused all the heartache.

As Ross drove toward Estelle Campbell's home, he tried to put everything else out of his mind, and it was the hardest thing he'd ever had to do.

Estelle lived in a downstairs apartment. Kids' toys littered the small yard. Ethan pulled the torn screen aside and tapped on the door. A woman in her fifties wearing jeans and a Dallas Cowboys T-shirt opened the door.

"Mrs. Estelle Campbell?"

"Yes."

"I'm Detective James and this is Detective Logan. Could we speak to you please?"

Her eyes narrowed. "What about?"

"Your son Rudy."

"He's in jail."

"We're aware of that. Could we come in, please?"

"I suppose." She moved aside and the first thing Ethan noticed was the smell—cigarette smoke. Cigarette butts filled an ashtray on a littered coffee table. Newspapers and magazines were piled high. Coke cans and an opened bag of potato chips were on one end.

The place was sparsely furnished. He and Ross sat on a stained brown sofa. The vinyl-square flooring had worn through to the cement in places. Two kids, a boy and girl of maybe four and three years old, played on the floor with a toy truck. The boy ran to the table, took a sip of Coke and reached for a handful of chips. The little girl soon followed. A baby sat in a Pack 'n Play playpen, where a bottle lay on the mat in a pool of milk. The one thing that seemed out of place was a big-screen TV. This was definitely the other side of the American dream.

"Mrs. Campbell, I'll get straight to the point. We have a witness who puts your car at the bank the same time Bryce Grundy was handed a large cash amount to represent your son and Devon."

"So?" She picked up a cigarette and lighter from the table. "I'm sure I'm not the only one with a Ford Taurus." She lit the cigarette, her hand shaking slightly. Blowing smoke through her nostrils, she placed the lighter back on the table.

"You're the only one with a dented and rusted rear fender. We saw it outside."

She plopped into a chair. "I didn't do anything wrong."

"We can arrest you on what we have."

"Arrest?" She sat up straight and took a puff. "For what?"

"Your son committed armed bank robbery where a man died. He then kidnapped two people and left them in the heat to die. He's going away for a long time and it doesn't matter to us if you go down for aiding and abetting him."

"Wait a damn minute. I had nothing to do with any of that."

The little boy ran to get a drink of Coke. "Who do the kids belong to?" Ross asked.

"My youngest daughter. We were on the HUD waiting list forever and we finally got this three-bedroom about two years ago. Then she got mixed up with a loser, got pregnant again and he moved in here. The HUD lady said he had to go. He wasn't on the lease." She took a drag on the cigarette. "She up and left with him and now I have the kids until she comes to her senses and comes back."

"When you go to jail, Child Protective Services will pick up the kids," Ross continued.

"Jail?" she squealed. "I'm not going to jail. I don't know anything."

"Tell us what you know then," Ethan pressed. "And you do

know something, Mrs. Campbell. We're not stupid. Your car was at that bank at the same time as Grundy's."

She kept puffing on the cigarette, not answering, as if she was weighing her options.

Ross reached for his phone on his belt and looked at Ethan. "Is it Violet or Carmen at CPS who works the day shift?"

Ethan glanced at his watch. "It's after five. Try Carmen."

As Ross tapped in a number, Estelle shouted, "No, wait."

Ross slipped his phone back into its case. "Tell us what you know."

Estelle snuffed out the cigarette in the ashtray, ashes spilling onto the table. "Okay. Rudy called me from jail and wanted to see me. I told him not to call me anymore when he gets into trouble, but I went anyway. He gave me a number and said to text *Lawyer or else* and sign it 'Rudy.' I asked him why he couldn't call himself. He said the cops were watching his every move, so I did it and thought that was it. After work on Thursday morning, I was fixing breakfast for the kids when my cell buzzed. I had a text message from that number. It said money was at the front door and gave instructions what to do with it. I followed them and parked where the message said. That's all I did."

Ethan clasped his hands. "Let me get this straight. Someone left twenty-five grand on your doorstep?"

"Twenty-five grand?" Her eyes grew big. "That case had that much money in it?"

"You didn't know?" Ross asked.

"Of course not."

She was lying. Ethan had interviewed suspects for a long time and Estelle was lying out both sides of her mouth. "What was the phone number?"

"I don't remember. Rudy told me to delete everything from my phone."

Ethan held out his hand. "May I see your phone?"

She pulled it out of her jeans pocket and handed it to him.

"Our tech might be able to find something on it."

"But I need my phone. I have to check on the kids from work."

"You work nights, right?" Ross asked.

"Yes."

"Who keeps them?"

"My neighbor's sixteen-year-old daughter. She likes to sleep here and watch the TV."

"Nice," Ethan commented. "Is it new?"

"I've had it about two months. The whole neighborhood wants to watch TV here."

Ethan wondered where she got the money to buy such an expensive item, but he'd save that question for later. Instead he asked, "Does the sixteen-year-old have a phone?"

"Oh, yeah."

"And you work with someone who has a phone?"

"Yeah."

"Then you can give the sixteen-year-old her number in case there's an emergency with the kids."

"I suppose."

Ethan got to his feet, as did Ross. "You can pick up your phone about ten in the morning at the police station. "He reached into his shirt pocket and handed her his card. "Call me if you think of anything else."

She looked at the card and then at his face. "Oh...you're the man..."

"Your son left to die? Yes. And one way or another I'm going to nail him. And, Mrs. Campbell, if you're lying to me, you're going down with him."

She shook her head. "I'm not. I told you everything."

Ethan nodded and Ross followed him out. Ross took the wheel and they drove away.

"What do you think?" Ross turned onto North Loop.

"I think she's in it up to her eyeballs."

"That's my feeling, too."

"The money wasn't left on her doorstep. She picked it up from someone."

"Mmm." Ross sped toward the station. "Now we have to take a really good look at that big ol' elephant sitting smack-dab in the middle of this case."

"Douglas Bauman?"

"Yes. If we could connect Mrs. Campbell to him, then maybe all the pieces would fall into place. Since tomorrow is Friday we're running out of time to make that happen."

Ethan moved restlessly, knowing he might not be able to make that connection. But in his gut he had that same feeling he had days ago—Abby had been the target on that Saturday morning.

CHAPTER TWENTY

BACK AT THE station, Ethan gave the cell to Jim, the tech who was a whiz at hacking a phone. Ethan told him what he wanted, and then he and Ross sat pouring over the files and evidence once again. "There has to be a connection between Rudy, his mom and Bauman."

"Yeah, but how in the hell are we going to find it?"

"By searching 'til our eyes cross." Ethan pulled out a file. "Beecher had something on that big ranch where we were left. Yeah, here it is. It's been for sale for four years. The last foreman said he hired Rudy one summer to haul hay. That's how Rudy knew about the ranch, and he probably noticed it was for sale and vacant."

"But the ranch has nothing to do with Bauman."

"Mmm. Damn, Beecher may be a pain in the ass, but he's thorough. He contacted the owners and they'd never heard of Rudy." Ethan closed the file. "So the ranch was a last-minute decision. That's what Rudy meant by a change of plans. Hostages weren't supposed to be taken."

"It was just supposed to be a bank robbery," Ross mused.

"They freaked when they heard the sirens."

Ross ran a hand through his hair. "None of this makes sense. They freak and instead of getting the hell out they take hostages?"

"Rudy grabbed Abby first, supposedly because he thought she'd pushed an alarm, but he had his eye on her from the start." Ethan slapped his hand on the desk. "What are we missing?"

Before Ross could answer, his cell buzzed. "Gotta go." Ross

got to his feet. "They found a body in a park off Congress Avenue."

Detectives were on an on-call rotation to respond to a homicide at all hours—twenty-four hours a day, including weekends. Since Ethan was on medical leave, he hadn't been put back in the rotation.

"Why don't you go home and rest, Ethan. We'll start fresh in the morning."

Ethan grunted. "You'll be dead on your feet in the morning."

"I'll get a couple of hours' sleep and be good to go."

They did that all the time, but they were getting older and Ethan now had a kid. As Ross left, he called home to talk to Kelsey. She chatted on and on about school. He wasn't sure when he made the decision, but when he talked to his dad he told him he was staying at the station for the night.

"You better tell the chatterbox."

Kelsey came on. "What's up, Dad?"

"I'm staying at the station tonight to work on the case."

"Oh. Where you gonna eat supper?"

"I'll pick up something."

"You have to eat, Dad."

"Okay. Okay."

"And, Dad, remember we have to get my dancing outfits this weekend. We can ask Abby to help us. She knows all about clothes."

"I'll see." But in light of everything that had happened he was sure that door was firmly closed. He'd tell Kelsey later.

Jim buzzed him so he strolled to the lab to see what he'd found.

"Here's a list." Jim handed him several sheets of paper and the phone. "Times and dates of texts Mrs. Campbell sent and the people who texted her. There were no deleted texts that I could find."

"She lied then?"

"Looks like it."

Jim stretched his shoulders. "If there's nothing else, I'm going home."

"Sure. Thanks, Jim."

Making his way back to his desk, Ethan mulled over the facts. Estelle was involved; he was sure. How did he prove it?

Before returning to all the paperwork, he went to his locker and got a protein bar. He kept them for when he didn't have time to eat. In the small kitchen he made a fresh pot of coffee and headed back to work.

It took him a while to go through all the texts and calls on the list. They were from family, people at work and neighbors. Jim had highlighted the call from Rudy, but there was no text from Estelle to anyone after that. How did she contact the other person? Nothing stuck out so he moved on.

He studied everything in the evidence box, and went through the timeline once again and sorted through all the information collected. Nothing jumped out at him and he grew frustrated. At two he could no longer focus, so he made his way to the sleeping quarters to crash.

He awoke at four and noticed Ross was crashed out in the next bunk. Very quietly, Ethan tiptoed to his locker for clean clothes and then hit the showers before getting back to work. All the while he'd been showering and dressing something had been tugging at his mind.

For there to be a connection to Douglas Bauman, Mrs. Campbell and Rudy would have to encounter him in some way. They didn't exactly move in the same circles. So how? Then it hit him. He quickly unlocked the drawer where he'd stored the files last night. He pulled out Mrs. Campbell's and Rudy's files and searched their work history.

In the past two years Rudy had worked as a roughneck on an oil rig, loaded feed at a feed store and mowed lawns for a lawn service. Ethan didn't see a connection to Bauman at those jobs.

Mrs. Campbell cleaned houses with another woman for eight months and then she was hired by a commercial cleaning service, B&B Services. *Commercial.* Ethan jumped up. That was it. It had to be.

He hurried to the lieutenant's office, but he wasn't in yet. It would take time to get a warrant to see B&B's customer list, but the lieutenant could use his clout to see if Bauman's offices were cleaned by B&B. He made more coffee and waited. Only the night crew was on duty, so the station was quiet.

Finishing his second cup, he saw the lieutenant come in. He was always at work by six. The man wore a suit, but after about thirty minutes in his office, the jacket came off. By mid-morning the tie was gone, and by lunch his shirtsleeves were rolled up to his elbows, which meant do not enter his office unless absolutely necessary.

Ethan gave him a few minutes then tapped on his door.

"What?" blasted through the door.

Ethan eased the door opened. "Can I ask a favor, sir?"

"No" came the sharp retort. "Not until I've had my coffee."

"Coming right up. I just made a pot." He dashed to the kitchen, filled a disposable cup and had it on the lieutenant's desk in less than a minute.

Craig took a couple of sips. "Now remember I haven't had any Tums yet so don't give me indigestion at this time of the morning. What is it?"

Ethan told him about the visit with Estelle and the phone. "She's the go-between for Rudy and this other person. The only viable suspect we have now is Douglas Bauman."

Craig's head jerked up. "Douglas Bauman? How much coffee have you had? The man's family owns banks, Ethan. Why the hell would be set up a robbery?"

"I haven't figured out a motive yet."

"Well, then you're blowing smoke up my pant leg."

"Sir, this is the first real lead we've had. Mrs. Campbell is involved and if we can tie her to Bauman, the motive will come out."

"How do you propose to do that?"

Ethan laid the sheet of paper he'd been holding on the lieu-tenant's desk. "Mrs. Campbell works for B&B Services. It does commercial cleaning."

"And you think they clean Bauman's office?"

"That's what I'd like to find out, but it's Friday and I'm run-ning out of time, sir. Could you call and use your clout to get their customer list?"

The lieutenant shrugged out of his jacket. "You do realize that if he's not on the list we'll have the wrath of the powerful Richard Bauman coming down on this department."

"Are you afraid of bad publicity, sir?"

"Get the hell out of my office and don't come back until I buzz you. I'll do my best to get the list. Go get breakfast or something and stay out of my hair."

"Yes, sir."

"Tell Ross to get his ass in here and fill Hal in before he comes in bitching about you ignoring his authority."

"Yes, sir."

As Ethan closed the door, he saw the lieutenant reaching for his bottle of Tums.

AFTER GIVING ROSS the lieutenant's message, Ethan went to breakfast as ordered. He walked because he needed the ex-ercise. The morning air was crisp and had an autumn feel to it. Dawn crept over Austin like a fluorescent light, getting brighter and brighter.

His thoughts turned to Abby, as they often did. He didn't know how something good could go so wrong. One minute he was in love and the next he had to make choices that would put that love in jeopardy. He'd screwed up and made the wrong choice. In his mind he thought she would understand, that she'd trusted him, but when things got rough her faith in him wa-vered. Not that he could blame her. He had put his job over her.

As the dewy morning continued to brighten, he wished he was lying in Abby's arms getting reacquainted with her body and those gorgeous breasts. He had to accept that wasn't ever going to happen again. Two months ago he didn't even know Abby Bauman, but now she was a part of him and always would be.

WHEN ETHAN RETURNED to the station, Ross was leaving. "Man, I'm sorry, I have to work this murder. Did you find anything last night?"

Ethan told him about Estelle and the cleaning service.

"That could be it, but if it isn't we're going to have to let the FBI take it from there. We just ran out of time."

"I'm not giving up yet."

"Didn't think so." Ross nodded. "I'll check in later."

Hal strolled in and Ethan gave him the lowdown. "So the lieutenant's making the call to B&B?"

"Yes, and I have orders to stay out of his office until he calls."

"Figures." Hal glanced toward the lieutenant's office. "This could take a while."

"I told him how badly we needed the information."

Hal slid into Ross's chair. "If this doesn't pan out, I'm closing the books and handing everything over to the FBI. And they will probably go over everything thoroughly and conclude that Rudy and Devon acted alone. Also, they'll conclude that due to the traumatic situation and stress you heard incorrectly."

"You know how to push my buttons, Hal, but I have more faith in the FBI. They're not going to ignore the money paid to Grundy."

Hal made a clicking sound with his teeth. "That's the kicker." Hal stood. "We at least have today…"

"James," the lieutenant bellowed. "In my office."

Ethan jumped up and was in the office in a flash. He expected Hal to follow him, but he didn't.

"Close the door."

Ethan did as ordered.

The lieutenant didn't waste time. "B&B is owned by a husband and wife, and they were reluctant to share anything about their customers until I mentioned we suspected one of their employees gained information through her job to aid a bank robbery and kidnapping case. If they cooperated with me, I'd try to keep their name out of it. If not, their business might be plastered across the front of a lot of newspapers and mentioned on TV stations. Funny, how that always does the trick." He laid a sheet of paper in front of Ethan.

It was the B&B customer list and Bauman Offices and Bauman Banks were highlighted. Ethan felt a moment of elation, but it was short-lived. They had to place Estelle as the person who cleaned Bauman's office.

"Sir…"

The lieutenant laid another sheet in front of him. "Is that what you need?" The sheet contained names of the people who cleaned the Bauman offices.

"That'll do it."

"Bring Estelle Campbell in and let's see what she has to say."

"She's coming in to pick up her cell. I'll be ready for her."

"Ethan, you have to get her to connect a lot of dots to implicate Douglas Bauman."

"Yeah." He realized that was going to be more than difficult.

"When Ms. Campbell comes in, I'll have them put her in interrogation room number two. Buzz me when it's all set. I want to watch, and, Ethan, I want this done by the book."

"Yes, sir. And thanks."

Back at his desk Ethan showed Hal the list of customers and employees.

"Hot damn, Ethan, we finally have a connection."

"I just wish we had more so we could start hammering the nails into her coffin." He picked up the list of employees. "The women Mrs. Campbell works with might know if she had personally met Bauman."

Hal grabbed the list. "I'll check 'em out. Since you met

Mrs. Campbell yesterday, you handle the interview. Ross is on a murder case and Steve is back on robbery. It's just you and me. With a little luck I'll be back before the interview is over."

"Hal," Ethan called before the man could charge away. "There's an expensive big-screen TV in Mrs. Campbell's home. Her coworkers might know how she got the money to buy it."

"I'm on it."

Ethan looked at all the files on his desk. *Motive.* There wasn't a shred of evidence for motive in any of them. Without motive they didn't have a case against Bauman. First, Ethan had to prove he was involved and hope the motive would follow.

He leaned back in his chair. "Why would Bauman hire someone to rob a bank? But, as they've thought all along, the robbery was a spur of the moment decision. So if Rudy and Devon weren't there to rob the bank, why were they there?" It had something to do with Abby. What did Bauman want them to do to her? His blood ran cold at the scenarios running through his mind.

An hour later the phone on his desk rang. Mrs. Campbell was in the interrogation room throwing a hissy fit.

The lieutenant came out of his office. "Where's Hal?"

"He's checking on a few things."

Ross came in and sat at his desk, writing in a file.

"Let's get this interview over with. Ross, you feel up to join-ing Ethan on the interview?" the lieutenant asked.

"Sure."

"Ethan, you take the lead. Ross, try not to fall asleep."

Ethan picked up the leather case with his information and the three men walked down the hall to the interrogation rooms. The lieutenant went into one room to watch and listen. Ethan and Ross entered interrogation room number two.

"What the hell they put me in here for?" Estelle demanded to know.

"Sit down, Mrs. Campbell. We have a few more questions."

"Why did they have to search me?"

"Standard procedure. Please have a seat."

She plopped into a chair at the table and crossed her arms over her chest. He sat at the end of the table and opened his folder. Ross sat at the other end.

Ethan now had to focus on the task ahead of him. He cleared his throat. "Mrs. Campbell, do you know Douglas Bauman?"

"Who? No." She quickly broke eye contact and fidgeted in the chair. She was lying.

He laid B&B's customers list in front of her. "Do you recognize this?"

She glanced at it briefly and shook her head. "No."

"Look again. You work for B&B Services and that's a record of the offices they clean. These are the offices that start with the letter *b*."

"So?"

He pointed to the highlighted section. "Bauman Offices are on it."

"So?"

He pulled the employee list out and placed it on top of the other one. "Now, I'm going to ask you again. Do you know Douglas Bauman?"

"Okay," she spat. "I clean his office."

"Mrs. Campbell—" Someone tapped at the door. "Hang on." Ethan and Ross got up and went into the hall. Hal was outside with the lieutenant.

"I spoke with the supervisor of Mrs. Campbell's crew." Hal looked down at his notes on his iPhone. "She said Mr. Bauman asked specifically for Estelle to clean his office. He liked her work. She didn't know where Estelle got the money for the TV, but she bought it at a Walmart near her house. I met with the store manager, and after a little checking he found that one had been purchased with cash the week before the robbery. Gotta love computers." He handed Ethan a receipt.

"Thanks, man."

"Tie it up, Ethan," the lieutenant ordered. "Get her to crack."

"I'm just going to be quiet," Ross said.

They went back in and Ethan laid the receipt on his case, facing Estelle so she could read it.

She took a brief look and glanced away.

"That's a receipt for a Samsung HDTV in the amount of two thousand four hundred and ninety-nine dollars plus tax. You have one in your apartment. Where did you get the money to buy the TV?"

She stared him square in the eye. "You can't prove I bought it."

"We can, Mrs. Campbell. The cashier will remember a cash purchase this big and the woman who purchased it. We're going to be pissed if you put us to all that trouble."

"Can I have a cigarette?" She ran her hands up her arms in a nervous gesture.

Ethan resumed his seat, as did Ross. "Sorry, it's a nonsmoking facility." He folded his hands across the folder on the table. "Mrs. Campbell, you're in this up to your eyeballs."

Color drained from her face and she ran a shaky hand through her hair, but she didn't respond.

He decided to move on from the TV. "You said Rudy gave you a number to text *Lawyer or else*. What did you use to send that text?"

"My cell."

"There are no deleted texts on your cell like you said." He pulled her phone from his leather case, opened it and saw there was some charge left on it. "I'll call Mr. Bauman's office and see if he takes your call."

She shrugged. "Go ahead. I don't care who you call. Can I leave? I need a cigarette."

"No." Before he could punch in the number he had for Bauman, a cell buzzed—in the room. It wasn't Ethan's or Ross's. The sound came from the floor and Mrs. Campbell's purse.

Ross reached for Estelle's purse and fished out a buzzing

phone. A prepaid phone. One she must have used to text Bauman. Ethan now knew where Rudy got his brains.

Ross shoved it across the table. "You want to explain this?"

Estelle twisted her hands and wouldn't look at him.

"We can get our tech to retrieve the numbers you called or texted on this phone, but it would be in your best interest to tell us."

Nothing but silence followed his words.

"Did Bauman tell you to buy a prepaid phone to contact him?"

Again, not a word left her mouth, so he tried another tactic. "Why would you bring it into the police station?" That baffled him.

"You took mine and I needed a phone to check on the kids. I didn't know you were going to question me."

"You thought you were home free?"

She looked down at the floor.

"Okay, Mrs. Campbell, I'm going to give you a chance to tell me the whole story. If you tell the truth, the D.A. might be willing to make a deal with you. If not, I'm going to tie this case up into a tidy little bow and you'll go down as hard as Rudy and Devon."

"I can't go to jail. I didn't do anything."

"You took the money to Grundy. No one left it on your doorstep. Where did you get it?"

She ran a hand through her hair again.

"You picked it up at Bauman's office, didn't you?"

She didn't answer.

"Did Bauman give you the money?"

She raised her head, her eyes narrowed.

"Ms. Campbell, you're looking at a lot of time in prison. How much time depends on how well you cooperate with us." He took a breath. "Now, I'm asking you again. Did Bauman give you the money?"

"Yes. Bauman gave it to me." For the first time her voice sounded defeated.

Ethan kept his emotions in check even though he could feel a crack in his composure starting to form. But he remained focused. He needed a motive and he intended to get it. He pulled out a small digital recorder from his case and placed it on the table. "This will record what you say. Then we'll have it typed up and you can sign it."

"Okay," she muttered.

"Start from the beginning, and tell me how all this started." He clicked on the recorder.

She drew a shaky breath. "Mr. Bauman is rarely in his office when we clean, but one night he came in to do some last-minute stuff, for his dad, he said. He told us to keep cleaning. I was finishing up when I got a call from Rudy. I ignored it because we're not supposed to be on our phones while working, and Mr. Bauman was there. I didn't want to lose my job. But he heard it and said he didn't mind if I took it. Rudy was in jail again and wanted me to get his bail. Mr. Bauman saw that I was upset and asked what was wrong. I told him I had a no-good son who was always in trouble and expected me to bail him out. Mr. Bauman was very nice and considerate. About a month later Mr. Bauman asked that I clean his office every time. He spoke to my supervisor."

She stopped speaking and Ethan asked, "Was there a reason for that?"

"I wasn't sure. Then one night he came in late to his office and wanted to speak to me."

"What did he want?"

"He...uh...said he had a job for Rudy and it had to be top secret. He'd give Rudy twenty-five hundred and me the same if I could get Rudy to do it."

"That's what you used to buy the TV?"

"Yes." She folded her arms across her chest again in a defensive manner.

"What did he want Rudy to do?" He held his breath as he waited for the answer.

"He…um…said his ex-wife was being difficult and he wanted to teach her a lesson."

"How?" he asked through clenched teeth.

"He wanted him to scare her, confront her at the bank as she got out of her car, touch her, make her feel uncomfortable and afraid."

That sorry son of a bitch. Ethan's control was hanging by a thread.

"It was just supposed to be that one little thing, but Rudy couldn't even get that right. His car broke down the day before, so he hooked up with his friend Devon, who got his dad's van. Rudy gave him half of the money and they did drugs most of the night. They decided since they were gonna be at a bank, they'd just rob it, get lots of money and really scare Ms. Bauman. The idiots found Halloween masks at Devon's. They got to the bank late, but just in time to push everyone inside. Then the sirens went off and Rudy lost it. He's always been stupid."

Ethan took a moment, trying to remain cool. "Where did Rudy get the Glocks?" He already knew they were stolen, but he wanted to hear her response.

"From a house burglary. Rudy had them stashed somewhere. He was going to sell them."

"Let me get this straight. Mr. Bauman wanted to teach his ex a lesson. Why?"

"He didn't tell me. That was his business."

"How did Mr. Bauman feel when the job was botched?"

"He was angry as hell. Told me to tell Rudy he was on his own."

Ethan pulled a sheet of paper out of his folder. "You saw Rudy the next day at the jail and delivered that message?"

"Yeah. Rudy said he wanted a lawyer and Mr. Bauman better pay or he was going to tell the cops why he was at the bank in the first place."

"You didn't use your phone to call Bauman because his number wasn't on there."

"No. Rudy told me to buy a prepaid one so Mr. Bauman would know Rudy wasn't going to finger him if he paid for a good lawyer."

"Rudy came up with the phone idea?"

"Yeah."

"Why not tell Bauman when you went to work?"

"Because he's not always there and Rudy wanted him to get the message fast."

"I see. When you called, how did Mr. Bauman respond?"

Estelle moved uneasily. "He threatened me and Rudy and said he didn't hire the other guy. That was Rudy's problem, but he didn't want his name mentioned. He was afraid his father would find out."

"So he paid the money?"

"Yeah."

Doug was one stupid dude. He just kept getting in deeper and deeper. If he had come forward, he could have saved himself a lot of trouble. Teaching Abby a lesson paled in significance to bank robbery, the death of Mr. Harmon and kidnapping. If he'd been man enough to step forward and admit he'd hired Rudy in the first place, he could have saved Abby a lot of misery. But then, maybe he wanted her to suffer. Doug's motive was still rather vague. Estelle's involvement was not.

"When you first visited Rudy in jail, did he tell you where he and Devon left Mrs. Bauman and me?"

"I had nothing to do with that."

Ethan frowned. A piece of the puzzle was missing. Rudy didn't have enough sense to think of a prepaid phone. And then it clicked in his mind.

He scooted forward. "Mrs. Campbell, did Rudy contact Mr. Bauman after the robbery?"

"Yeah."

"How? Mr. Bauman's number wasn't on his cell."

"He gave me one of those prepaid phones to give to Rudy. He had one, too. Rudy tossed his in Houston."

"Wait a minute." He held up the prepaid phone on the desk. "You called Bauman's prepaid phone with this?"

"Yes."

"Let's get back to Rudy's call after the robbery. What did he tell Mr. Bauman?"

"I don't know…"

"What did Rudy tell Mr. Bauman?" he shouted.

"I need a cigarette."

"Did Rudy tell Mr. Bauman where he'd left his ex-wife?"

"Yes, okay. I'm not answering any more questions. Can I go?"

"No," he snapped, wanting to reach over and shake her. "What did Rudy tell you he told Mr. Bauman?"

"He…um—" she chewed nervously on a fingernail for a second "—told him his ex was on the Old Mill Ranch and he could now play the hero."

Ethan swallowed his anger. "But he didn't play the hero, did he? And neither did you. You could have called from a payphone, or anywhere to let the police know where we were, but you played the coward, just like Mr. Bauman. Do you know what it's like being burned alive, Mrs. Campbell?"

"Ethan." Ross clicked off the tape recorder, but Ethan was focused on Estelle.

"I…I…um…"

"How much did Bauman offer to pay you to keep quiet?"

"I…um…"

He slapped his hand on the table. "How much?"

"Another twenty-five hundred for me and the same for Rudy, but…"

"What about Devon?"

"Rudy said to tell him the lawyer had been hired and to keep his mouth shut."

"Devon didn't know he wasn't getting a dime?"

"No."

"Honor among thieves," Ethan murmured. His and Abby's lives were worth a lousy twenty-five hundred dollars each. His gut churned with renewed anger.

"Listen, I didn't know all those bad things were going to happen. I'm sorry."

Two uniformed officers stepped into the room. Ross started reading Estelle her rights.

"What's happening? What's going on?"

"You're under arrest, Mrs. Campbell," Ethan said, closing his case and getting to his feet. "Welcome to hell."

"I can't go to jail." She tried to pull away from the officer. "I have grandkids to pick up."

"CPS will get them," Ross told her. "And they will locate your daughter."

"No, no, no, you can't do this!" she screamed as the officers dragged her from the room.

Ethan walked out, spent and more disillusioned than he'd ever been in his life. How could something like this happen? He didn't have time to dwell on it. The lieutenant slapped a warrant into his hand.

"Make the arrest. It's your collar. Take two uniform cops with you. Keep it quiet and legal." He glanced at Hal. "You going?"

"Nah. This is Ethan's show."

The lieutenant turned to Ross. "You?"

"Damn straight."

"I'm proud of the way you guys worked together. You did a great job."

"I'm still not clear about Bauman's motive," Ethan said.

"It'll fall into place." The lieutenant returned to his office and he and Ross headed for the door.

"Just a minute." He reached for his phone and called Abby. Even though she didn't want to speak to him, he had to let her

know. It rang and rang. *Answer, Abby. Answer.* She didn't. It
went to voice mail. Damn it!

"It's Ethan. Call me. It's important."

Call me, Abby. Please.

CHAPTER TWENTY-ONE

AFTER A JOG, Abby took a quick shower. Wrapping a towel around her, she went into her bedroom and sat at her dressing table, rubbing lotion onto her legs and arms. She planned to pick up Chloe early and spend some time with her dad and Gayle.

She'd thought the interview with the police might push Gayle off the deep end, but it had accomplished just the opposite. It had prompted her dad to have a long talk with his wife. They had agreed to be more open with their communication and that Gayle would stop smothering Abby and Chloe. Abby had seen them yesterday and they were giggling and teasing each other like teenagers. If Abby didn't love them it would be quite sickening. But she was very happy they had found a balance to make their marriage work.

Removing the towel, she picked up a thong from the bed. She'd bought a few new sets of underwear on Tuesday, and had thought Ethan would get a kick out of them. They were pink and *Taste Me* was written in red on the triangle in front. Wadding them into a ball, she tucked them away in a drawer and reached for another pair. She slipped her feet through the holes and vowed she wouldn't think about Ethan.

Hooking her bra, she refused to let Wynken, Blynken and Nod cross her mind. When a tiny sob left her throat she knew she'd failed. She quickly grabbed slacks and a top and sat at her dressing table, brushing her hair. As she applied lip gloss, her cell buzzed. She glanced at the caller ID. *Ethan.*

Why was he calling? Should she answer? No. If she heard

his voice… The phone stopped and then there was a beep. He'd left a message.

Her hand shook slightly as she touched a button to listen. "It's Ethan. Call me. It's important."

Important? His voice sounded stressed. Something was wrong. Before she could call him back, someone pounded loudly on her door. And kept pounding. What the…? She ran to see who was at her door. It could be Ethan. She hated herself for the way her heart raced at the thought.

Looking through the peephole, she saw it was Doug. Damn! She yanked opened the door. "What are you doing?"

"Let's go." His hair was tousled as if he'd been running his hands through it, which was odd because his hair was always impeccable.

"What?"

"Let's go, Abby."

"What are you talking about? I'm not going anywhere with you."

"Fine. Chloe and I will go without you."

"Chloe?" That shook her.

"She's in the car."

"How did you get her?"

"I picked her up from day care. I am her father."

"They're not supposed to let her go with anyone without my permission."

He turned toward the stairs as if she hadn't spoken. "We're leaving. You can come or not." He took the stairs two at a time.

"Doug. Doug!" She slammed the door and ran after him. He wasn't taking her child anywhere.

He backed out of a parking spot and she opened the passenger door and jumped in. He shot out into the street. Buckling her seat belt, she glanced to the back. Her heart stopped. Chloe lay limply in her car seat, not moving. Her skin was so pale.

"What have you done to her?"

"I gave her some liquid Tylenol. She's sleeping. That's all."

"Why would you give her Tylenol? She's not sick."

"She was screaming, wanting her mommy, so I had to give her something to keep her quiet."

"And you just happened to have Tylenol?"

"Yes. I have to keep it because she always cries wanting to go home. My daughter doesn't want to spend any time with me because you've turned her against me."

"So you've been drugging her?" Anger churned inside her.

"It's the only way I can get that damn doll away from her. Dad said she has to learn discipline."

"You are a lousy excuse for a father." She glanced at Chloe. "Something is wrong with her, can't you see that?" She unbuckled her seat belt, intending to get to her baby any way she could.

When she attempted to crawl between the leather seats, Doug pushed her back and grabbed a small handgun from the console.

Pointing it at her, he said in a cold voice she didn't recognize, "Sit back and buckle up or I'll kill all of us."

ETHAN, ROSS AND two officers took the elevator up to the top floor of the Bauman building. It opened into a large reception area. Ethan walked up to the woman at the desk.

"We're looking for Douglas Bauman."

She eyed them warily. "His office is down the hall to the left, but he's not in."

"Where is he?"

"He left for a vacation about twenty minutes ago. He and his ex are getting remarried and they're taking their little girl with them on a second honeymoon."

Son of a bitch. He was too late.

He turned to Ross. "Get info on his car and I'll call Abby to verify this crap." But Ethan already knew the answer.

"I better call Mr. Richard Bauman." The receptionist poked a number on her desk phone.

"You do that, sweetie," Ross said.

Ethan stepped aside to call Abby. It rang and rang and went to voice mail. He then called Abby's father. "Mr. Baines, this is Ethan James. Is Abby there?"

"No. Why do you want to know?"

"Could you please give me the name of Chloe's day care?" he asked, ignoring the question.

"Not until you tell me what's going on."

He drew a deep breath. "Is Abby getting back together with Doug?"

"No."

"Mr. Baines, I will have someone contact you later, but right now we need to verify Abby's and Chloe's whereabouts. This is urgent."

He must have gotten through to him because he rattled off the number. "Just let me know my girls are safe."

"I will." Ethan immediately called the number. A woman answered.

"This is Detective Ethan James with the Austin Police Department. Is Chloe Bauman in your class?"

"Yes."

"Is she there?"

"No. Her father picked her up about fifteen minutes ago."

Damn it. He had them.

Ross hurried over. "I called the lieutenant and he's putting out an APB on Bauman and he's getting a chopper in the air. He wants to know where Bauman is headed."

Before Ethan could respond, Richard Bauman charged in. "What's going on here?"

Ethan pulled the arrest warrant out of his shirt pocket and slapped it against Mr. Bauman's pristine white shirt. "That's an arrest warrant for Douglas Bauman. Where is he?"

"You must be mistaken."

"Where is he?" Ethan shouted.

Mr. Bauman took a step backward. "He's...on vacation with

his ex-wife and daughter. They're putting their marriage back together and I couldn't be happier."

"He lied to you."

"No." Richard shook his head. "He wouldn't do that. He knows what's at stake."

"What would that be?"

"I told him to get his life straight with Abby or he could kiss the CEO position goodbye. I want a family man at the helm, not a playboy."

And the last piece of the puzzle, the motive, fell into place. Anger gnawed at him once again.

"Mr. Bauman, you'll be happy to hear that your son followed your orders." He tapped the warrant again on his chest. "Read this. Doug hired two thugs to scare Abby, misguidedly thinking she'd be so afraid she'd run back to him, I suppose. But the thugs decided to rob the bank and take hostages. I think you know the rest of the story."

The man paled. "No. That can't be true."

"Where is Doug going on vacation?"

"To Italy. He rented a villa there."

"Let me guess. You have a company jet?"

"Yes."

"Where is it hangared?"

"Austin-Bergstrom International Airport."

Ross was immediately on the phone to the lieutenant.

"Mr. Bauman, I'd advise you to corral all the lawyers on your payroll because your son is going to need them. To add to the other charges, he has now kidnapped Abby and Chloe. He's going down with the other scumballs he hired."

THE CAR STEADILY moved down I-35. Abby had no idea where he intended to take them. Her only concern was Chloe. Doug held the gun in his right hand and it rested on his thigh. If she tried to grab it, they'd swerve into traffic, hurting innocent people, not to mention themselves. She had to try something else.

"Doug, please. Pull over. Let's talk. I'll do anything you want. Just let me go to Chloe. Please."

"How does it feel to beg, Abby? I've been begging you for months and you've ignored me. I shouldn't have to do these things. We should be together."

"I don't love you anymore and you don't love me either. What kind of marriage would we have? It wasn't good the first time."

"Love?" He grunted. "I was in lust with you, but you were this demure, cold bitch I could never get close to. Dad said I had to marry you. You were the perfect wife for me."

"Your dad told you to marry me?" She was aghast.

"Yes."

Abby fought to control her temper and it wasn't easy. She took a couple of deep breaths. "Pull this car over and let me and Chloe out. Do you hear me?"

"I can't. I've gone too far and I can't stop now."

"What do you mean?"

"Nothing. The jet is waiting for us. I've taken care of everything. We'll fly away to Italy and get reacquainted. In a couple of weeks we'll return as a family and Dad will appoint me the new CEO and everything will be just like it should be."

"You're insane, Doug." She calmly released her seat belt. "Now I'm going to my daughter. Shoot me if you have to, but I don't believe you have the guts. You're a yellow-livered daddy's boy."

As she rose out of her seat, he lifted the gun. She knocked his hand away but he quickly brought it back and hit her against the head with the barrel. She felt the cold steel, heard the window pop where her head landed. A searing pain shot through her and everything went black.

ETHAN SLID INTO the driver's seat of their unmarked squad car. Ross took the passenger side, still on the phone.

"The lieutenant said to head back to the station. Chopper's

in the air, the highway patrol and all police units have been notified. They'll locate Bauman." Ross clicked off.

Ethan listened closely to the police radio. "Highway patrol spotted a gray BMW headed south on I-35. That's it." He backed up and sped out of the parking lot, heading for the interstate.

"Uh, Ethan. The station is the other way."

"I know."

"Damn. I knew you weren't going to let this go. Sometimes I feel like we're Butch Cassidy and the Sundance Kid. And in case you're wondering, I'm the good-looking one with all the hair."

"Yeah, right. Hold on."

"I wasn't thinking of doing anything else."

Ethan zoomed in and out of traffic.

"The BMW is turning onto Texas 71 headed east" came over the radio.

"He's probably headed for US-183 near the airport," Ethan said. "We have to cut him off before he gets there." He wove in and out until he reached a string of cop cars driving side by side.

"We can't get through," Ross pointed out.

"Yeah. A minor inconvenience." He let his window down, reached for the red flashing light and slammed it onto the top of the car, then hit the siren. A loud wail echoed. He picked up the radio receiver. "This is Detective Ethan James. I have a warrant for the arrest of Douglas Bauman. Let me through. I'm right behind you in a black sedan."

"Ethan, what the hell are you doing?" the lieutenant's voice blasted through the receiver.

"It's my collar, sir." He kept up his tough stance, but he meant it.

Voices mumbled on the radio, but Ethan couldn't make out what was being said. The lieutenant was talking to someone.

The police had all civilian cars stop. Ethan continued to

follow the caravan of cop cars. He was just waiting for one to slow down so he could zip through.

"This is Chief Alveraz" came through loud and clear on the radio.

"Shit, we're toast," Ross quipped.

"Make sure all civilian cars are stopped and out of harm's way," the chief continued. "Let Detective James through, but be prepared to back him up. And, James, don't you screw this up."

"Thank you, sir." He and Ross high-fived.

The patrol cars slowly shifted into single file. He zoomed by, waving his thanks. The gray BMW was up ahead.

"I'm driving past him and making a roadblock with the car. Hold on."

"Let 'er go!" Ross shouted.

Ethan pushed his boot down on the accelerator. They whizzed by the BMW, Ethan slammed on the brakes and the sedan spun to a halt on the highway. The BMW was forced to stop. He and Ross jumped out, guns drawn. Ethan ran to the driver's side, Ross to the passenger's side.

Ethan yanked opened the door and everything came to a complete stop. Doug had his right arm around Abby's neck and a gun held to her head with his left. Blood matted her blond hair. His heart crashed against his ribs in fury.

"Back off or I'll shoot her," Doug warned.

Ethan kept his cool. "Let her go, Doug. It's over."

"Tell everyone to back off and let me through to the plane or I will kill her." He pushed the end of the barrel against the side Abby's face. She moaned.

He shut out the sound. "That would defeat your purpose, Doug. You did all this to get Abby back into your life."

"Just let us go to the plane. This is between Abby and me."

"You're wrong there. You involved nefarious people in your scheme and it backfired. Estelle Campbell gave you up. Your dad was more than shocked to hear about your illegal activities."

"You told my father." Doug's eyes glazed over with fear. "Why'd you do that?"

Ethan had his gun pointed at Doug's head, but he couldn't figure out a way to get to the man without Abby getting hurt.

"Have you told Abby the truth, Doug?"

"Shut up."

"C'mon, man. Tell her everything you did to force her back into your life."

"What did you do?" Abby asked, her eyes wide.

"He hired Rudy to teach you a lesson." Ethan didn't want to tell her this way, but he hoped if he did, it would save her life. He had to keep Doug distracted enough so he wouldn't pull the trigger. "And it backfired."

"Shut up!" Doug shouted, losing his grip on the gun. "He's lying!"

"Afraid not. Like I told you, Estelle Campbell ratted you out and we have a warrant for your arrest in connection with the bank robbery, the death of Mr. Harmon, kidnapping and a whole lot of other charges."

"Oh, my God!" Abby began to struggle. "How could you?"

Doug had a stranglehold on Abby, and she coughed from the pressure. "It wasn't meant to turn out like that. The idiot was only supposed to scare you. Remember when you were in college and that guy was stalking you? You called me and I took care of it. You needed me, and I was there for you. I would have done the same this time, but that stupid bastard decided to rob the bank."

"I would have never called you," Abby growled. "I would have called the police."

"No, you would have reached out to me. You know I can protect you."

"Never, Doug. Never."

"Tell her what else you did," Ethan prompted, his eye on the gun, waiting for an opening.

"I didn't do anything else." Sweat beaded on his forehead.

"Sure you did," Ethan kept on. "Rudy told his mother where he and Devon left us, and she told you. Being the coward that you are, you decided to keep that information to yourself. You didn't want dear ol' dad to find out what you'd done, so you left us out in the searing heat to die of thirst and be incinerated in a fire. Besides, if Abby died, you'd be a grieving single father and your dad couldn't fault you for that. Right? He'd hand over that CEO job without any more demands."

"Shut up, man. I couldn't stop anything. I couldn't, Abby."

"You selfish, egotistical…"

Abby was trying to wiggle her left arm free, which was wedged between her and Doug. He had to keep Doug's attention.

"I didn't mean for you to get hurt," Doug said. Sweat trickled down the side of his face.

"You just didn't want daddy to find out." Ethan kept up the pressure.

"You didn't have to tell my father." Doug's attention was completely on Ethan.

Now, Abby, now. Knock the gun away. He silently willed her to act.

"Oh, he knows every—"

Abby's arm came up and shoved the gun toward Doug. The revolver tumbled to the floorboard. Ethan yanked Doug out onto the pavement while Ross took care of Abby. Cops converged on Doug and he was in handcuffs in seconds.

"Abby!" Doug called. "Tell my father I didn't mean to hurt you."

Ethan shoved his gun into its holster. "Read the bastard his rights."

Abby cried out and he dashed around the car to her. She held a limp Chloe. The child's head fell backward over Abby's arm, her arms and legs dangling lifelessly.

"What happened?"

"Doug drugged her." She kissed Chloe's cheek. "Wake up, baby. It's Mommy."

Ethan reached for the child's neck to find a pulse. He couldn't find one. Fear congealed in his throat. Oh, God, no!

"Ross!" he shouted. "Call the lieutenant and get the chopper back. This baby needs to get to a hospital. Now!"

Ross ran for the squad car. Several officers gathered round to see if they could help.

"Abby, I have to give her CPR," he said gently.

"Oh," she choked out, but handed Chloe to him. Someone pulled a child's blanket from the car and Ethan laid Chloe on it. The September sun beamed down and the pavement was hot, but no one noticed.

Ethan tilted Chloe's head, held her tiny nose and blew into her mouth. He did it over and over until he felt her small chest move. "She's breathing."

Abby gathered her child into her arms. "Wake up, baby. Wake up."

"The chopper's coming!" Ross yelled. "Get the patrol cars out of the way so it can land."

The officers immediately went into action and a large part of the highway was cleared. As they waited, Ethan said to Ross, "Get a car to pick up Abby's parents and bring them to the hospital."

"Will do."

In less than a minute the chopper was on the ground. "I'll carry her," Ethan offered.

"I'm not letting her go," Abby said with tears in her eyes. He swallowed hard and they ran for the helicopter. Ethan lifted them inside. Luckily, the helicopter wasn't a two-seater. A small cargo space was behind the seats. Abby held Chloe, softly talking to her.

"Call the hospital and let them know we're on the way," Ethan told the pilot as they took off.

"The lieutenant already has," the man replied.

"What did Doug give her?" he asked Abby.

"He said Tylenol, but I've given her Tylenol before and she's never had this kind of reaction. He must have given her too much. How could he do this to his own child?"

"Shh." He tucked her hair behind her ear, eyeing the matted bloody hair. "Did he hit you?"

"Yeah. With the gun. He...he wouldn't let me go to Chloe."

Ethan's hands curled into fists. He wanted to break something. Preferably Douglas Bauman's head.

"We're landing," the pilot called. "E.R. team is waiting."

The doors flew open and Chloe was placed on a gurney and rushed into the E.R. He and Abby ran behind. The doctor and nurses tried to keep Abby out of the room, but soon found they couldn't keep the mother from her child. He paced outside, waiting.

Everett and Gayle Baines rushed in. "Is it true? Doug is behind everything?" Everett asked.

"Yes. He drugged Chloe and the doctors are working on her. He also hit Abby. They both need medical attention."

"Oh, my poor babies," Gayle cried, and they both hurried into the room. He heard sobbing. It was Abby and he steeled himself not to go in. She had her parents. He kept waiting, though. Waiting for Chloe to cry or wake up.

Wake up, Chloe. Please.

Ross walked in. "How are they?"

"They're still working on Chloe." He paced back and forth. "She has to wake up."

"She will. Did the Baineses make it?"

"Yeah. They're in there."

Wake up, Chloe. The longer she was out, the more danger she was in. Suddenly, a loud cry echoed through the E.R. followed by a faint, "Mommy. Mommy."

Ethan let out a long agonizing breath. "Thank God, she's okay."

"Are you coming to the station? They're booking Bauman."

"I'm not leaving here until I know they're okay." He ran a hand through his hair. "I should have listened to the lieutenant and stayed off this case. Then I would have been there to protect her and that bastard wouldn't have been able to hurt her again."

"Come on, Ethan. This isn't your fault."

"Oh, yeah? How many times did I lose my perspective, Ross? How many times did you warn me? How many times did Hal warn me?"

"I don't care if you were on the case or off it. You couldn't have stopped Bauman until we had all the facts and you're the one who got those. You stopped him from getting on that plane with her. Enough with the guilt. I'm heading back to the station, but I'll be back."

Ethan continued to pace until a doctor came out of the room. "How are they?"

The doctor looked at him and then at his badge. "Did you bring them in?"

"Yes."

The doctor closed the chart he was holding. "You got them here just in time. The little girl has been given more Tylenol than any three-year-old should have. We had to pump her stomach and she's fine now. She just wants her mommy. We're going to keep her overnight for observation. They'll take her to a room in about an hour."

"And Abby?"

"The nurse is dressing her wound now. It's just a bad bruise. She'll be fine, too. Hope you got the guy who did this."

"Yes. He'll be locked up for a while."

"Good." The doctor walked off and Ethan continued to pace. He wasn't sure why. They were fine so he should go, but he couldn't make himself leave.

"Ethan."

He swung around to see Abby standing there, a small bandage on her hairline.

"Why are you still here?"

"I wanted to make sure you and Chloe were okay."

"We're fine."

He stared at her, the sadness and pain in her beautiful eyes tearing at his heart. "I'm sorry, Abby. For everything."

"Me, too." She looked down at her hands. "I'm numb inside. And angry. And disillusioned. At what I allowed Doug and his dad to do to my life. I have only myself to blame for being so naive, stupid and trusting. You see…" She blinked back a tear. "I kept believing in love. In the fantasy."

"Abby…"

She held up a hand to stop him. "Then I met you. Even the robbery and the fire couldn't stop me weaving a fantasy about you. The connection was so strong and I wanted it to be real, but it wasn't. I have to step back now and take control of my life. I have to live in the real world where love and trust are just an illusion. And through this mess I have to find me. Never again will I allow anyone to take advantage of me."

Her face suddenly softened. "I will always be grateful for what you did for me and I'll never forget you. Goodbye, Ethan."

"Goodbye, Abby." He walked away. He'd always heard that strong men didn't cry. Cowboys didn't cry. Cops didn't cry. So he wasn't sure what the wet stuff was on his face.

He took a cab back to the station and went straight into the lieutenant's office. He took off his badge and laid it on the desk. "I'm done. I quit."

"What's wrong with you?"

He turned and left without another word.

"Ethan."

He didn't look back. There was no need. His job meant nothing to him now. He got into his truck and headed for the only place he'd ever found peace.

He went home.

CHAPTER TWENTY-TWO

THE NEXT FEW days were rough for Abby. She wanted to hide beneath the covers and never come out. But even though she had that debilitating feeling inside, she wouldn't hide. She would not let her daughter down, and Chloe needed her. She became agitated when Abby was out of her sight. Abby had to undo all the damage Doug had caused.

Her dad and Gayle wanted her to stay at their house again for a while, but she refused. She had to stand on her own two feet and in the weeks that followed she found she had more strength than she'd ever imagined. Reporters were a nuisance, wanting interviews. She gave a statement and asked that they please respect her family's privacy. After that, they left her alone. Occasionally, there'd be a guy with a camera trying to get a photo of her and Chloe. She ignored them.

The lady from the day care visited and apologized profusely for what had happened. They'd hired a new girl and she hadn't had time to familiarize herself with the files. She went on to say Doug was very persuasive, saying they were going on a family vacation and that Chloe was glad to see her father. The woman never suspected a thing was amiss. Abby knew how persuasive Doug could be and she couldn't blame the day care. He would have found a way to take Chloe. She accepted the woman's apology, but wasn't sure if Chloe would return. Their world had once again been turned upside down and Abby was struggling to make a stable home for them.

She received three calls from Richard Bauman wanting her to see Doug. He was asking for her. She told him in no uncertain terms that she would never see Doug again. Nor would Chloe. He had never reached out with an apology. Just demands.

Then he called to ask if she would testify that Doug meant her and Chloe no harm. She hung up on him.

He called again to ask if he and Celeste could see Chloe. She told him no, and that she would be hiring a new lawyer to make sure that never happened. She just didn't know where she was going to find a lawyer to take on the Baumans.

So she enlisted Holly's help. After asking around, Holly came up with two names. One had the personality of a potato and Abby knew the Bauman lawyers would shred him like confetti. The second one suggested she agree to a huge settlement and allow them to see Chloe every now and then. She told him where he could stick that idea.

"What am I going to do, Hol?" she asked that afternoon in her apartment. She sat cross-legged on the rug while Holly lounged on the sofa. "There aren't any good lawyers willing to take my case, or should I say take on the Baumans."

"You might have to hire someone from Houston or Dallas."

"I'd like to know something about them first."

Holly reached for Abby's laptop on the coffee table. "Let's do a search and see what happens." Her hands flew over the keyboard. "You know, this would be a good question to ask Ethan. He probably knows the good, the bad and the ugly of lawyers."

"Hol, I cannot involve Ethan in my life anymore."

Holly stopped typing and looked at her. "Why?"

"I just can't, okay? It's complicated."

"Uncomplicate it."

"Ethan is married to his job." Her words came out sounding hurt and she didn't mean them that way. Or maybe she did.

"Ah, I see. Solving the case was more important to him than you?"

"It's not that," she denied. "We got in too deep, too fast. We didn't even know each other."

"But you knew what was important. He risked his life to save yours and you trusted him. Ah." Holly eyes widened as if she'd discovered something important. "He broke that trust."

"It's more than that. Ethan has a twelve-year-old daughter he's trying to be a father to. I have a three-year-old who's been traumatized. And the girls do not like each other. Both girls need the love and reassurance of their parents. What kind of parents would we be if we put our feelings before theirs?" She shook her head. "Ethan and I weren't meant to be."

"Abby, there are divorced couples all over the world with kids and they adjust."

"Could we talk about something else, please?"

"Sure." Holly went back to the laptop and Abby searched for lawyers on her phone.

"Did you know Ethan quit the force?"

"What? When?" Holly had her full attention and she was sure that's exactly the reaction her friend had intended.

"Right after Doug was arrested. Rumor is he turned in his badge and said he was done."

"Why?"

"I heard he said he lost his perspective and made bad choices."

"Oh." She was dumbstruck. Ethan loved his job and he was good at it. They both had made so many mistakes, but she never wanted him to give up something he loved.

The doorbell rang and she leaped to her feet to answer it before it woke Chloe. She'd been whiny and clingy all day.

Her parents stood there and Abby smiled. "Checking up on me, huh?"

"Yes." Gayle hugged her and her dad kissed her cheek.

"We thought we'd take you and Chloe to get ice cream and go to the park so Chloe can play."

"Thanks, Dad, but Chloe's down for a nap and Holly and I

are searching for lawyers. I can't find one in Austin willing to seek full custody so Holly and I were thinking we might need to look in Houston or Dallas."

Holly scooted over, and Gayle and her dad sat on the sofa. "That's going to be expensive," Everett said.

"I know." Abby sank into the comfy chair. "I can get a loan at the bank and…"

"Nonsense," Gayle interrupted, digging in her purse. "I'll sign a blank check and…"

"Gayle." Her dad stopped her.

"Don't worry, Everett. I won't use my money. I'll write it on our account."

Her father laughed out loud, and Abby hadn't heard him do that in a long time. He put an arm around Gayle. "I love you."

Gayle kissed him. "I know, honey."

"Please." Holly made a face. "Don't make me barf."

Everett grinned. "Now you young girls need to find a nice young man."

"You're preaching to the choir," Holly told him.

The room was full of love and happiness, and Abby felt it in relation to her father and Gayle. It had been a long, hard road, but they were now a family.

"Thank you, Gayle, for the offer and I might take you up on it, but I don't know what a lawyer is going to cost. I have to find one first."

"If I had known Doug had caused you all that misery, I would have beaten him with Everett's golf club that day he tried to take Chloe."

"My tiger." Everett squeezed Gayle.

"Mommy. Mommy!" Chloe screeched from the bedroom.

Abby and Gayle were on their feet at the same time. "I'll get her." Gayle took off down the hall and Abby let her. She wanted to see how Chloe did with someone else. Standing in the hall, she listened closely.

"Grandma."

"Hi, sweetie. How's my baby?"

"'Kay."

"Let's wash your face and fix your hair."

"'Kay."

Abby stepped back as they went into the bathroom.

"Would you like to go to the park and get ice cream with Grandpa and me?"

"Yeah. Can I go on the big slide?"

Abby went back to her chair, happy her child was doing better. She wasn't screaming for her mommy.

In a few minutes, Chloe crawled into her lap. "I'm gonna go to the park with Grandma and Grandpa."

Abby kissed her. "Have fun. Mommy will be here with Holly."

As they left, Abby whispered to her father, "If she cries…"

"Don't worry. I'll have her back here in a flash."

Abby went back to searching for lawyers with Holly, wondering how long Chloe would stand being away from her. But her baby was better. That was the important thing.

A few minutes later there was another knock at the door. Abby glanced at her watch. "Ten minutes. That didn't take long."

"Ten minute is ten minutes." Holly raised her head from the computer. "She's just a baby and wants her mommy."

Abby opened the door to a dark-haired woman in a business suit, not her parents with Chloe. Handing Abby a card, she said, "I'm Lissa Malone, an attorney. I read about your situation in the paper. If you want custody of your daughter, I'll do my best to make that happen. My number is on the card." She turned and headed for the stairs.

"Wait," she called. "Come in, please."

"There's no need for discussion until you make up your mind."

"I need an attorney. Come in so we can talk."

Ms. Malone stepped into the apartment with a Louis Vuitton bag over her shoulder and an equally expensive briefcase in her hand.

"This is Holly, my friend." Abby made the introductions.

"I've heard of you," Holly said. "You're a child advocate. You fight for the rights of children."

"Yes."

"Ms. Malone, you're an answer to my prayers, but I don't understand why you're willing to take my case."

"As your friend said, I fight for the child. I've lived in Austin for a long time and I know the Bauman name and their family's power. I just wanted to offer my services if you need them."

"Yes. Yes."

Within minutes, Abby had hired Lissa Malone to represent her and Chloe. "How much will this cost me?"

"I don't talk price until the case is finished. If I lose, you don't owe me a dime. If I win, we'll talk price."

"That doesn't seem right."

"I'm not in this for the money. I'm here to help your daughter."

"Are you for real?" Abby had the feeling she'd conjured this woman up out of thin air.

"You'll find out in the next few days." Ms. Malone looked at her Rolex. "I would like to meet your daughter in the morning at ten and then we'll go over every last detail of this case. What you expect from me and what I expect from you."

"Okay."

Abby danced around the apartment in excitement. Out of the blue, her prayers had been answered. "Wait a minute." She stopped dancing. "Things like this don't happen for no reason. Do you think the Baumans sent her here to give me a false sense of security? I mean, did you notice her clothes and purse? They were expensive. How does she afford that?"

Holly resumed her seat on the sofa. "I don't know much about her, just her work. Maybe we can find something on the internet. But she doesn't seem like a person who can be bought." Holly sat with the laptop cradled on her legs. Abby knelt on the floor as her friend searched.

"She has a law degree from UT. Married a wealthy stock-broker fifteen years her senior. He died five years ago. That would account for her expensive taste. Uh-oh."

"What? She has a connection to Richard Bauman?"

"No. She was born in Willow Creek, Texas."

Abby sat back on her heels. *Ethan had sent her.*

"Please don't blow this out of proportion. You need Ms. Malone."

Abby got to her feet. "I'm not stupid, Holly. I don't care who sent her. I want custody of my child." She remembered Ethan talking about a killer attorney who had gotten custody of Kelsey for him. It must have been Lissa Malone.

LATER, HER PARENTS came back with Chloe, and her daughter was excited that Grandpa had let her go down the big slide by herself. After her parents left, Abby fixed dinner and bathed Chloe, putting her down for the night in her own bed. She'd been sleeping with Abby and that could not continue.

She didn't quiz her daughter much about what had happened. There were blue marks on her neck where Doug had forcefully held her. Every time she saw those it angered her. Chloe had never even been spanked.

Chloe had only said that Daddy made her drink some stuff and she didn't want to. She'd started to cry, wanting Mommy, and he had told her to shut up. Then she got scared and she was still scared. Abby was at a loss at how to make her feel safe. But today was a big start.

That night so many problems weighed upon her but she knew she had to keep fighting for Chloe and herself.

As much as she tried to take steps away from Ethan, something kept pulling her toward him. He knew she needed help and he made sure she got it in the form of Ms. Malone. She moved her head on the pillow and remembered the morning they'd spent in this room. All the emotion and passion they'd shared was forever.

Then the unthinkable happen. He chose his job over her and broke her heart. The thought hung in her mind for a moment and something clicked. He didn't choose his job over her; he did his job because of her, no matter how much it hurt him. And Doug was behind bars because of that.

Oh, Ethan.

ETHAN SPENT HIS days in turmoil. His daughter was his only bright spot. He took her to school and picked her up, which was at varying times because she was in so many activities now. His daughter was becoming a social butterfly.

He went into the kitchen to get a glass of ice water. Sometimes at night he'd feel the heat from the fire and the water helped. He wondered if Abby still felt it, too. Oh, God, he had to stop thinking about her. But that was difficult when she filled his every waking thought and all of his dreams.

As he got a glass out of the cabinet, he heard voices coming from Kelsey's room. It was after ten-thirty. She should be asleep. He walked into her room and flipped on the light. Propped up in bed on several pillows, she was talking on her cell.

"Gotta go," she said into the phone and slid down into the bed.

He held his hand out for the phone.

"Ah, Dad," she grumbled, but placed it in his hand. "I get it back in the morning, right?"

"Depends how I feel in the morning. You broke the rules. You're supposed to be in bed at ten and not on the phone."

"But Cathy called me. There's a football game tomorrow and we're trying to decide what we're going to do afterward. Sleep over at her house or mine."

"This is the first I've heard of a sleepover. After the game, you'll be coming home with Grandpa and me."

"Jeez." She flopped over in bed. "When are you going back to work? You're getting as grouchy as Grandpa."

He was. He felt as if his nerves were tied up with barbed wire.

"We'll talk in the morning."

On his way back to the kitchen, he heard a knock at the door. Who could that be? It was almost eleven now.

Levi stood on the doorstep. "I saw the light and knew you were still up."

"You saw the light from your house? Down the road and two miles away?"

"Of course not. I just got back into town and Pop said you haven't gone back to work."

"So you thought you would come nag me?"

"Maybe." Levi followed him into the kitchen. "You talking to someone?" Levi pointed to the phone in Ethan's hand.

"It's Kelsey's. I had to take it away from her for talking when she's supposed to be asleep."

"Oh. How's the parent thing going?" Levi removed his Stetson and took a seat at the table.

"So-so." He laid the phone on the counter and got two Coors out of the refrigerator. Handing one to Levi, he added, "I let her get away with a lot of stuff. I have to start disciplining her."

Levi popped the top on the can and took a swallow. "In your present mood that shouldn't be too hard."

He sank into a chair and took a swig from his can. "Don't start, Levi."

"Why haven't you gone back to work?"

"Because I quit."

Levi gave him one of his classic you're-not-fooling-me looks. "I've known you since we were knee-high to a grasshopper, as Pop would say. What's eating at you?"

He ran his thumb across the wetness of the can and wanted to throw it against the wall. "I screwed up, man. If I'd made better choices, Abby wouldn't have gone through another terrifying experience. And Chloe would never have been harmed."

"How do you figure that?"

"I fought the lieutenant to stay on the case. But he was right.
I had too much personally invested in it. I should have let Hal
handle the whole thing."

"And Douglas Bauman would probably have gotten away
with what he'd done."

"What?"

"No one would have dug through every little detail like you
did. They're swamped with a heavy caseload. Even Ross would
have stopped. But you kept going because you were up against
the clock. If you hadn't, Abby and her little girl would be in
Italy somewhere and you would have a hell of a time finding
them. From what Ross told me, Bauman was determined to
make things happen his way."

Ethan took a gulp of beer. "Why do you have to be right?"

"Why do you have to feel so much guilt?"

"Because I love her, and I hurt her." The words had just
flown out of his mouth. Obviously, he'd needed to get that off
his chest.

"Then do something about it. Talk to her."

"I did. At the hospital." He stood and ran both hands through
his hair. "I don't know how much more she can take. She's
hurt, angry and disillusioned. She said she had to sort out her
life and then she said goodbye in a way that I knew was final."

"I'm sorry, man."

"But it's not over for her. The Baumans aren't going to give
her time to catch her breath before they file a custody amendment. With Doug in jail, they'll want the right to see their
granddaughter, and that will be hard for Abby."

"Yeah. So what are you going to do about it?"

Ethan leaned against the cabinet. "I called Lissa."

Levi chuckled. "She certainly won't be afraid to go head-
to-head with the Bauman lawyers."

"I just hope Abby hires her."

"Uh…Abby doesn't know that you're acquainted with Lissa."

"No. I just told Lissa about the case and thought she might be interested. She'd already read about it."

Levi took the last swig of his beer and stood. "You're not going back to work because you want to be available in case Abby needs you."

"Man—" Ethan drove a fist into his hand "—I can't stand the thought of the Baumans hurting her again."

"Then why aren't you with her?"

"Uh…she said we got too involved too quickly and what she felt for me was gratitude. It wasn't real, but she would always remember me."

"Ouch." Levi reached for his hat. "Remind me to never fall in love. Now I'm going home to sleep for about twelve hours." He headed for the door and turned. "If you need me, you know my number."

"Yeah. Thanks."

Ethan threw the cans in the trash and went to bed. Lying awake in the darkness, he could feel her soft skin against his, smell the sweet scent of her and experienced a deep longing inside that was as real as it got.

It was real, Abby.

It is real.

THE FIRST THING Abby learned about Ms. Malone was that she was direct and thorough. They spent many hours going over every aspect of her relationship with Doug and his parents.

Chloe was reticent about talking to her. She hid her face against Abby and refused to speak. Her baby was no longer the happy child who used to laugh and run through the house. Now she was very quiet. But Abby noticed as each day passed that Chloe was slowly getting better, especially after the outing with her parents. She would play in her room for short periods of time alone without needing to see Abby, which was good because Lissa was coming over to discuss their case. She and Lissa were now on a first-name basis. Abby liked the mysterious, serious attorney.

Lissa had filed papers to amend the custody agreement, granting Abby legal and physical custody. The Baumans had quickly answered, contesting the filing. In two weeks, a judge would hear both sides and rule. That morning they sat at Abby's dining table, going over details.

"I have to be honest, Abby," Lissa said, flipping through a pile of notes. "I have to prove that it's detrimental to Chloe's well-being for her to spend time with the Baumans. All I have is Richard's diabolical manipulation of Douglas. I have to show he and his wife would treat Chloe the same way."

"Doug was always telling me snide comments of his father's. Richard said Chloe was too old to cling to a doll and I needed to take Baby, a doll she takes everywhere, away from her. And I know they take the doll from her when she's there because Chloe tells me. Richard says children shouldn't be mollycoddled. It makes them weak."

"This is good." Lissa scribbled on a pad. "Anything else that I can prove?"

"When Doug was ten, they sent him away to boarding school because Richard wasn't pleased with his grades. He couldn't come home until they were up to Richard's standards."

"This is even better. Douglas's life has been constantly manipulated by his father."

"Yes. Getting his father's approval was the most important thing to Doug."

"Even marrying a woman of his father's choosing."

"Yes." Abby resisted the urge to squirm. "I can't believe how gullible I was."

"Don't beat yourself up, honey. Richard and Douglas Bauman are master manipulators." Lissa pulled out a paper from the file. "Lieutenant Eagon was nice enough to let me see the robbery file."

That made Abby think of Ethan and she suddenly had to know. "May I ask you a personal question?"

"No. I don't do personal."

Abby refused to be put off. "It's not about you. Do you know Ethan James?"

"Yes." Head down, Lissa continued to read.

"Did he ask you to take my case?"

"No." Again, she kept reading. Finally, Lissa looked up. "Is that important?"

Yes. Very.

"No" was what came out of her mouth. "I was just curious."

Lissa leaned back in her chair. "I've known Ethan a long time, and every now and then he calls me if there's a case with a child involved who might need my help. I read about you in the paper and saw a lot of your ordeal on TV. The decision to offer my help was mine alone. Okay?"

"Okay." The woman was certainly an enigma and Abby was happy to have her on her side.

Lissa pushed bright pink reading glasses up the bridge of her nose. "There's something about the robbery that's very vague to me."

"What?"

"From the report it says Douglas hired Rudy to scare you so you'd call him for help like you did in college. Why was he so certain you'd call him?"

"What? No, that's not right. I didn't call—" She wove her fingers through her hair in distress. "That's not how it happened."

Lissa picked up a legal pad and pen. "Tell me what happened with Bradley Cummins in college. Were you dating Douglas at the time?"

"I had broken up with Doug."

"Why?"

"He belonged to a fraternity that had really wild parties that made me feel uncomfortable—a lot of drinking, smoking pot and drugs. That wasn't my scene and I told Doug we weren't suited for each other and broke up with him. He called for several days apologizing, but then he finally gave up."

"When did Bradley Cummins become a problem?"

"I don't know. Maybe two weeks later. I had an accounting class with him. He started making a point of sitting by me, and everywhere I went he was there. He began making crude remarks, such as he'd love to fondle my breasts or he couldn't wait for me to wrap my legs around him. I told him to cut it out or I was calling the police. Then one night I was studying at the library with a friend. It was late when we came out. She ran to her car and I ran to mine. I dropped my keys. All of a sudden Bradley was there. He pushed me against the car and I shoved him hard. He fell down, giving me time to get in my car and drive away."

"Then you called the police?"

"No. My cell was in my purse and I had slung it into the car. It was on the passenger floorboard and I couldn't reach it. I wasn't stopping to get it. I rushed to my dorm to call them. I was shaking so bad I had to calm down first. Before I could, Doug called and he wanted to know what was wrong. I sounded stressed, he said. I told him to get him off the phone. He said he'd be right there and he was. He called the police and took care of everything. I never had a problem with Bradley again."

Abby ran her hands over her face as those events became crystal clear. "Oh, my God! *Doug called me.* I didn't call him. He already knew what had happened. I'm almost certain he put Bradley up to it. I have to be the stupidest woman alive."

"Just trusting. After that, you gave Douglas another chance?"

"Yes. He was my hero. My prince charming. I think I need to go throw up." She took a deep breath. "Doug was hoping for the same thing happening this time. After Rudy supposedly frightened me, I'd go into the bank and he'd call apologizing for not showing up that morning. And I'd be ever so grateful to have him take care of my little harassment."

Lissa placed files in her briefcase. "I have facts to verify, but I believe I have enough to put doubt in the judge's mind about entrusting Chloe to the Baumans' care." She reached for her purse and stood. "Do you mind if I enlist Ethan's help?"

"Uh…no. Why?"

"I don't believe a man can do anything better than a woman, but dealing with Mr. Cummins might take a rougher hand than mine. And I need to be in my office preparing the facts that will support the theory that Chloe's welfare is at stake, and the only conclusion is to give you total custody. I will press strongly for no visitation, but ultimately that will be the judge's decision."

"I understand." Abby walked her to the door. "Could we get the names changed at the same time?" Abby had decided to have their last names changed to Baines.

"We can certainly get yours changed, but we'll have to wait for the judge's ruling before we can consider changing Chloe's name."

"Thanks, Lissa."

"Keep your phone handy in case I need to ask a question."

Abby closed the door and went to check on Chloe. She'd been quiet for some time. She was sound asleep, curled up on the floor with Baby. That worried Abby. Since the overdose of Tylenol, Chloe slept too much. Abby would have to ask the doctor about that.

She picked the toddler up and carried her into the living room. Sitting in the big comfy chair, she cradled her daughter close. If the judge granted the Baumans visitation rights, Abby didn't know what she was going to do. She'd take Chloe and leave the country before she'd let them spend one minute with her. She and Chloe had been put through enough.

Her stomach twisted at the enormous task ahead of her. Her primary goal was to protect her child. She couldn't fail.

She stared out the French doors to the gray October sky.

Ethan would help with the case. At the thought, her stomach settled down. After all the doubts and hurt feelings, she still trusted him.

CHAPTER TWENTY-THREE

As SOON AS Ethan got the call from Lissa he was on the job and in a better mood. It didn't take him long to find Bradley Cummins. He was a CPA in Georgetown, Texas, not far out of Austin. After getting the truth out of Mr. Cummins, he got the man to sign a statement to the fact that Douglas Bauman had paid him to harass Abby in college.

From Lissa's office, he went to the station and apologized to the lieutenant. He told him he wasn't ready to return to work. He needed more time. But he did sit down with Ross and Hal to go over some details from the robbery. Hal didn't object. They had a solid case for the D.A, because homicide, robbery and the FBI had worked together.

Ethan nursed a cup of coffee. "Did you guys wonder why Bauman was so sure Abby would call him after Rudy accosted her?"

"Yeah." Hal scratched his head. "That was a little puzzling since they were divorced, but we really don't need all the answers to nail that bastard."

"Lissa Malone…"

"A courier just brought a large envelope from her," Hal interrupted. "I haven't opened it yet."

"She's attempting to gain legal and physical custody of Chloe for Abby without any visitation rights to Doug or the Baumans."

Ross shook his head. "Bauman's attorneys will not let that happen."

"Don't underestimate Lissa or Abby. In one of their many

talks Abby remembered something very crucial. Lissa has sent you copies of what she discovered. After the incident in college, Abby did not call Doug as Doug had stated. He called Abby because he set up the whole thing to get Abby back after she'd broken up with him."

"Now that makes sense." Ross nodded. "Doug planned to call Abby when she got into the bank and come to her rescue, but it blew up in his face."

Ethan took a quick swallow of coffee. "That's about it. Once the bad stuff started happening he didn't have the guts to stop it. In his warped mind, if Abby made it out alive, he'd be the consoling ex. If she died, he'd be the grieving ex and a single father, which was sure to draw his father's sympathies. With money to pay off Rudy and Estelle, he felt safe behind his manipulations." He downed the rest of the coffee. "How'd the bail hearing go?"

"The judge is holding firm on no bail," Ross said. "He's too big of a flight risk, but Baumans' attorneys are in there trying. The last I heard they were petitioning to have him evaluated by a psychologist in a hospital environment. That didn't fly either. He's being evaluated, but not in a hospital. The D.A. is keeping him locked up tight."

"I agree he's insane, but he knew right from wrong and he did it anyway." Ethan got to his feet. "I better go before I get my blood pressure bubbling."

"Nice seeing you, Ethan," Hal called as he walked away.

Ross fell into step beside him. "When are you coming back? I'm paired with Holby and it's not the same."

"I don't know. I told the lieutenant the same thing. I'm trying to sort out the future for me and my kid."

"And Abby?"

"I don't know, man, if she can even see a future after the hell Doug has put her through. And if the Baumans are allowed visitation, I'm not sure what she'll do."

"But you'll be there to help her."

"I'm not sure she wants that."

"Good luck," Ross said as Ethan went through the door.

Ross was right. He'd be there for Abby to the bitter end whether she wanted him to be or not.

ABBY FINALLY GOT Chloe down for the night and put her in her own bed, hoping she'd stay there and not wake up at midnight screaming for Mommy. It disrupted the night for both of them. Soon, though, she prayed Chloe would make it through the night in her own bed.

Abby planned to watch a movie, but before she could make it to the living room her cell buzzed. It was Lissa, and she came straight to the point, as always.

"Abby, I've obtained the medical reports from when you and Ethan were brought in and also when you and Chloe were taken by helicopter to the hospital. Were you aware that Chloe wasn't breathing when you pulled her from the car?"

Abby began to tremble and she had to sit down. "Yes. She was so pale and limp I knew something was terribly wrong. Then Ethan took her and performed CPR. He said she was breathing and then the chopper arrived. It happened very quickly. The doctor said we got to the hospital just in time."

"If Ethan hadn't given her CPR, she would have been DOA."

Abby gasped.

"I'm not saying that to be cruel," Lissa hastened to add.

"It's okay," Abby told her. "Like I told you, Doug was regularly giving Chloe Tylenol, which I was unaware of, when she stayed with him. He said she always cried for Mommy and it was the only way to keep her quiet. I was stunned when he told me and I wanted to kill him with my bare hands."

"Well, I've heard all I need to hear. I'm filing a petition to terminate Douglas Bauman's paternal rights."

"Can you do that?"

"I have more than enough horrifying evidence for the judge

to take a long look at it. And if the judge grants it, then we don't have to worry about the Baumans."

"Oh, Lissa."

"Don't get your hopes up too high. The judge will look at all the evidence and decide if Chloe will be better off without her father in her life. A man who drugs and almost kills his child is a no-brainer to me, but either way I'll be in there fighting for you and Chloe."

"Thank you, Lissa."

For the first time Abby could see a ray of light in her dismal situation. There was hope. And Ethan was a big part of that hope. She'd heard from Lissa that Ethan had gotten Bradley to admit that Doug had paid him to frighten her, just as she'd thought. She wanted to thank him. She fiddled with her phone. It wasn't only about the thanks. She wanted to hear his voice, to be with him. Laying the phone aside, she wasn't sure that was even possible now.

TWO DAYS BEFORE the hearing, the judge wanted to visit with Chloe. Abby was hesitant about this, but Lissa said it was absolutely necessary. If they had a chance for the judge to grant the petition, she had to assess Chloe's mental health herself, even though the custody evaluator and a child psychologist had already visited Abby and Chloe. It was unusual for a judge to ask this so Lissa felt it was a good sign.

There was a playroom at family court and Abby waited with Chloe to meet Judge Judith Seaton. Chloe investigated all the toys then sat in a red rocker, holding Baby. Abby took a seat in a straight-backed chair, feeling queasy.

As soon as the door opened, Chloe flew to her and hid her face against Abby.

"Good morning, I'm Judith," the judge introduced herself informally.

"I'm Abby, and this is my daughter."

The judge pulled a chair closer and sat down. "What a pretty little girl. What's your name?"

Chloe didn't respond.

"Tell the lady your name," Abby urged.

"Chloe," she barely whispered.

"How old are you Chloe?"

Chloe held up three fingers.

"Next year you'll go to school. Would you like that?"

"Yes." Chloe raised her head. The judge had her full attention. "I'm gonna go to school like Kelsey."

Abby did a double take. She didn't even know Chloe remembered Kelsey.

"Who's Kelsey?" the judge asked.

"My friend. She calls me twerp."

"Why does she call you twerp?"

"'Cause she likes me."

"I see."

Abby tried hard not to smile. It was an endearment, after all. At least to Chloe.

"Who's this?" The judge pointed to the doll Chloe was holding.

"Baby, my dolly. I hold her when I'm sad."

"I see. You like Baby?"

Chloe nodded.

"Do you like Mommy?"

"I love Mommy."

"Do you love Daddy?"

Chloe burrowed against her, turning her face away from the judge.

"Do you love your daddy?" the judge repeated.

"No," Chloe spat and literally began to climb Abby. "Wanna go home. Wanna go home."

Abby grabbed her with both hands, pulling her back into her lap. "Mommy's here. It's okay." She kissed her face over and over.

After Chloe had calmed down, the judge asked very gently, "Chloe, may I ask you one more question? And Mommy's right here. She's not going anywhere."

Chloe nodded with tear-filled eyes.

"Do you love Grandfather and CeCe?"

Chloe shook her head. "They take Baby, and I cry 'cause I scared."

"Thank you, Chloe. I really enjoyed talking to you." Without another word, the judge left the room.

She hugged Chloe. "Let's go to Grandma and Grandpa's."

"Okay." Chloe crawled down and Abby took her hand. She wanted to ask about Kelsey but decided not to. Chloe had had a fascination with Kelsey ever since she'd met her. Just as Abby had a fascination with Kelsey's father.

So she decided to leave that door closed—for now.

THE HEARING DAY arrived and Abby was all nerves. Lissa and the Baumans' attorney met with the judge in the morning to present their arguments. At three in the afternoon the judge would render her decision. Abby didn't attend the morning session as Lissa said it was unnecessary, but Lissa wanted her there for the ruling. There was no way Abby would be anywhere else.

Holly took off work to be there, and Abby was grateful to have her friend's support. Her parents had Chloe in the playroom. It didn't even seem odd that she thought of Gayle as her parent because she was now, in every sense of the word.

The courtroom was small, paneled in dark wood. There was a stern, official feel to it, with the United States and Texas flags standing in a corner. Abby sat with Lissa on the right and the Baumans were with their attorney on the left. Glancing back, she nodded to Holly, but she was really looking for Ethan. She thought he would be here. She needed him to be here.

"I just wanted you to know I visited with Douglas at the jail," Lissa said as they waited.

"Why?"

"I thought he had a right to hear from me that I was trying to terminate his parental rights. I was hoping the bastard would have a conscience and do the honorable thing."

"He didn't?"

"No, so we're on our own today. Keep positive thoughts."

Abby's attention was on the judge as she took her seat. "Good afternoon, everyone." Judge Seaton folded her hands over a larger folder. An iPad was to her right. "I have spent a great deal of time reviewing the evidence that supports terminating Douglas Bauman's rights as a father. Fatherhood is a God-given gift and no one should have the power to interfere with that. Of course, there are extenuating circumstances in this case. Mr. Bauman did some bad things, but is that enough to sever his ties to his daughter?"

Oh, no. Abby gripped her hands in her lap until they were numb. The judge's words didn't sound positive.

"My main concern is three-year-old Chloe and her welfare and her future. There's no doubt she's been traumatized by her father's actions, but she's young and the bad memories will fade. Children are very forgiving. So I had to ask myself, in the years ahead would Chloe want to see her father? Would she want to have a relationship with him?"

Abby moved restlessly. She couldn't take much more of this. Lissa shot her a consoling glance.

The judge opened the file and pulled out something. It looked like a photo. "Every time I asked myself those questions I came back to this photo. It was taken with an officer's phone seconds after Chloe was pulled from the car by her mother." She motioned to the Baumans' attorney and he stepped forward to take it. "According to the officer's deposition, Chloe was not breathing. Detective Ethan James performed CPR on the highway and brought her back, but the doctor's report said she once again stopped breathing in the E.R. There are bruises on her neck where she was held by force.

"This bothered me a great deal. Chloe is alive because good people acted quickly." She paused for a second. "Douglas Bauman forfeited his paternal rights when he forced Tylenol down his daughter's throat. Today I'm making it official. Douglas Bauman's paternal rights to Chloe Bauman are terminated. Full legal and physical custody is awarded to Abigail…Baines. I'm also granting the name change for Abigail and Chloe."

"This is an outrage." Richard Bauman was on his feet.

"Yes, it is, Mr. Bauman," the judge replied. "I suggest you get counseling for your son, yourself and your wife. This case is adjourned."

Abby jumped up and hugged Lissa. "Thank you! Thank you!"

The Baumans walked out without a word.

Holly ran up and grabbed her, and then her parents and Chloe came in. They hugged and kissed and everyone was smiling. Chloe didn't have a clue what was going on, but she was smiling, too. Abby picked her up and held her tight. All she wanted was for her baby to be happy. The judge had given her that chance and Abby was ecstatic.

She raised her head and saw Ethan standing in the doorway. Her heart soared. He nodded and walked away. No. No. No! She handed Chloe to Gayle. "Stay with Grandma. Mommy'll be right back."

She ran for the entrance, but she didn't know which way he had gone. The parking lot was the logical place. Her heels made clickety-clack sounds on the pavement. She stopped when she saw him opening his truck door.

"Ethan!"

He turned, his handsome face marred with sadness.

"Ethan," she breathed and took off running. He held out his arms and she flew into them. Her body molded to his until they were one mass of quivering need. "I'm sorry." She stroked his face, his hair. "I got derailed by all the pain."

"I'm sorry, too."

"Ethan…"

"Shh." His lips found hers and the world righted itself for the first time in months. "I love you, lady," he whispered into her mouth.

"I love you, too." They held on, just needing to touch each other.

He rested his forehead against hers. "Congratulations."

"It's over and I can breathe again." She kissed him briefly. "I can't stand to be away from you another night. What are we going to do? You have a twelve-year-old you're just getting to know. I have a traumatized three-year-old. How can we ever be together?"

"We get married" was his shocking yet delightful answer.

"Do we dare?"

"Just trust me."

"E-tan, E-tan," Chloe cried, running toward them.

Ethan caught her. "Hey, cutie."

"Where's Kelsey?" Chloe asked.

"In school. How would you and your mommy like to go with me to pick her up?"

"Can we, Mommy? Can we?"

"Since we came with Grandpa, I don't see why not."

"I'll get the car seat out of the back of my car," her dad said.

Within minutes they had Chloe buckled in. Abby hugged Holly and her parents. Gayle hung on a little longer. "Just be happy."

"I am." She smiled and climbed into the passenger's seat. "I'm finally getting to ride in this big silver truck."

"Yep."

"Don't rear-end anyone."

"As long as a beautiful blonde doesn't stop dead in front of me." He grinned and pulled out into traffic. Glancing at her, he asked, "Ready for a new adventure?"

"Yes." She gazed into his warm, warm brown eyes and

knew whatever they had to face down the road they would face it together.

Love was all they needed, after all. And a little trust.

EPILOGUE

One year later...

ETHAN JAMES BELIEVED in real love and happy endings. And if someone pressed him, he might even admit to believing in fairy tales—reality style.

The hard-nosed cop had been tamed.

He spooned a sleeping Abby, kissing her warm neck. "Time to get up. Your parents are coming for lunch."

"Five more minutes," she begged.

His wife was not an early riser. During the week when the alarm went off, she got up, but on weekends she liked to laze in bed. With two active daughters, that was an indulgence.

"You got it." He kissed her cheek and rested his face against hers.

The past year had been a frenzy of activities, some emotional and some tearful, but the marriage was working. No one tried harder than Abby to create a loving family.

They were married a week after the hearing in the small church where Chloe used to go to day care. Gayle outdid herself with a reception in her home. The day was perfect except for the two kids, who seemed to dislike each other. Or, he had to admit, it was his kid causing all the problems. He had thrown a lot at her at one time, and he kept hoping she'd adjust. It didn't happen overnight, though.

They talked for a solid week about where they were going to live. Abby's apartment was too small, and Ethan refused to uproot Kelsey, as Sheryl had done so many times. So Ethan talked to his dad, and Abby and Chloe moved in. There was one problem, though. Where was Chloe going to sleep? He'd promised Kelsey she wouldn't have to give up her room, so that was out.

In the end, they put a small bed in their room for Chloe with stuffed animals and toys. Abby found a colorful partition at a thrift store and Chloe had her own space, close to her mother. Sometimes at night Chloe would wake up and crawl into their bed. It was a terrible arrangement. He met with a contractor, Abby picked out house plans and construction started on their own home next door to Walt.

One morning they awoke to Chloe crying. Abby was out of bed in an instant, but Chloe wasn't in her bed. The crying was coming from Kelsey's room. Before Abby could charge in, Ethan grabbed her.

"Let's listen first."

"Ethan, I can't stand it when Kelsey makes Chloe cry. I can't."

"Shh." He held her tight, hoping the girls could work out whatever was wrong without the adults interfering.

"What did you get in my bed for?" Kelsey asked.

"I wanted Mommy." Chloe hiccupped.

"She's not in here."

Chloe started crying again. "You're mean."

"Stop crying, twerp. You gonna wake up our parents."

"My...my daddy did something bad."

Total silence followed, and he had to physically restrain Abby from bursting into the room.

"I heard." He'd told Kelsey everything that had happened. "Sometimes adults do stupid things."

"They do?" Chloe hiccupped again.

"Yeah. My mom did something stupid, too. I don't see her anymore."

"I don't want to see my daddy."

"You don't have to."

"Oh."

"If you have any questions, just ask me. I know lots of stuff."

"You do?"

"Yep. I got your back, twerp. You don't have to worry. I'll take care of you."

"You will?"

"Yeah, and you can sleep in my room now."

"Oh, boy. I'll get Baby."

Chloe darted out and Abby caught her. "I've been looking for you."

"I was with Kelsey." She wiggled down. "Gotta go."

Kelsey came out of her room. "Dad, I've made a decision."

"About what?"

"Chloe can sleep with me, but when I have friends over she has to sleep with you."

"Deal." He hugged her until his arms hurt. His kid had come through.

Abby hugged her, too. "Thank you, Kelsey."

After that, the tension lessened, and Kelsey and Chloe bonded in a way they hadn't expected, but they still had tiffs. He supposed that was typical of all sisters.

Abby felt she needed to talk to Chloe about her father. She told Chloe that Doug had to go away and he wasn't coming back. That was all Chloe needed to hear—that her father wasn't coming back to get her. They'd never realized how much she feared that.

Doug had sent a letter through Lissa that he wanted them to give Chloe when she was older. It was very simple. He admitted to everything he'd done, said how sorry he was and that he wasn't cut out to be a father. He added that when he got out of prison, he was leaving the United States and starting a new life. He wished her happiness. Abby put it in a safety-deposit box for Chloe when she turned twenty-one.

Ethan adopted Chloe and Lissa drew up papers to make

Abby Kelsey's legal guardian if anything happened to him. They were a real family.

The past year had been so busy with him back at work, Abby in school to finish her degree to teach, and keeping up with the girls. They were glad to see each other at the end of the day. In the fall, Abby would teach kindergarten in Willow Creek. Against the odds, they had made it work.

"Wake up, beautiful lady." He slid his hand beneath the sheet to caress Wynken and Blynken.

Abby caught his hand. "Don't even think about Nod, mister." She turned and stared at him with sleepy blue eyes. "I know what you're thinking."

He laughed. "That's a no-brainer." His hand moved lower.

"The girls will be up at any minute."

He kissed her slowly, loving the way she moaned as he deepened the kiss.

"Come back here, twerp. I'm gonna kill you."

Ethan groaned, pulling his lips away. "The alarm just went off."

The door burst opened and Chloe jumped onto the bed in nothing but her Barbie panties, holding one of Kelsey's bras. Kelsey quickly appeared with murder in her eye.

Ethan and Abby sat up. Abby nodded at him, which meant she'd take this one.

"Give me that." Kelsey made a dive for the bra.

Chloe jumped away. "No. I want to wear it."

"You don't have any breasts," Kelsey pointed out.

"I got breasts." Chloe pushed out her chest.

"Give me that."

Chloe danced away but her mother caught her, taking the bra from her. "What are you doing in Kelsey's room? You have a room of your own, now."

"Uh…" Chloe had a hard time lying or she hadn't learned the skill yet. "Uh…we listened to Kelsey's iPod and danced."

"When you were supposed to be asleep?"

"But, Mom, it wasn't a school night," Kelsey hastened to explain.

Ethan loved it when she slipped and called Abby "Mom." She was doing that more and more.

"We were listening to Justin Bieber," Chloe added. "Kelsey has a crush on him."

"You're such a twerp." Kelsey grabbed her and started tickling her. Giggling fits ensued. They rolled from the bed to the floor.

"Daddy, help," Chloe cried.

"What's going on in here?" Walt stood in the doorway.

Kelsey jumped up and hugged him. "Good morning, Grandpa." Chloe latched on around his knees.

"C'mon. I'll fix you girls breakfast." He looked at Chloe. "Where's your clothes, little bit?"

"I not little bit. I'm a big bit."

"You're not even two bits."

"I can count, Grandpa. Wanna hear?"

"Okay, but let's find your clothes first."

Ethan and Abby rolled out of bed and slipped into shorts and T-shirts. "I think Walt misses us. He's over here three or four times a day."

"It'll wear off." He slipped into a pair of Crocs.

"Ethan."

"Hmm?" He looked up to see a dreamy expression on her face and he knew he was fixing to get knocked six ways to Sunday.

"We have an extra bedroom now and I was thinking it would be nice to have another child."

Yep. That knocked him sideways. "You want to bring a baby into the mix?"

"Yes. I'd like to have another child—your child. Not right now, but maybe in a year or so."

He pulled her into his arms and held her. "Whatever you want, lady. I just want you to be happy for the rest of your life."

Cupping her face, he kissed her until there was no doubt about his feelings for her. He rested his forehead against hers. "You have brought so much life to my ho-hum existence."

"Probably more than you bargained for."

"The robbery? Yeah. The wildfire? Yeah. But it brought me you so I'm not complaining."

She stroked his hair. "I love you, Ethan."

"Good, 'cause we're in debt up to our eyeballs, but I have a feeling our lives are going to be filled with a lot of love, excitement and craziness." He took her hand and they walked to the kitchen. They suddenly stopped short.

Walt stood in the middle of the kitchen staring down at a gallon of milk he'd obviously dropped because milk was splattered all over their barely used tiled floor.

Kelsey stood at the sink, her mouth opened as she gaped at the milk on her feet.

"Shazam," Walt said.

Chloe stood on one of the new bar stools at the island, milk dripping from her chin, looking at the mess. "Shih Tzu, Grandpa!" she shouted.

Yep. Craziness.

* * * * *

Watch for the next book in Linda Warren's
WILLOW CREEK, TEXAS, *miniseries,*
A TEXAS FAMILY, coming October 2013
only from Harlequin Superromance!

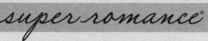

COMING NEXT MONTH FROM

HARLEQUIN

super romance

Available August 6, 2013

#1866 WHAT HAPPENS BETWEEN FRIENDS
In Shady Grove • by Beth Andrews

James Montesano has always been Sadie Nixon's soft place to land. Isn't that what friends are for? But something has changed. Instead of helping her pick up the pieces of her life, James is complicating things by confessing his feelings...for her! Suddenly she sees him in a whole *new* way.

#1867 FROM THIS DAY ON
by Janice Kay Johnson

The opening of a college time capsule is supposed to be fun. But for Amy Nilsson, the contents upend her world. In the midst of that chaos, Amy finds comfort in the most unexpected place—Jakob. Once the kid who tormented her, now he's the only one she can trust!

#1868 STAYING AT JOE'S
by Kathy Altman

Joe Gallahan ruined Allison Kincaid's career—and she broke his heart. Now reconnecting a year later, they're each looking for their own form of payback. But revenge would be so much easier if love didn't keep getting in the way!

#1869 A MAN LIKE HIM
by Rachel Brimble

Angela Taylor came to Templeton Cove to start over. But when the press photographs her in Chris Forrester's arms during a flood rescue, it's only a matter of time before her peaceful new life takes a frightening turn....

#1870 HER ROAD HOME
by Laura Drake

Samantha Crozier prefers the temporary. Her life is on the road, stopping long enough to renovate a house, then moving on. But her latest place in California is different. And that might have something to do with Nick Pinelli. As tempting as he is, though, she's not sure she can stay....

#1871 SECOND TIME'S THE CHARM
Shelter Valley Stories • by Tara Taylor Quinn

A single father, Jon Swartz does everything he can to make a good life for his son. That's why he's here in Shelter Valley attending college. When he meets Lillie Henderson, Jon begins to hope that this could be his second chance to have the family he's always wanted.

YOU CAN FIND MORE INFORMATION ON UPCOMING HARLEQUIN® TITLES, FREE EXCERPTS AND MORE AT WWW.HARLEQUIN.COM.

HSRCNM0713

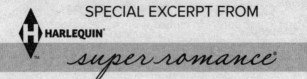
Staying at Joe's
By Kathy Altman

On sale August 6

Allison Kincaid must convince Joe Gallahan to
return to the advertising agency he quit a year
ago—and to do so, she must overlook their
history. But when she tracks him down at the
motel he's renovating, he has a few demands
of his own.... Read on for an exciting excerpt of
STAYING AT JOE'S by Kathy Altman.

Allison tapped her fingers against her upper arm as she turned
over his conditions in her mind. No matter how she looked
at it, she had zero negotiating room. "So. We're stuck with
each other."

"Looks that way." Joe's expression was stony.

"I didn't come prepared to stay, let alone work," she said.

"I can see that." He looked askance at her outfit. "You'll
need work boots. I suggest you make a run to the hardware
store. Get something sturdy. No hot-pink rubber rain gear."

"I'm assuming you have a separate room for me. One with
clean sheets and a working toilet."

"You'll get your own room." In four steps he was across the lobby and at the door. He pushed it open. "Hardware store's on State Street. You can't miss it."

When she made to walk past him, he stopped her with a hand on her arm. His nearness, his scent, the warmth of his fingers and their movement over the silk of her blouse made her shiver. *Damn it.*

Don't look at his mouth, don't look at his mouth, don't look—

Her gaze lowered. His lips formed a smug curve, and for one desperate, self-hating moment she considered running. But she'd be running from the only solution to her problems. "If I'm going back to the agency and delaying renovations for a month," he said, "then I get two full weeks of labor from you. No complaints, no backtracking, no games. Agreed?"

She shrugged free of his touch. "Don't worry, I'll do my part. Your part is to keep your hands to yourself."

"You might change your mind about that."

Will they keep their hands to themselves?
Or will two weeks together resurrect the past?
Find out in STAYING AT JOE'S
by Kathy Altman, available August 2013 from
Harlequin® Superromance®.

REQUEST YOUR FREE BOOKS!
2 FREE NOVELS PLUS 2 FREE GIFTS!

◆HARLEQUIN®

super romance®

More Story...More Romance

YES! Please send me 2 FREE Harlequin® Superromance® novels and my 2 FREE gifts (gifts are worth about $10). After receiving them, if I don't wish to receive any more books, I can return the shipping statement marked "cancel." If I don't cancel, I will receive 6 brand-new novels every month and be billed just $4.94 per book in the U.S. or $5.24 per book in Canada. That's a savings of at least 14% off the cover price! It's quite a bargain! Shipping and handling is just 50¢ per book in the U.S. and 75¢ per book in Canada.* I understand that accepting the 2 free books and gifts places me under no obligation to buy anything. I can always return a shipment and cancel at any time. Even if I never buy another book, the two free books and gifts are mine to keep forever.

135/336 HDN F46N

Name	(PLEASE PRINT)	
Address		Apt. #
City	State/Prov.	Zip/Postal Code

Signature (if under 18, a parent or guardian must sign)

Mail to the Harlequin® Reader Service:
IN U.S.A.: P.O. Box 1867, Buffalo, NY 14240-1867
IN CANADA: P.O. Box 609, Fort Erie, Ontario L2A 5X3

**Are you a current subscriber to Harlequin Superromance books
and want to receive the larger-print edition?
Call 1-800-873-8635 or visit www.ReaderService.com.**

* Terms and prices subject to change without notice. Prices do not include applicable taxes. Sales tax applicable in N.Y. Canadian residents will be charged applicable taxes. Offer not valid in Quebec. This offer is limited to one order per household. Not valid for current subscribers to Harlequin Superromance books. All orders subject to credit approval. Credit or debit balances in a customer's account(s) may be offset by any other outstanding balance owed by or to the customer. Please allow 4 to 6 weeks for delivery. Offer available while quantities last.

> **Your Privacy**—The Harlequin® Reader Service is committed to protecting your privacy. Our Privacy Policy is available online at www.ReaderService.com or upon request from the Harlequin Reader Service.
>
> We make a portion of our mailing list available to reputable third parties that offer products we believe may interest you. If you prefer that we not exchange your name with third parties, or if you wish to clarify or modify your communication preferences, please visit us at www.ReaderService.com/consumerchoice or write to us at Harlequin Reader Service Preference Service, P.O. Box 9062, Buffalo, NY 14269. Include your complete name and address.

HSR13R

SADDLE UP AND READ 'EM!

This summer, get your fix of Western reads and pick up a cowboy from some of your favorite authors!

In August look for:

CANYON by Brenda Jackson
The Westmorelands
Harlequin Desire

THE HEART WON'T LIE by Vicki Lewis Thompson
Sons of Chance
Harlequin Blaze

TAKING AIM by Elle James
Covert Cowboys Inc.
Harlequin Intrigue

THE LONG, HOT TEXAS SUMMER by Cathy Gillen Thacker
McCabe Homecoming
Harlequin American Romance

Look for these great Western reads AND MORE available wherever books are sold or visit
www.Harlequin.com/Westerns

The clock is ticking for Angela Taylor

Angela Taylor came to Templeton Cove to start over. But when the press photographs her in Chris Forrester's arms during a flood rescue, it's only a matter of time before her peaceful new life takes a frightening turn....

Suspense and romance collide in this sensational story!

A Man Like Him
by Rachel Brimble

AVAILABLE IN AUGUST